RIDE DIRTY, COWBOY

DIRTY COWBOY #2

ELLE THORPE

WWW.ELLETHORPE.COM/NEWSLETTER

For my beautiful sister-in-law, Merinda. Because you're a kickass Aboriginal woman, just like Addie.

PROLOGUE

KAI

*B*lood dripped on my hand. For a long moment, that was all I allowed myself to notice.

Not the screaming.

Not the flurry of activity outside the mangled wreck of the car.

Not even my best friend, who lay dying on the back seat.

I blocked it all out.

Everything, except the drip.

Drip. Drip. Drip.

But it couldn't be kept at bay forever. Too soon, reality punched through, the chaos focusing into crisp, clear pictures, breaking down the walls I'd been trying to build around myself.

I wished it hadn't.

Because it wasn't my blood.

I twisted, my gaze raking over Addie's silent form in the passenger seat beside me. Her head slumped forward, chin to her chest. Instinct told me not to look farther. Not to look into the back seat again. Not to *ever* look there again, even though I couldn't quite remember why.

"Addie," I rasped. The blood staining my hand and arm fell from a gash that ran the length of her face. My stomach rolled at the sight of the open wound, and her lifeless, unconscious body.

The arm I'd slung across her chest at the moment of impact trembled, and I forced myself to move it, fumbling for the release button on my seat belt.

"Addie." I tried again, my voice stronger this time. "Addie, wake up."

I shook her shoulder, which did nothing but bobble her head around. Panic and adrenaline hit me all at once.

"Addie!" I yanked the handle on my door and shoved it open with my shoulder. My legs didn't want to hold my weight, and I leaned heavily on the hood, half running, half limping around the broken metal shell.

I had to get her out.

Steam hissed from beneath the hood, and bile rose in my throat at the ticking sound that filled my ears.

On the other side of the car I stopped dead.

"No," I whispered.

The entire back section of the passenger side was crumpled in, wrapped around a traffic light pole.

Don't look. Don't look. Just get her out.

But the front section hadn't fared much better. My fingers found the cold, twisted metal of her door handle, and I jerked it with everything I had, but it didn't budge. Sirens wailed in the distance.

Too far. They were too far away.

Reaching through the broken glass, I pushed two fingers to the vein running down her neck and prayed to feel the steady beat that would tell me she was still alive.

Still with me.

But there was nothing. Not a thump. Not a beat. Not a pulse.

"No," I whispered, shoving my fingers harder into her delicate skin. "No!"

I wouldn't let her go.

Not like this.

Not ever.

1

KAI

*I*t was supposed to rain at funerals.

Gray skies, black clothes, water falling from the sky that matched the tears falling from red-rimmed eyes. It all went together so perfectly. Just like in the movies.

But I'd been in Australia for the past three months, and I could count on one hand how many times I'd seen rain. I'd spent my days riding in the sunshine, thankful for all that good weather. But not today. Today it was too bright. Too hot. Too happy.

Nothing about today should be happy.

Around me, people popped black umbrellas, but it wasn't to keep themselves dry from a gloomy, cloud-filled sky that would have fit the occasion. It was to keep off the unrelenting summer sun. The middle-aged woman beside me offered to share hers, but I politely refused, then ducked my head, hiding beneath the brim of the Stetson I didn't dare take off.

A rodeo buckle on the woman's belt gave her away as a fan, and I didn't want anyone recognizing me. Not when I wasn't even supposed to be here.

A black limousine pulled to a stop on the road, and a ripple of murmurs ran through the crowd around me. Rodeo security moved in and opened the back doors for the people inside.

Brad Pruitt, head of the World Bull Riding Association, stepped out first. A sneer threatened to curl my lip at the very sight of him. As always, his tall, broad-shouldered presence was overbearing. He towered over the people milling around, in a dark shirt rolled to his elbows, and black dress pants, despite the scorching temperature. But my attention was drawn back to the car before I could dwell on my dislike for the big man who signed my pay checks.

Bowen Barclay was next out of the door, stopping to hold out a hand to his fiancée, Paisley. I watched the two of them join hands, my breathing stuttering. That's how they'd been that night, too. Had it really only been a few weeks ago that we'd been at a bar, celebrating Bowen winning the Australian championship? It somehow seemed like a year had passed in that time.

Except the weight of my guilt hadn't diminished one iota. And I knew it never would.

I waited for Paisley or one of the security guards to close the door, but then a long, dark-brown leg appeared from within the depths of the limousine. Her foot was enclosed in red pumps, and my gaze traveled up the shapely curve of her calf. Inch by inch, a black knee-length dress became evident, then more of her, until the most beautiful woman I'd ever seen in my life sat perched on the edge of the seat.

Addie.

Shock punched me in the gut, stealing my breath. She wasn't supposed to be here, either. I'd called the hospital just this morning to check on her. Just like I had every morning since she'd woken up. They hadn't said anything about her leaving.

Paisley held out her hand, and once Addie had her heels digging into the soft dirt, she wrapped her fingers around Paisley's and gingerly lifted herself into a standing position. Her legs wobbled.

On instinct, I lurched forward, as if I could get through the ten-person-deep crowd quick enough to catch her. Bowen stepped in, grasping her other arm, and I planted my feet heavy on the ground once more. But it was an effort to force them to stay still, when all I wanted to do was rush to her side and make sure she was okay. She turned her face, and I caught sight of the white bandages covering one cheek and the side of her neck. My breath rushed out in a harsh exhale as guilt took its place.

"I don't know about this," Paisley said, her voice carrying over quiet whispers of the crowd watching on. She bit her bottom lip and cast a worried eye over Addie, who held tightly to Bowen's arm. "I think we should take you back to the hospital. We should have at least brought a wheelchair."

I nodded, agreeing with Paisley. Then I realized what I was doing and ducked my head again, hoping no one had noticed me eavesdropping. But I couldn't keep my gaze on the ground long. It was only moments before I was seeking Addie out again.

"No," she insisted with steel in her tone. "I need to be here. I'm not going back."

I ground my molars together. She needed to be in a damn hospital bed. What kind of crackpot doctor let her leave after she'd been so badly injured? Was *still* so badly injured?

Paisley and Bowen, with matching frowns of concern,

supported Addie across the uneven ground to a line of waiting people, all wanting to express their condolences.

"I'm so sorry for your loss."

I recognized the wife of one of the other riders when she stepped forward and squeezed Addie's hands. Addie nodded, thanking her, and forced a tiny smile for the woman's husband who gave her a one-armed hug and said sadly, "We miss him."

The couple moved aside, ready to let the next in line take their place. Addie's expression remained serious through every awkward hug and every pat on the arm. She thanked each person for coming with lips that barely opened.

A muscle ticked in the side of my jaw. I knew her expression. It was the one she got when she was bothered by something and wanted to be alone. Sunny, with his overly extroverted personality, hadn't always noticed when she'd gotten that way. But I had. And just like then, I wanted to storm over there and tell those people to back off and give the woman some room to breathe.

But I hadn't said anything then. And I wouldn't say anything now. It had never been my place. Still wasn't.

Eventually Bowen noticed as well and announced Addie needed to sit and rest. Paisley guided her to the front row of white chairs which had been reserved for close friends and family. As they approached, a wave of WBRA bull riders stood in unison, some pulling off their hats in respect and nodding to her before sitting back down.

That was where I should have been. Standing up there, paying my respects beside the guys I rode with. But instead, I was at the back of the crowd, hiding. Like a pussy.

Addie smiled at them, but it didn't reach her eyes. In fact, it was barely more than a grimace. Her shoulders were stiff, and her gaze wandered. I took another step back, making sure I was well hidden in the crowd, but with the tiniest of gaps so I could still watch her.

"Where's Kai?" she asked.

My heart stopped.

"Flew back to the States already." Bowen's mouth pulled into a hard line.

Addie recoiled as if Bowen had physically slapped her. "What? When? He needs to be here."

"All I know is I got a message from him yesterday saying he was going home, and he'd see me on the American leg of the tour if I made it out there."

Addie went quiet. But a frown creased Paisley's forehead as she questioned her fiancé further. "He was Sunny's best friend. He couldn't wait one more day and come to his memorial service?"

Pain sliced through me, quick and sharp, opening up the internal wounds I'd barely begun to heal from. Paisley was right. I was a grade A asshole. But I just couldn't face them. Not after what I'd done. I didn't deserve to sit up there with Sunny's friends and fans like I had a right to be there.

Like I hadn't been the one who'd killed him.

Brad stepped forward to a microphone on a stand and adjusted it to suit his towering frame. The low murmur of conversation stopped, and the crowd gave him their attention.

"I'd like to thank you all for coming today. It is with heavy hearts that we pay our last respects to Sunny Burke. Sunny's death in a tragic car accident late last year saddens us all and devastates our rodeo family. We thank the Lord for keeping two other riders safe—Kai Hunt and Deacon Ashford, as well as Miss Stacey Burns and Sunny's girl-friend, Miss Addie St. Clair."

I dug my toe into the dirt, praying it would open and swallow me whole. This was exactly why I'd told everyone I wasn't going to the memorial. I didn't want anyone focusing on me, when they should have been focusing on my best friend, who was still lying in a morgue, waiting to be sent back home to his mother in Texas so she could bury his body. There was nothing that could be done about that, but this day was supposed to be about him and remembering the amazing guy he'd been.

Not thanking the Lord because I was still alive when I had no right to be breathing.

It should have been me who'd died. I *wished* it had been me.

Brad called Bowen and Deacon up to the microphone, and the two of them launched into reminiscing about good times with Sunny—about the time he'd gotten bucked clear over the safety rail but somehow managed to land on his feet. About the times we'd spent hanging out and barbecuing around a firepit at Bowen's place in the country. About how happy he'd been when Addie had agreed to go out with him that first time.

I let the words wash over me, allowing myself to remember all those good times, because I'd been there with Sunny through them all. Each one ripped me open inside, but I welcomed it. I listened intently to every memory the two guys shared, then mentally added more of my own. From the first time Sunny and I had met as stupid fifteen-year-olds on the junior circuit. To the last moments, when I'd looked in the rearview mirror as the car spun out of control and seen the fear in my best friend's eyes.

My lungs and chest ached, and I realized with a jolt that I'd been holding my breath. I'd found myself doing that often since the accident. I let it out, then gulped in a lungful of fresh, clean air, almost hating I was able to when he wasn't.

The weight of someone watching forced me to look up, and my gaze collided with Addie's through the gap of people. Her deep-brown, intelligent eyes flashed in recognition, then widened in surprise. She raised her hand and opened her mouth to call out to me.

And like the pathetic coward I was, I turned and stalked away.

2

ADDIE

*P*aisley and Bowen hovered in the hall until I'd managed to get my apartment door open. Paisley worried her bottom lip with her teeth, biting down on it hard enough I was concerned she'd draw blood.

"Seriously. I'll be fine," I assured her.

Her expression didn't change, but she stepped in and gave me a tight hug. "We're just a phone call away if you need us, okay? You make sure you call if you need so much as the TV remote passed to you."

"Thank you. You guys have been too good to me." They really had.

I'd spent the long drive from the city, sleeping on the back seat of Bowen's four-wheel drive. They'd carried my bags, bought me food, and now they were here clucking over me like mother hens.

Bowen stretched his arms above his head. "I'm so glad to be out of the city. I miss my bulls and fresh air."

I had no affinity for bulls but I agreed about the fresh air. The thought surprised me. All through the years I'd lived in tiny, dead-end Lorrington, I'd dreamed about getting out.

All I'd wanted to do was move to the city and leave my past in the dusty dirt of the country town I'd always hated.

A stab of guilt hit me in the gut, and a little voice in my head questioned—not for the first time—if that was why I'd agreed to date Sunny in the first place. He'd swept into my life, a whirlwind of confidence and personality. He was tall, handsome, and wealthy. He was everything I wasn't and yet somehow still interested in me.

I'd convinced myself there could be something more than friendship between us. Because I had wanted to believe that. So badly. I'd wanted an epic romance, and a Prince Charming who stole me away from the drudgery of small-town life.

Bowen was looking at me oddly, and I realized it had been too long since I'd spoken. They probably wanted to get back to their kids, and I really wanted to be alone. My legs were getting wobbly again, and a headache built behind my eyes. I needed to lie down.

I wrapped my shaky fingers around the wood of the open door and faked a yawn that quickly turned into a real one.

Paisley got the hint immediately. She grabbed Bowen by the hand and tugged him toward the exit. But her gaze pinned me as she moved. "I mean it. You call me. You are not being a bother. We're only a thirty-minute drive away at the ranch."

I nodded to appease her, though I knew I wouldn't call. I closed the door and just in time, because my legs suddenly felt like they were made from lead. Avoiding my reflection in the mirror opposite the door, I slid down the wall, collapsing on the thick-pile carpet in relief, without even turning on a light.

My head thunked back against the wood, and I closed

my eyes, wishing I could just sleep there. Getting to the bedroom, and out of these uncomfortable funeral clothes, seemed like a Herculean task in my current state. My energy was at flat battery levels, despite the fact I'd slept for eight hours on the drive home from the city.

Images of Kai's piercing gaze flashed behind my eyelids. Those deep-blue eyes, so full of mixed emotions it was impossible to tell what he was actually feeling. Had it really been him I'd seen through the crowd?

He should have been back in the States. Or at least on a plane somewhere over the ocean. A long sigh fell from my lips, and I pressed the heels of my hands into my eyes, careful to avoid my still healing wounds, and tried to relieve the pressure of the headache.

And the images of Kai's too handsome face.

It couldn't have been him. I'd probably still had traces of painkiller in my system at the service this morning. Whatever the hospital had me doped up on had been strong. I'd spent days after the accident, drifting in and out of consciousness, and I'd seen Kai's face during that time, too. So that had to be it. The drugs made me hallucinate. And I'd hallucinated Kai.

Great. Trust my subconscious to be conjuring up images of the one man on earth who couldn't stand the sight of me.

I dragged myself to my feet and stumbled across the small living area to my single bedroom. It took twice as long as it should have, and when I got to the bed, I decided sleeping in the dress I'd worn to the memorial was actually a viable option. And maybe I'd just take the tiniest of naps before I bothered taking off my heels...

The shrill ringtone of my phone woke me sometime later. I sat up, blinked a few times, trying to clear the fuzz from my eyes, and vaguely noted it was still dark. I hadn't even bothered closing the blinds before I'd fallen into bed, and the sky had changed from that deep, dark, middle-of-the-night black, to a predawn indigo. I fumbled around the bed, searching for my phone, wishing like hell the obnoxious thing would shut up. I couldn't imagine who would be ringing me this early anyway. Except perhaps for Paisley, but when I finally found the phone and saw the name *Tony* on the caller display, I straightened my spine.

"Addison?" he asked after I hit the answer button. He hadn't even let me say hello.

"Yes?" A flicker of nervous excitement cleared the last of sleep from my foggy brain. My boss didn't make a habit of calling me when it wasn't even light outside. That had only happened a handful of times in the three years I'd worked for him. And each time, it was because a big news story had broken, and he'd needed me to report on it. But living in little Lorrington—breaking news didn't happen all that often. So mostly, my job was nine-to-five. "Is everything okay, Tony?"

His reply was brisk. "I know you're on sick leave, and I respect that. Truly, I do. So this offer comes with no expectations."

I squinted into the darkness. "Uh, okay?"

"You know we're owned by a multi-national mass media corporation?" He didn't wait for me to answer, because he knew I knew. It wasn't some dirty little secret. The corporation's logo was stamped all over our office. On our stationery, our coffee mugs, on certificates that hung in crooked frames in the reception area. "Well, one of the big bosses emailed me today. They heard about the accident."

My shoulders slumped. "And they want to do a story?" They weren't the first ones to contact me about an interview. "Look, I spoke to Deacon—he was one of the other...

survivors. He said he was going to get the WBRA to handle all of this sort of stuff."

A clicking noise came down the line, and I knew Tony was playing with the lid on his pen. He always did that when he was on the phone. I'd worked for the local newspaper and website from the time I'd left school, and we were a tiny team of four. I knew all of Tony's tics. Just like he and the other two guys we worked with knew mine.

"Yeah, see, thing is, you aren't going to want them handling this. This isn't an interview request. Well, not exactly."

I sighed. Another thing I knew about Tony was that he was a rambler, and if you didn't get him to the point quickly, you'd be stuck there all day. "So what did they want?"

"They do want the story. Rodeo is big in many parts of the US, Australia, and Brazil. But this story has gone beyond the rodeo crowd. There's been interest from outside those circles, too. People want to know what happened. It's morbid, but the accident, along with other recent events on the Australian tour, has brought the sport more attention."

I knew what he was talking about. Bowen and Paisley had been the talk of the Australian tour. Their romance, and Bowen's scuffle with a journalist which had landed him in jail, had been broadcast all over the WBRA's YouTube. Other media outlets had picked it up, and it went viral.

I shook my head even though Tony couldn't see it. "I don't think—"

"Wait! Before you say no, hear me out. They want you to write it. But not just the story of the crash. They want someone to do a yearlong feature, following the bull riders through the US tour. You'd have a spot on the US website, to talk about the rodeo, behind-the-scenes interest type stuff, how the riders are coping after losing such a prominent figure from their community..."

"A gossip column? Is that what you're saying?"

Tony's pen fiddling switched to a tapping noise. I would have bet he was at his desk, stained coffee mugs littering the surface and his inbox overflowing without me there to sort it out for him.

"Well, that's not exactly how they pitched it, but I guess so. They want you to do it, since you already have the trust and sympathy of the other riders. They're willing to send you around with the team to each event of the US leg."

My eyes widened. "The US leg runs almost a full calendar year. The finals aren't until November!"

"I didn't think that would be a problem for you. You've always talked about wanting to leave Lorrington, ever since I've known you."

I ran a hand through my messed-up hair. "Shit, Tony. Thanks for springing all this on me. Your timing isn't the best."

"I know. I know. Like I said, if you don't want it..."

I mulled over the offer for a moment. Then realized I was being ridiculous. They were going to pay me to go work in the US for almost a whole year? When else would I ever get another opportunity like this? What would I do if I said no? Wait a few more weeks until I got fully back on my feet, then return to the same boring life I'd had pre-Sunny? Desperation coursed through my veins. I didn't want to be stuck in this oppressive small town, wallowing, while everyone else went on with their lives around me.

Guilt stabbed me in the stomach again. Yeah, I'd get to go to America and travel around, write my stories, and be published on a website that actually got more traffic than the seventeen people who got their daily weather report from *The Lorrington Times*.

But Sunny wouldn't. Sunny was never going anywhere again. I didn't want to turn his death into some sort of spectacle. I didn't want to spill secrets on the people I'd made friends with, in the short time Sunny and I had been together.

"Everyone is going to say I'm selling out."

Tony sighed. His voice changed from boss to stand-in father, a role he'd played in my life more than once. "Look, Addie. Here's the thing. This is going ahead whether you say yes or no. Brad Pruitt has paid them a lot of money to take advantage of the hype already building around this. And he wants to capitalize on it as much as he can. You say no, they'll just hire someone else. You'll do this job with more compassion and respect than a stranger would. Do it. Go, and get the wanderlust out of your system. And then come back. If you want. Or don't. I don't want to lose you, but I've never thought you were made to stay here either."

I tried to imagine reading a column written by some heartless, random reporter, who didn't know or care about the guys in the rodeo. Tried to imagine someone else writing about Sunny's death, or the bond he'd had with Kai, or trying to make sense of the relationship between Sunny and me.

Tony was right. I didn't have to turn this into some gossip rag. It would be a tribute.

A stirring of excitement swirled in my belly. I liked that idea. A tribute to the man we'd lost, tasteful and informative, but fun behind-the-scenes stories about my friends who were still here. And Kai. Because Kai and I had never really been able to call ourselves friends.

Doubt crept back in. Touring with the WBRA meant

being stuck in the same hotels, same planes, same tour bus, same everything as Kai. I opened my mouth to refuse again, but Tony cut me off.

"Great! So you'll do it!"

I squeezed my eyes tight then opened them, pushing away the memory of the stony look on Kai's face the last time I'd seen him...the night he got behind the wheel of Sunny's car. No, I wasn't going to miss out on the opportunity of a lifetime just because it would mean seeing him every day. I wouldn't let him have that much power over me.

"I'm in." I glanced around the room, and for the first time, noted the complete lack of personal touches. No photos of friends. No trinkets from trips taken. I'd never really made this place a home. I wouldn't miss it in the least. "When do I leave?"

"That's the other thing," Tony said with an edge of hesitation in his voice. "You need to fly out tomorrow."

*O*n the other side of the room, groans chorused from the group of riders waiting to get back to the States. A tinny voice had just announced over the speakers that our flight was delayed by an hour, and nobody was happy about sitting in an uncomfortable airport chair any longer than they had to. Especially when we'd be sitting on planes for the best part of the next twenty-four hours, on our flight out of Australia.

I slumped in my seat, deliberately chosen for its distance from everyone else, and shoved my AirPods in my ears. I drummed my fingers on the arms of the chair, restless. Even blasting heavy rock through my skull did little to erase the thoughts of Addie. My skin felt tight, and I itched to release some of the pent-up energy. I needed to ride a bull. Or run. Or...I needed sex.

That suddenly seemed like a great idea. I just needed to screw someone else and get the inappropriate thoughts about Addie out of my head once and for all.

I switched apps and scrolled way down, looking for a

number I hadn't used in a long time. Before I could change my mind, I tapped in a message.

Flying into New York. Want to have a drink?

The three little dots that indicated a response being typed bubbled up on the screen. I waited, my breath stalling in my lungs.

Sure thing, Cowboy. Anytime. Anyplace.

Fuck.

I imagined myself rolling around the sheets with the cute redhead I'd met when I was on tour last year. It did nothing for me. And I suddenly wished I hadn't sent it at all. This was probably going to be a mistake of epic proportions that would make me feel worse than I already did. But hell. Was that even possible? Trusting my initial gut instinct, I sent back the details of the hotel I was staying at, telling her to meet me there when my flight got in.

The woman, Angeline, was a rodeo groupie. We'd had a fun couple of days, but that had been it. The tour had moved on, and I'd gone with it, leaving Angeline behind.

I hadn't thought much about her since, and I assumed she hadn't thought about me either. We'd both known what it was. A hookup. I hadn't planned to repeat it.

But hell. I couldn't stop thinking about Addie. And I needed to do something. I needed to do *someone*.

Stashing my phone away, I pulled out an iPad, balancing it on my lap. I brought up a video and hit the play button, the footage rolling on the screen. A bucking bull spun in circles, trying to dislodge the rider on its back. I let the video run through to the end, then stopped it, dragged my finger back along the progress bar and started it again, this time pausing it throughout the eight-second ride, studying the rider's form.

"Watching videos of yourself again?"

I snapped my head up. Even over the calls of the announcers in the video, with plugs in my ears, I'd heard her. And I'd recognized her voice instantly. I stared up at Addie, a small suitcase with wheels sitting beside her on the floor and a backpack slung over her shoulder. There were dark circles beneath her big eyes and gaunt hollows shaping her cheeks. My gaze drifted to the fresh gauze bandages taped to one side of her face, before I refocused.

I stared, shocked, for a good long minute. "What are you doing here?" The words came out more of a growl than I'd intended them to.

Addie visibly bristled. "Excuse me?"

I couldn't imagine a reason for her being at the airport at nearly midnight, two days after she was released from hospital. Hell, it had been barely been any time since she'd woken up from an accident that had her in and out of consciousness for days. She shouldn't even be vertical right now. She should have had nurses and doctors checking her stats and her friends fussing over her.

"I said, what are you doing here?" I forced myself to stay seated, but I had half a mind to stand, gather her up in my arms, and get the first Uber back to the hospital. And once I got there, I'd strap her to the damn hospital bed so she couldn't leave again. Not until she was one-hundred-percent well.

Addie's fingers tightened on the handle of her bag. "Catching a plane, if that wasn't obvious from the bags, the tickets in my hand, and the fact we're at an airport. But that's beside the point. What are *you* doing here?"

My leg bounced, and I closed the cover on my iPad and put it on the seat beside me to avoid dropping it onto the floor. "Waiting for my flight home. The US leg of the tour starts in a few days."

"I'm well aware of that. My point was, what are you still doing in Sydney? Bowen said you went back home already. You didn't come to the memorial..."

I shifted uncomfortably on my seat.

Her eyes narrowed. "It was you I saw, wasn't it? Why didn't you sit with the rest of us?"

I didn't say anything. What was there to say? *I didn't come sit with you because it's my fault your face is covered in bandages?*? How about how I didn't want to feel the weight of judgment from every single person in that crowd, who all knew I'd killed my best friend?

Addie huffed out a sigh when it became apparent she wasn't going to get a response from me. "Fine." She spun around and stalked away, dragging her luggage with her.

I was on my feet before I even realized what I was doing. Three long steps, and I caught up to her, yanking the suitcase out of her hand.

"Hey!" She spun around to face me and grabbed at her bags again.

My skin sparked as our fingers touched, and a jolt ran through my whole body. I snatched my hand away as if I'd been branded.

"What do you want, Kai?"

"I want you to go home. You shouldn't be here."

Her fingers balled into fists. "You're such an asshole."

People were turning in our direction. I shoved my hands in my pockets because I was afraid they might have had a mind of their own, just like my feet seemed to. I cursed myself for chasing after her in the first place. But I was right. Even now, she was swaying slightly on her feet and leaning on the handle of her suitcase so hard I thought it would collapse and she'd go down with it. Her skin was clammy, tiny beads of perspiration on her forehead, despite the cold air-conditioning. "Can you please sit down?"

But that was obviously the wrong thing to say as well.

"I think I'll stand, actually."

I ground my molars together. She was so infuriating. But short of actually throwing her over my shoulder or tying her to a seat, there really wasn't anything I could do. "Fine," I gritted out. "Suit yourself." I forced myself to turn around and take a step toward the seat where I'd abandoned my belongings.

Her angry gaze burned a hole in my back. "You're going to have to get over it," she spat at me.

I froze.

This was it. The moment I'd been dreading ever since Sunny had introduced me to her.

I'd tried so hard to hide it. But the minute I'd laid eyes on her, my heart had stopped. My mouth had dried, and Sunny had laughed and explained that my lack of words was just my personality. "We call him Frost," he'd explained to his beautiful new girlfriend. "Because he doesn't talk much to anyone. Except me."

I closed my eyes and remembered the weight of Sunny's arm over my shoulders, his other hand linked through Addie's fingers. She was so beautiful, with her long dark hair and brown skin. Her eyes were big and framed by doll-like black eyelashes. Her cheekbones were high, and her lips... fuck. I'd had so many dreams about her lips I couldn't even stand it.

But from the first moment we'd met, I'd known there was more to her than a banging body and a face that should have been on magazine covers. Her presence sparked something deep inside me. She was sweet. And kind. And her laugh was contagious.

Sunny had made her laugh all the time, and I'd let that noise rain down over me like some sort of magic potion. Even the nights where I rode like shit, when we went to a bar afterward, and she was there, everything seemed just that little bit better.

Except that it also made the whole thing worse. Because I was a dog for even allowing myself to think like that.

She was my best friend's girl. And I'd been in love with her from the minute I'd seen her. I squeezed my eyes tighter before opening them again. "Get over what?" I didn't dare turn around and face her. I was too damn ashamed.

"I know you hate me. You always have, and that's fine. He's gone, and you don't have to pretend to like me anymore."

My eyes widened. Hate her? I'd never hated anyone less in my life. I couldn't comprehend how she could think that anyone could even remotely dislike her.

I schooled my features into something colder and harder as realization spread through me. It was better like this. Better if she thought I hated her. Because I didn't ever want to see the look on her face—on anyone's face—if they realized the truth. "We're just different people." My words were as stiff and forced as the rigid muscles in my back and shoulders.

She shifted behind me, and I longed to turn around and look at her. I was worried about how long she'd been standing, and a new wave of guilt consumed me. She would have sat down already if I'd just left her alone.

We'd all be better off if I just left her alone.

"You're going to have to get used to seeing me."

I whirled around, no longer able to keep my back to her. Panic churned in my gut. "What does that mean?"

Her mouth pulled into a tight line. "You'll see soon enough."

With that, she walked away to a cluster of seats by a window. This time, I let her go.

4

ADDIE

*L*ong flights weren't something I had any experience with. It wasn't like any of my foster parents had ever nudged me awake one morning with a bright smile and excitedly whispered, "Guess what, sweetheart? We're going on holiday!"

The best I could hope for in those days was a shove and a grunted, "Get out of bed. I'm not driving you to school if you miss the bus."

The first and only time I'd ever been on a plane was when Sunny had taken me away to a rodeo in Melbourne. But that flight had been so short, I'd barely had a chance to look out the window and then we were there.

This flight, though? This was the flight that never ended. The sun rose over the ocean, and I marveled at its beauty, but my delight had been short-lived. The hours seemed to stretch out to double the regular length, and nothing I tried made the minutes pass any quicker. I shifted and twisted in my seat, my tailbone aching and my muscles cramped. I'd tried to read, but I couldn't focus on the words. I'd tried doing a bit of writing on my laptop, but the sentences I tapped in were bland. And I'd tried sleeping. I was so tired. But every time I closed my eyes, all I saw was Kai's scowling face.

He was a few rows behind me—I knew because I'd caught a glimpse of him when I'd gone to the bathroom. But I'd quickly looked away, refusing to make eye contact. Even though I couldn't see him from my seat, I could *feel* him. He was so close, and trying to sleep, knowing he was there, was the most distracting thing in the world. Was he sleeping? Watching more of his rides? Was he thinking about me?

I swallowed thickly. He'd made it pretty clear that if he was thinking about me, it wasn't in a friendly way. I pulled my shoulders back. It didn't matter what he thought about me anyway. I was here to do a job. And I was going to do it well.

As soon as I'd found a bed and slept for a hundred hours.

I'd never felt more relieved than when we touched down at Newark Airport. The bump and grind of the wheels hitting the runway on US soil was music to my ears. The moment the safety light blinked off, I unclicked my seat belt and hauled my carry-on luggage out of the overhead compartment. Uncaring if I seemed rude, I made a beeline for the exit. My breath came in short rasps. As if my body realized I would soon be out in the big wide world again, the plane suddenly felt tiny and suffocating. I tugged at the neck of my hoodie, heat prickling at my skin.

"You okay, love?" an older woman with a British accent asked. She had kind eyes, lined at the corners with age. Her gaze raked over me, true concern furrowing her brow.

I nodded, but my tongue was thick, and I couldn't form a reply. Hot air swirled around me as I edged toward the doors, only increasing the stuffy atmosphere. Once I made it into the tunnels that took us inside the airport, I breathed a little easier, but my steps were slow and my feet as heavy as lead. I shuffled along in the crowd, grateful when they led me to the baggage claim because I hadn't had the energy to work out where that was.

Realization hit me, sharp and dizzying. Without any sort of planning, I'd hopped on a plane and traveled across to the other side of the world. My knees buckled at the enormity of that realization. And though exhaustion kept threatening to pull me down, I knew I had to keep moving. I just had to put one foot in front of the other and get to...get to where, exactly? I stopped and glanced around. People bustled everywhere, and they all seemed to know exactly what they were doing. While I stood alone, staring with eyes the size of saucers and a sinking gut feeling that I'd bitten off more than I could chew. I tried to take a deep breath, but it ended up being more like a short gasp for air. I dropped my backpack from my shoulder, too wobbly to hold it there any longer. Shit. I *really* needed to get to my hotel.

A warm hand brushed mine, making me jump. My backpack was pulled from my grasp, and I spun, ready to take on whoever was trying to rob me, when I recognized Kai's handsome profile. He didn't say anything. Didn't even look at me. Just hoisted my bag onto his back and gently pried the suitcase from my other hand.

I followed him through customs, without saying a word. I was more tired and weak than I'd ever been in my life, and while I didn't normally need anyone taking care of me, I wasn't naïve enough to think I had this situation under control. I'd only been released from hospital a few days ago, and in those few days, I'd attended a memorial for someone I cared about deeply, and then a day later, I'd jumped on a twenty-hour flight. Not exactly everyday occurrences. So I cut myself some slack. And I let Kai help me.

"Thank you," I said quietly, as he set my bags down outside in a pickup area.

He finally glanced over at me. "Please don't."

"Don't thank you?"

He nodded.

"Why not?"

He shoved his hands in his pockets again. "Because I don't deserve it."

I didn't know what he meant by that, and my foggy brain struggled to think it through. Why was he always so confusing? He spoke in riddles I never had the answers to.

Pain pierced through my skull, and I rocked backward, catching myself at the last moment.

"Whoa." Kai's strong fingers wrapped around my upper arm.

I glanced down at his pale hand, so different to my own. I wondered how he spent so much time outdoors, yet never seemed to have much of a tan. I swayed in his grasp again, my head swimming.

"I need to find my hotel...so tired..."

Black spots danced at the edges of my vision, and the last thing I saw before my eyes rolled back was Kai's panic. It was the same expression I'd seen on his face the night we got in a car together. The same night that car had crashed, killing my boyfriend, and his best friend. But my brain tapped out, and my worries fled.

5

ADDIE

*B*lurry. Everything was blurry. I blinked a few times experimentally, but grit coated my eyes, and my lids were too heavy to keep open. I tried lifting a hand, but a tug, followed by a sharp sting, made that too much effort. Instead, I dropped my arm, and it bounced off something soft. Flashes of light pricked behind my eyelids, and my heart sped up.

It was happening again.

The flash of the other car's headlights and the sickening crunch and spin as we were hit. Screams in the back seat, and Kai...that look on Kai's face as he reached for me.

A band tightened around my chest, choking off my oxygen supply. I gasped for air but I couldn't breathe. I tried to see through the darkness, but there was nothing. Fear churned my stomach, until I wanted to vomit just to ease the sensation.

"Hey, ssshh. You're okay," a familiar voice said through the haze of dark and light and terror.

Kai.

Déjà vu rushed in on me. His voice was always there in

the void. I blinked again, and his features swam in front of me, just like they had so many times before. He smiled, and my heart slowed down. Every time I saw his face through the haze, the band around my chest eased a little. But I knew now that he wasn't *really* here. Kai wouldn't have smiled at me in real life.

But he felt real in my head.

"You're always here," I murmured.

His face moved closer. His jaw was strong and stubbled. His eyes so blue. So different to mine. But I'd always thought them beautiful. They suited him. Sunny and the other guys called him Frost. Frost and his frosty blue eyes. "You're always here when I'm hurt," I repeated.

His presence inside my head was like a warm blanket, wrapping around me and keeping me safe. I liked it.

But when I blinked again, his beautiful smile had turned dark. His lips pulled tight, then down, and he backed away until I could only see him out of the corner of my eye.

The room came back into focus in a blinding blur, but when it cleared, it focused on Kai, hunched in a chair. He wouldn't meet my eye.

I groaned as pain slammed around my skull. Lifting one hand to my aching head, I realized the tug and sting I'd felt before was a cannula and an attached IV tube. I ripped it out.

"What?" I asked at Kai's disapproving look. That was more like it. The only expression he wore around me was grump.

"You needed that. You were dehydrated."

I shifted back against the stiff white pillows and glanced down my body, relieved to find I was still dressed in the hoodie and leggings I'd worn on the plane. I ignored Kai's comment. "What happened? Last thing I remember is waiting for a cab and then…this." I prodded at my head and winced.

Kai's eyes were stormy. "You passed out. I didn't catch you quick enough, and you hit your head on the concrete."

I gazed around at my surroundings, taking in the white walls and the row of portable machines lined against one wall. "So you brought me to the hospital? In America?" The last part of the sentence came out slightly hysterical.

Kai folded his arms across his chest. "Would you have preferred I just step over you and go on my merry way?"

I scowled back at him. "Of course not." But I was shuddering to think how much this was going to cost. Did my contract with the WBRA cover hospital visits on the very first day? Did I have some sort of travel insurance? Hell. I didn't even officially start until tomorrow. I sighed heavily and sank back into the mattress.

As soon as my head hit the pillow, though, I jerked upright. The hazy state I'd been in as I'd first woken up… I'd been talking. And I'd seen Kai's face… Heat rose in my cheeks. Shit. What had I said?

Kai was still doing that intense watching thing he did while studying bulls. I'd always found it fascinating when he'd gone into these little trances. Once, Sunny and I had had a full conversation across him, poking fun of the way he concentrated so hard while everybody around him was goofing around and having a good time. It seemed silly and immature now, when he stared at me with that same intensity.

"Do you know where my phone is?" I asked, desperate for something to do with my hands. And equally keen for a reason to look away from him. "I need to check my work emails. What time is it?"

"Eight-ish. You were out for a while."

I blanched. "Have you been here that whole time?"

He shrugged.

"Sorry. You probably had plans. I'm sure sitting in the hospital all day babysitting me wasn't part of them."

"It's fine. My plans were easily canceled."

He seemed sincere, but I felt bad anyway. He lifted my purse from the back of his chair. "You should call your folks. I tried, but your phone is locked, and I didn't know the password."

"No need. No one to call."

I riffled through my purse and pulled out my phone, using my thumbprint to turn off the lock.

"Oh, I'm sorry." Kai's voice was polite. "I didn't realize they'd passed."

I shrugged. "They haven't. Well, maybe they have, I don't know. I grew up in foster care. I never met my real parents. Not that I can remember anyway."

"You never mentioned that before."

"Not exactly something I bring up at the pub after the rodeo."

He was shaking his head. "No, but Sunny never said anything..."

"Sunny didn't know either."

He cocked his head but remained silent.

I didn't have anything more to say about that, and I didn't dare look up at Kai's expression. It would either be the permanently grumpy scowl he always wore around me. Or he'd pity me like everybody else did, when they found out my parents had abandoned me at a local fire station when I was barely a month old. Nobody liked hearing the story of the little aboriginal girl who grew up, bouncing from house to house, never really finding a home with any of them. I'd been on the receiving end of those stares my entire life, and they did nothing but piss me off. I might have had nothing and come from no one, but that wasn't going to be my future. That was why I'd taken the job at the newspaper, and why I'd accepted this assignment. This was my chance. I was on the other side of the world, in a huge country full of possibilities, with real options for the first time in my life.

So I didn't need Kai's or anyone else's pity. I just needed to write amazing pieces each week and make a name for myself. That I could do.

I poked the email app, and as I'd expected, there was an inbox full of mail from Tony. The first one was a forward from our head office, with Interview Subjects as the title.

I opened the email eagerly and skimmed over the polite opening paragraph. *Below, please find a list of interviews we'd like you to set up and conduct while you're on the tour.*

The very first name—Kai Hunt.

I blew out a heavy breath through my teeth and glanced over at the man in question. Of course Kai was the first on the list. He was at the center of the entire drama, and I'd known this was coming. Might as well get it over with.

"Kai, I—"

"Hello, Miss St. Clair. I'm Dr. Lyons. Gave yourself a nasty bump on the head there, didn't you?"

I reluctantly turned to the middle-aged doctor and forced a smile. "Guess so."

"So we just need to take you down for a CT scan—"

"Ah, no thanks."

The doctor's bushy gray eyebrows pulled together in a frown. I would have put money on Kai's expression matching, if I'd been game to peer over at him. Which I wasn't.

"It is a little loud and uncomfortable, but it's important to take precautions to ensure there's no bleeding on your brain." The doctor had obviously practiced his disappointed parent face earlier and had no qualms about using it on me now.

Dollar signs swam in front of my eyes. Dollars I didn't have. I didn't dare get any tests done until I spoke to Tony and worked out whether my medical bills would be covered.

I threw the white hospital blankets off and swung my legs over the side of the bed. Where the hell were my shoes? I ignored Kai, whose disapproval practically vibrated off him. The doctor watched in quiet confusion while I hunted around the floor for my sneakers.

"I need to leave," I explained. "Just give me whatever papers you need me to sign and I'll be out of your hair."

"No," the doctor and Kai said at the same time.

Irritation with the two of them rose from the soles of my bare feet and spread through me like a wildfire. I glared at Kai.

"Thank you for bringing me in, but you have no say in what I do." I turned back to the doctor before Kai's expression could change. "I'll come straight back if anything weird happens, okay? I feel fine." Apart from the stabbing headache, but whatever.

The doctor frowned again, but with unease stamped all over his forehead, he pulled some papers from the back of a clipboard attached the foot of my bed. He gave me a stern look. "Fine. But at the first sign of nausea, dizziness—anything out of the ordinary—you come straight back."

"Deal."

"And you have someone stay with you. You shouldn't be alone."

"There's no one—"

"I'll do it."

My mouth dropped open. "No, you—"

"Great," the doctor said, nodding at Kai as if I hadn't

even spoken. "She shouldn't be alone for the next twenty-four hours."

"Excuse me, but—"

"Not a problem." Kai stood from his chair and crossed the space, holding a hand out for the doctor to shake.

"Does anybody care what I want here?" I demanded.

"No," the doctor and Kai said in unison.

Dr. Lyons' lips curled up in the corner like the whole situation amused him. But Kai's expression was as rigid as ever. I huffed out a breath and shoved my feet into my sneakers. Kai picked up our bags, like it was no big deal, and stalked out the door without another glance in my direction. I snatched my purse up and stomped over to where the doctor held a pen and clipboard, ready for me to sign my life away. He reeked of smugness.

"You do realize what you've done here, don't you?" I muttered.

The older man grinned. "Just making sure my patient doesn't die from stubbornness."

I glared at him and hurried to sign my name before shoving it back in his direction. "You've just created my worst nightmare."

6

KAI

*B*y the time Addie made it out to the street, I already had a cab waiting. She slid into the back seat and slammed the door, while the driver and I tossed bags into the trunk. One look at her expression through the lightly tinted windows told me I'd get my hand bitten off if I dared to sit beside her, so instead, I made a beeline for the passenger seat.

"Where to?"

I let Addie answer, since I had no idea of her travel plans. "Paragon Hotel."

Surprise had me cocking an eyebrow. Well, that worked out well. Because it was the same hotel the WBRA had booked for the riders on the tour. I didn't dare tell Addie, though, because with the way her eyes burned a hole in my back, she might just change her reservation. If I could keep her close, perhaps I could keep an eye on her longer than just tonight.

For Sunny's sake. He would have wanted me to watch out for her.

The driver kept up a steady stream of conversation,

which was good, because I didn't feel like talking. And Addie was about as talkative as a rock in the back seat, though her silent anger spoke volumes. My phone kept buzzing with questions from Angeline over why I'd canceled our hookup plans, but I ignored them all. It had been a ridiculous idea anyway.

We arrived at our destination, and I tipped the driver before grabbing the luggage from the rear of the car. I let Addie snatch her pull-along suitcase because she wouldn't have to shoulder the weight, but she huffed loudly when I wouldn't give up her backpack. Even if she hadn't been under the weather, my mom had taught me manners.

She stalked up the steps, disappearing through the glass doors. I caught up to her at reception, waiting while she checked in, then followed her to the elevators. With an outstretched finger, she jabbed the button, and the doors slid shut, enclosing the two of us in a metal box.

I forced myself to stare straight ahead, but it was a battle I was scared I was going to lose. Just like every other time I'd been alone with her, that urge to reach out and take her hand, or brush a strand of hair from her face was strong. It was why I'd always avoided being alone with her. I would never betray my best friend, but something about her drew me in like a magnet. And it ate me up inside that I could harbor feelings for her. Feelings that were all fucking wrong.

I squeezed my eyes shut. But even with my eyes closed, I still knew exactly how beautiful she was. I still knew the way her hair curled slightly when it brushed over her shoulders. I knew the sweet flare of her hips when she wore a tight dress to a nightclub. I knew the sparkle she got in her deep-brown eyes when she was teasing me and thought I hadn't noticed.

But I always noticed. I noticed everything about her.

Everything you shouldn't notice about a woman your best friend liked. Or maybe loved. Had Sunny loved Addie? I had no idea. Fuck, what did it matter? She was his, even now.

The bell on the elevator chimed at the exact same second my heart splintered. I was never going to see her again after tonight. Why would I? She'd go back to Australia at the end of her trip, and I'd keep touring through the US until I won the championship. Or until a bull took me out. Whichever came first.

I was so lost in my thoughts; Addie was halfway down the hallway before I caught up to her. I stopped while she swiped her access card, and after she opened the door, I followed her inside the dimly lit room. It was late afternoon, and through large windows, the neighboring skyscrapers cast long shadows. I placed our bags down by a small kitchenette and went back to close the door behind me.

"What are you doing?" Addie demanded.

My hand paused on the handle. "Closing the door?"

"Why are you closing it with you on this side, though?"

I sighed. "Because I'm staying with you. You heard the doctor."

"I heard you and the doctor making decisions and not giving me a say in them."

"We gave you a say. You had the choice to stay, get your head checked, and have professional medical staff keep an eye on you. You didn't take it, so now you're stuck with me for twenty-four hours."

Her mouth dropped open. "You can't be serious."

"Have you ever known me to joke?" I was hardly known for my sense of humor.

She threw her hands up in the air. "You're impossible."

I pressed my lips together. If anyone was impossible it

was her. I shut the door firmly, while she folded her arms over her chest.

"There's only one bed."

"Happy to sleep on the couch."

We both looked over at it. It was a small love seat.

I knew instantly that my six foot one frame was never going to fit on it. "Or the floor."

She rolled her eyes. "Suit yourself. I'm going to bed."

"You're tired? That's not good."

She held up a hand. "Don't even, Dr. Kai. It's not a concussion. I just didn't get any rest on the plane, so apart from however long I was unconscious, I haven't slept in days. I'm going to sleep."

"Fine."

"Fine!"

Fantastic. We'd resorted to twelve-year-old-style arguing. Great start. Addie riffled through her suitcase and after pulling some clothes out, made her way to the only door in the room, which presumably led to the bathroom. I sank down on the couch and groaned at how hard it was. Behind the closed door, the shower turned on, and I let my head fall back, staring at the ceiling, refusing to think about Addie getting naked, water dripping down her lithe body...

Shit. It was going to be a long night.

7

ADDIE

*M*y hotel room wasn't exactly big to begin with, but with Kai's oversized body hanging around, it felt even smaller. I was still annoyed he'd followed me home like a stray dog, but after a hot shower, where I finally got to wash all the plane grime from my body, I was minutely less testy with him. After all, he had spent hours sitting in the hospital with me, and now he was here, trying to look after me even though he had to have other things to do.

I ignored my rumbling stomach and slid down into the silky sheets of the bed, hissing in pleasure at how good they felt. I could eat later. Right now, all that mattered was sleep. I was vaguely aware of Kai taking a shower, but I was completely dead to the world by the time he emerged.

Sometime later, a delicious scent wafted around my nose, waking me from my dreams. My stomach rumbled so loud I wouldn't have been surprised if they'd heard it back home in Australia. I blinked sleepily and caught sight of a man hovering over me.

I skittered backward, pulling the sheet up around my

chin, even though I was fully dressed in long-sleeved pajamas beneath it. "What are you doing!"

Kai held up one hand in mock surrender, but the other held a takeout container with a plastic fork sticking out of the top. "Your stomach sounds like a jet engine revving up for takeoff. I could hear it from the couch. So I ordered food."

"Oh my God, is that Chinese?"

He nodded, holding it in my direction.

"For me?"

He nodded again.

"Oh my God, I love you." I scampered across the bed and snatched it from his hands. Delicious chicken covered in thick, sweet syrup sat in the box, just waiting for me to devour it. I scarfed it down, barely stopping to chew. "Best meal ever," I mumbled in between sticky mouthfuls.

I made short work of almost the entire container before I stopped and realized he was watching me. Reluctantly, I held it out to him. "Sorry. Did you want some? I should have already asked that. But honey chicken is my favorite."

The corner of his mouth lifted. "I know. "

There was a beat of silence between us. Then he rushed to fill it. "Anyway, that's why I had it hovering under your nose. When the delivery guy knocking on the door didn't wake you, I got worried you might have passed out again."

"And you thought chicken might revive me?" I grinned, then stabbed another forkful of fried meat.

He shrugged, red flushing his pale cheeks. "I didn't think you'd appreciate me shaking you awake."

He was probably right there.

"How are you feeling?"

"Tired still." I held up my hand. "But before you get all frowny again, I feel good otherwise. Headache is gone."

"That's something."

I nodded and glanced around the room. It was darker than when I'd gone to sleep. The only light now was cast by two lamps on hallway tables. "What time is it?"

"Late."

"It's still the fifteenth, though, right?"

"Barely."

My eyelids were getting heavy again, now that my belly was full. "I've got to get up for work in a few hours."

Kai took the empty container from my hand and walked it back to the silver garbage can in the kitchen. "I've got a meeting in the morning, too. My alarm is set for seven. That work for you?"

His meeting was likely the same one I was going to...the one downstairs in the conference room, where Brad Pruitt would inform all the riders I was tagging along for the next few months, in order to spill all the behind-the-scenes secrets. Knowing Brad, he'd put some sort of spin on it that made it sound like a great opportunity. Some of the group wouldn't mind. Many of the guys were young and all over social media. They'd welcome the chance to grab more Instagram followers.

But Kai wouldn't.

I bit my lip. I should tell him. But what was I supposed to say? *Hey, you're stuck with me for months, while I write a big exposé, primarily focused on you and the fact you were driving the car when your best friend was killed!*

I couldn't tell him that. Not at midnight, after he'd spent all day caring for me. He'd actually sort of cracked a smile just now. Though I knew it was gutless, I was just too tired to get into another argument with him. So instead, I confirmed that seven was fine for the alarm and laid back down in my bed. Kai padded over to the lamps and switched them off, plunging the room into a near complete darkness.

But as tired as I was, sleep wouldn't come easily this time. I stared at the ceiling, mind whirling and gut churning with nerves about tomorrow and how my new assignment would be received. Guilt ate away at me, and I questioned once more if I'd done the right thing. Tony's warning that if I didn't write it, someone else would, kept coming back to me, and again, I convinced myself this was the right thing to do. Not just for me but for everyone.

Kai tossing and turning on a too-small couch only intensified my guilt. I hated what I was going to do to him. I knew he would despise any sort of media attention. He barely tolerated it when it was solely focused on his rides. Any focus on his personal life would be an automatic no go. I knew that. He was so different from Sunny. Sunny would have lapped it up. But I knew it was only going to push Kai deeper into his shell.

"Kai?" I said into the darkness.

The writhing on the couch stopped. "I thought you were asleep."

"No."

"You should be."

"You should be, too." I paused. "Will you please just come sleep in the bed? You're about a foot too long for that couch, and I feel horrible about it."

There was a beat of silence, then, "I'm fine."

I blew out a breath through my teeth. He wasn't fine. He'd been in an accident recently, and though I'd been unconscious at the time, Paisley had told me he'd had a pretty severe case of whiplash that had resulted in a neck brace for a few days. Sleeping on a cramped couch couldn't be doing anything good to that injury.

"You're not. Just come sleep in the bed, would you? It's big, and if you're really that worried about sleeping next to me, I'll build a pillow wall between us."

A soft snort came from his dark shadow, but then he was moving toward me. The closer he came, the more of him I could see, illuminated only by the tiny strip of outside light coming in around the edge of the blackout curtains. His sweatpants were loose and I swallowed hard when I realized he didn't have a shirt on. Light from the city street outside fell over his bare chest and abs, and I scooted away from him to the far side of the bed. I grabbed an extra pillow, wedging it in the middle.

He raised an eyebrow. "You weren't joking about the pillow wall, then?"

I shook my head but didn't reply because I was suddenly finding it hard to form words. I couldn't remember ever seeing him without a shirt on. Like all the guys, he lived in a uniform of dusty blue jeans, boots, and T-shirts. It wasn't like he was bull riding bare-chested...though something deep within me warmed at that thought. He would look damn good on the back of a bull, with his abs contracting and his biceps popping.

I squeezed my eyes tight shut as the mattress dipped on his side. What was wrong with me? It'd barely been a month since I'd lost Sunny, and here I was, checking out his best friend. I was the worst sort of person. Who did that?

The sort of person who was never in love, a voice whispered in my head. And I knew it was right. Sunny and I hadn't been in love. We'd never promised each other anything. We'd had fun, and I liked him, a lot. But that was all we'd been. There was a reason neither of us had ever said I love you. There was a reason neither of us had ever pinned the other one down for a commitment. He'd never called me his girlfriend. For a little while, I'd thought I'd wanted that. But as we got to know each other, it had become more and more apparent that we were great friends, who fell into bed together.

Then, he'd died.

Kai lay down beside me, on his side of the pillow wall. At last, he was still, his big body stretching almost the full length of the bed. But it was a long time before either of us fell asleep.

8

KAI

$\mathcal{F}$ ighting through a blurry haze, I blinked my eyes open. I couldn't have been asleep long, because the room was still as dark as when I'd crawled into Addie's bed at midnight. But something had woken me. I tried shifting on the mattress, but I was pinned down by a weight that hadn't been there as I'd drifted off. One side of my body was warmer than the other.

I inhaled sharply.

Addie.

Our pillow wall had disappeared, and she was tucked against my chest, her head on my biceps. I widened my eyes, staring down at her. I didn't dare move. Instead, I just let my gaze wander over her. Her long hair spilled around her head and over my skin, soft as freaking silk. I longed to pick up strands of it and swirl it through my fingers. Her dark lashes fanned out over her cheeks, and the scent of the hotel shampoo, mixed with something that I'd always associated with Addie, swirled around my nose. My heart constricted. The heating in the room wasn't great, and I knew she'd likely gotten cold, unconsciously seeking out a heat source. I always got hot when I slept, which was why, even in winter, I slept naked. Not that I was going to do that in Addie's room, so I'd fished out a pair of sweats. But now I wished I'd put a T-shirt on, too. Because the feel of her hands resting on my bare skin was almost more than I could handle. My dick was so hard, it was probably tenting the sheets. I shifted my hips away from her, mortified to think she might wake up and find me like that.

Shit. What was I supposed to do? I should move her, shouldn't I? This was all sorts of wrong.

But she needed sleep, and I hated the thought she might have been cold. I closed my eyes and tried to still the pounding of my heart. I was such a liar. They weren't the only reasons I didn't want to move.

I liked having her wrapped around me. I liked she was so close I could feel her warm breath misting over my skin.

Right or wrong, I wasn't moving. So I let the feel of Addie pressed to my chest send me off to sleep.

Hours later, the alarm went off, blaring a painfully annoying beeping sound straight through my skull. I jolted, blindly reaching out to shut off the offending device. With a rush, last night came back to me. Addie curled up against me. Long limbs draped over mine. Her plump lips mere inches from my skin. My eyes flew open, light flooding in, blinding me. But as the glare cleared, there was no beautiful woman in the bed beside me. The spot she'd lain in last night was now nothing but rumpled sheets. I smoothed a hand over them, but they were cold.

"Addie?" I called into the silence. I listened for running water in the bathroom, but there was nothing. I got up and stumbled toward the door, but when I knocked, there was no reply.

She was gone.

I sighed. It was probably better. I needed to get ready for a meeting with the rest of the team anyway. And if she wasn't here, that meant she was conscious and walking around, so maybe she didn't need those head scans after all.

I showered, dressed, and then hung around the room until the very last second, in the hope she might come back. At two minutes to nine, I gave up any chance of seeing her again and headed for the elevators that would take me downstairs to the conference room. I'd have to go back to her room later to pick up my luggage, so maybe if I timed it right, I'd get a glimpse of her then.

I berated myself as I walked. She had a meeting at nine. It was stupid to have hung around so long that I almost made myself late. I wondered what her work assignment was. She worked for a local newspaper. I read her articles on their website each week. She reported on things like football team matchups, and a local resident who had celebrated her one hundredth birthday. Those things could have bored me to tears, but she wrote with compassion and heart, and somehow, always managed to make me feel something, even over the most mundane of local topics.

Wandering into the conference room, I picked up a cinnamon roll from a table and nodded gratefully when a hotel employee offered to pour me a cup of coffee. I slunk into a seat at the back of the room and chewed my pastry, trying to clear my mind of all things Addie St. Clair. For the first time since landing back on US soil, I turned my thoughts to the whole reason I'd come home. The new bull riding season would kick off at Madison Square Garden in two days' time. And I had every intention of winning the round and starting my year right.

The other guys milled around me, some of them clapping me on the shoulder and saying hello. I nodded to each of them but didn't strike up a conversation. This was nothing new, and they were used to it. The only one who had never taken my silences at face value had been Sunny. He'd plonked himself down beside me the day we'd met and talked my damn ear off. Never once had he thought I might not want to be his friend. He just assumed we were and went on telling me his every secret until I knew more about him than I did anyone else. And somewhere along the way, I'd started telling him about me, too. I glanced over at the empty seat next to me. We were never going to do that again. He'd never slide in the chair I'd kept for him, his long legs all gangly like a newborn foal. He was never going to talk my ear off while Brad droned on about whatever bull riding business we were there to discuss. Tears pricked the backs of my eyes, and I looked away. Next time, I'd sit somewhere else. With Johnny or Deacon or one of the other guys. Anything to avoid having an empty seat beside me.

At the front of the room, Brad clapped his big hands together. "All right."

His drawl was so Southern I was sure sometimes he put it on. I was from the Southern states, too, but his accent was overstated. Just like he was. Everything about Brad Pruitt was larger than life and over the top.

"Now, I hope you had a good break and are ready to get back into it. You weren't all in Australia, but I dare say you've heard about Sunny by now, so this shouldn't come as a surprise. I want to have a minute's silence in respect of the loss of one of our own. Sunny was a damn good bull rider and a crowd favorite. I know they're all going to miss him, just as each and every one of us here will."

Around me, heads nodded. Some were probably swiveling in my direction. My stomach churned, and I stared down at my hands, determined not to make eye contact with anyone. I feared what I'd find there. Pity? Anger? I didn't know which was worse. My skin prickled with rising anxiety.

The minute of silence felt like forever, and I was glad, for once, when Brad started talking again.

"Now, in the face of this tragedy, I want us all to rise up, stronger than ever. The accident and Sunny's death has brought a lot of curiosity. And instead of letting rumors flare, I wanted to get ahead of the beast. *Daily News International* reached out over the break and expressed interest in what we're doing here. They wanted press access to do some stories. Behind-the-scenes type stuff, that will bring you all more publicity. And more publicity means bigger sponsorship deals. And what does that mean? Yep. More money in your back pocket."

What the fuck? Irritation burned hot at the back of my neck. The room broke out into ripples of chatter, mostly from the younger guys who would lap up the attention. I sought out some of the more seasoned riders, to take in their reactions, but none of them seemed particularly upset by this news either.

It was just me. I wasn't naïve. I read between Brad's well-thought-out lines.

They wanted to do a gossip segment. And considering my accident was the biggest news in rodeo right now, I could guess where they would want to start. Bubbles of anger boiled in my veins. Brad had to be kidding if he thought I was going to agree to this. Because I wasn't.

As if he'd read my mind, he searched around the crowd, his gaze landing on me, and said, "I'll expect all of you to be on your best behavior and to answer any questions they might have. Don't forget, you all signed contracts, saying you would help promote the sport. This is part of that."

My upper lip curled in disgust. On the Australian tour, Brad had played Paisley and Bowen like a fiddle, all for the sake of publicity. And I hadn't liked it one bit, but it hadn't directly affected me, so I'd kept my mouth shut. This was different. If Brad thought he could let some reporter come in and start snooping around...

"With all that said," Brad continued, "many of you know Addie St. Clair as Sunny's girlfriend. Addie, stand on up, please."

Shock jolted through me, and I twisted my fingers into the denim of my jeans. Puzzle pieces slid into place in my head. Addie being on the same plane as the rest of the team. Addie having a room in this hotel, of all the hotels in the city. Addie saying she was here for work...

She stood slowly from a seat in the second row, and I wondered how I hadn't noticed her earlier. With reluctant steps, she walked to the front of the room to stand beside Brad, the small wave she gave to the assembled crowd awkward. She scanned the rows, freezing when she locked eyes with me. White teeth bit down on her plump bottom lip.

"Addie already worked for the media group who wanted to do the story, so she seemed like the perfect person to bring on tour with us. Whatever she wants, you give it to her, understood? If she wants to know anything from your bull riding history, right down to the color of your underwear, I don't care. You give it to her. These highlights are going to help bring people to the rodeo. And that's a good thing for all of us."

A ripple of "Yes, boss" echoed around the crowd, but I couldn't tear my eyes away from Addie. Her mouth was pulled into a grim line.

People stood and began leaving, the room rapidly emptying, but I didn't move.

The look on her face was clear for me to read.

I'm sorry.

Every muscle in my body tightened. Sorry, my ass. I pushed to my feet and stormed out of the room, not caring that the head of the WBRA was yelling my name as I did.

Whatever she wants, just give it to her.

Brad's words rolled around my head as I shoved through doors and past people who walked too slowly. When I finally made it out on the street, I sucked in a lungful of cold, New York air.

No way in hell was I giving Addie St. Clair, or anyone else, full access to my life story.

Not now. Not ever.

9

ADDIE

*T*urning my phone over in my hand, I hovered a finger between the call and message icons. I needed to interview Kai. It was the main reason I'd been sent here, but after the way he'd left the meeting this morning, I wasn't sure how that was ever going to happen.

I folded my arms on the table in my hotel room and laid my head down on top. Even hours later, I still felt like being sick every time I recalled the expression on Kai's face. I'd known he wasn't going to be happy about the extra media attention. But I hadn't anticipated the storm out, or the look of disappointment and anger he'd worn as he'd left.

I hated this. I wanted to be his friend, even though I really didn't know why. It had always bugged me that we'd never gotten along. For Sunny's sake, I'd tried to get him to open up to me. But I'd been shut down every time I'd managed to get Kai alone.

I straightened and pulled my shoulders back. I had to let all that go—this stupid need to be liked. I knew it stemmed from the way my parents had abandoned me as a baby. I'd spent my entire life trying to make people like me as a result, hoping if I could just be likable enough, maybe people wouldn't continue to leave me. I knew it wasn't healthy. But I couldn't seem to stop. And Kai was like an itch I just had to keep scratching at.

He was going to have to get used to the fact I was going to be around for a while, whether he liked me or not. I had a column to write. And he was the one rider the public would be most interested in. So that was what I was going to give them.

But I was still too chicken to call him. Instead, I brought up the message app and quickly typed in a short paragraph, asking him when we could meet for an interview. I stared at the phone for a long moment, stupidly waiting for a reply. When the screen remained blank, I sighed and put the phone down on the table.

A loud knock at the door made me jump. I scrambled over to it, a tiny ray of hope creeping in. Maybe it was Kai. I swung the door open, slightly breathless.

"Hi, Addie."

My hope blew away. Not Kai. Instead, two very tall, very handsome men stood outside my room. They both had the same dark hair, though one wore his longer, tendrils curling slightly at the back of his neck. The other had his shorn close to his scalp. They both had three-day-stubble beards, and their broad shoulders filled the doorway. When they smiled, there was a definite family resemblance.

The one who'd spoken, with the longer hair, stuck out his hand. "I'm Rem James." He jerked a thumb in the direction of the other man. "That's my brother, Abel. We're here for our interview?"

"Right! You're the, uh..." I checked my notes. "The rodeo

clowns, right? Come in." I pushed the door wider and waved a flustered hand around in the direction of the little table and the extra chairs I'd asked room service to bring me earlier.

Rem eyed me as he walked by. "You okay? If now is a bad time, we can come back..."

I smiled brightly at him. "No, don't be silly. We had an appointment. I just lost track of time." Lost track of time stressing over Kai, that was. I darted a glance to my phone, but it was still obnoxiously blank.

We all settled into chairs, and I hit record on my phone before putting it down in the center of the table. "So, rodeo clowns, huh? How does that work?"

Rem gave me an easy smile. "Actually, the term is bull-fighter."

"Oh, I'm sorry. You don't actually fight the bulls, though, right?"

Abel shook his head. "No, definitely not. Our sole job is distracting them once a rider comes off."

"I've seen you out there. You're crazier than the guys riding."

Rem grinned, brown hair flopping in his eye. "I'm not sure they all see it that way, but yeah, you have to be a bit of an adrenaline junkie to run in front of a bull who's hell-bent on goring someone."

I laughed at his casual attitude. "Is that why you do it? The rush?"

They both shrugged in unison, but it was Rem who spoke. "Good money, too. Plus, it's fun being down there. The crowd screaming, the bright lights, the traveling around and seeing the country." Rem elbowed Abel. "That, and I get to hang out with my asshole brother every day."

Abel shoved him back, but it was all in jest.

"It's really nice the two of you get to work together. And you seem to be making a bit of a splash, too. You two are popular from what I can tell. Growing quite the fan base of your own."

"It's been a gradual thing over the last few years. But yeah, we're signing autographs alongside the riders now." Abel went a faded shade of pink. "Well, a handful of autographs anyway. They were probably superfans."

I nodded, making a note on a pad of paper. "Makes sense. You guys are out in the ring the entire time. The riders are only out there for a few minutes. That's why I wanted to interview you. It's so dangerous, and there's real interest in what you do."

"The WBRA seem to think so, too. They give us microphones and headcams and everything now." Abel still looked a bit embarrassed. "Don't really know why they'd want to listen to either of us huffing and puffing when we're trying not to get poked in the ass by a horn, but the crowds seem to like it."

"What about the injuries, though, you must have had some? Any serious ones?"

They both went quiet, looking down at their hands.

Abel cleared his throat. "Yeah, Rem took a pretty bad hit a few years back."

I reached out a hand to squeeze Abel's arm, realizing I'd hit a raw nerve. "Sorry. You don't have to talk about it if you don't want to."

Rem shook his head. "Nah, it's not that. He's just a big cry baby."

That seemed to lighten the mood, and Abel rolled his eyes. "He nearly fucking died, and he calls me the cry baby.

If it had been me, I would have just gotten up outta the dirt and brushed myself off."

Rem groaned, and Abel and I both laughed. But I was interested in Abel's initial reaction. "He nearly died?"

He nodded, sobering, then swallowed hard.

Rem slung an arm around his shoulders. "Come on. I'm fine now. Quit being sensitive about it."

Abel shrugged off Rem's arm and turned to me. "Sorry. He fucking jokes about it all the time, but it's still raw for me. I had to watch them load him into an ambulance, not knowing if he'd even make it to the hospital alive. Worst night of my life."

I nodded, reliving my own worst night. Though I didn't remember the ride to the hospital. I was grateful when Abel kept talking because I wasn't sure I could have got any words out right at that minute. My memories were cutting off my throat.

"I'd only just gotten him back when it happened."

I raised an eyebrow.

"We're half brothers. Different moms. Our dad disappeared when I was five. Rem was six. And our moms raised us on opposite sides of the country."

Rem cut in. "Our mothers hated each other." He laughed. "Still do. You should see them carry on if they happen to both turn up to the same rodeo. So we lost contact. We're only back in each other's lives because I hired an investigator to find him."

Abel smiled at his brother. "Best day of my life, when that investigator found me and said my brother wanted to meet up again."

Rem groaned. "Don't say stuff like that. The whole nation will realize how sappy you are."

But Abel kept his gaze trained on me, ignoring his brother. "So that's why I still get choked up over that night, even though, as you can see, he's perfectly annoying to be around again. I don't really care if people think I'm a sap. I can own that."

"I think it's really nice, actually. I wish I had a sibling who cared about me that much."

Rem frowned. "Your siblings wouldn't care if a five hundred pound bull tried to take you out?"

I laughed. "I don't have any siblings. Well, none I know of anyway."

"What do you mean?"

"I grew up in foster care. Never knew my birth family."

Rem leaned forward. "You could have a whole host of siblings then. Could be ten of them out there. You ever look for them?"

I tapped my pen against the notepad, making little blue dots in the corner. "No."

"You must have thought about it, though?"

I shrugged.

Rem sat back in his seat. "Sorry. I'm prying, and we're not here for me to interview you, are we?"

I laughed, a little relieved. I wasn't used to being on the other end of the questions.

Rem held up his hands. "I promise not to pry anymore. But finding Abel again was the best thing I ever did. I can get you the number of the private investigator I used, if you want?"

My mouth dropped open, thoughts swarming my head. Was that what I wanted? I'd be lying if I said I hadn't thought about looking for my birth parents. But I'd always worried I'd just end up disappointed. After all, they'd abandoned me. Left me at the fire station like I was a puppy they got for Christmas but lost interest in by the new year. I'd never really considered they might have gone on to have more children. I could have a brother or sister out there somewhere. Someone who had never been given the choice to be in my life. Someone who was family but hadn't rejected me like my parents had.

I nodded to Rem. "Actually, I think I'd like that."

10

ADDIE

*O*utside the hotel windows, the light faded, but I'd been writing the story about Rem and Abel and refused to get up to turn on the light. I knew if I did, I'd notice Kai's bags, still sitting on the floor beneath the switch.

I groaned at my silent phone for the five hundredth time since sending Kai that message. He still hadn't written back. All afternoon, I'd been on edge, thinking he would have to show up at some point to collect his things. He still had the second key to my room, so I hadn't wanted to leave, in case I missed him.

But that meant I'd skipped lunch. I'd buried myself in my work and ignored my rumbling stomach, just wanting to get the piece about the bullfighting brothers out of me. But now I was starving. And I was sick of the sight of this room.

"Screw it," I muttered. I shut my laptop and decided to get dressed up and take myself out for dinner. Too much sitting around in this hotel room was lame. And I was in New York City. We'd be moving on after tomorrow's rodeo, and I didn't want to miss my chance to see at least a little of what the city had to offer.

I changed into one of the few decent outfits I'd brought with me and pulled my hair into a messy, high ponytail. I caught a glimpse of my reflection in the small bathroom mirror, then looked away. That was what I did now. Ever since the accident, I avoided mirrors wherever I could. But tonight, something stopped me. I rolled my head from side to side, trying to ease the sudden tension in my neck. "Stop being such a chicken," I whispered to the empty room. With a deliberate step, I forced myself to face the mirror, and this time I really took in my reflection.

Tears welled in the backs of my eyes. From the left, nothing had changed. Same brown skin. Same full lips and wide nose I'd hated as a kid but had made peace with once I'd grown into it at about fifteen. My eyes were still deep and brown, my eyelashes still dark and long.

I twisted my face a half inch to one side, taking in my bandages. I hadn't looked beneath them, always changing them by feel alone. But it was time. Sucking in a deep breath, I tried to calm the nausea rising in my stomach, and then I peeled back the edges of the tape, holding the gauze pieces to my face.

I dropped them into the trash can, then with agonizing slowness, lifted my gaze to my reflection. And there it was. A great ugly scar, accompanied by two smaller ones, marring one whole side of my face. The edges were raw, even though my surgeon back home had seemed pleased with his work. He'd assured me it would get better with time, but examining it now, I really wasn't so sure.

I blinked hard and turned away from the mirror, berating myself for being vain. What did a scar matter, when Sunny had lost his life in the very same accident? I decided then and there, I wasn't covering it up anymore. I didn't care who saw.

I strode to the door of my room and yanked it open. "Holy shit!" I yelped when there was a person on the other side.

Rem shot out a hand, helping to steady me. "Whoa, sorry!"

"You scared me. I was just on my way out."

He cast his gaze over me. "I see. You look...good."

I shifted my purse up my shoulder. "Thank you."

We hovered in the doorway, neither of us saying anything, just smiling at each other. I liked Rem, and his brother. But the silence that drew out between us quickly became awkward.

"Um, did you stop by for a reason?"

"Right!" Rem jumped as if I'd startled him. He patted the pockets of his jeans, then shoved his hand inside. "I have something for you."

Down the hall, the elevator doors opened, and a flash of red plaid beneath a wide-brimmed hat caught my eye. Kai's ice-blue eyes froze when he saw me standing there with Rem. Our gazes locked, and awareness prickled over my skin. I opened my mouth to call out to him—

"Here you go," Rem said, shoving a piece of paper in front of me.

Distracted, I broke the standoff with Kai. I shook my head in confusion. "Sorry, what's this?" I asked Rem. But before he'd even answered, my attention was drifting back in Kai's direction. My heart pounded at the sight of him, and I told myself it was just adrenaline from nerves about the apology I owed him.

"The phone number you wanted," Rem said, though his words barely registered.

Kai's mouth flattened into a straight line. He spun on his heel and stormed toward the elevators again.

"Kai! Wait!" I yelled. Then turned back to Rem and grabbed the phone number of the private investigator he'd used to find his brother. "Thank you. I really appreciate it, but I need to talk to Kai."

Rem didn't comment when I slammed my door and took off down the hall. "Kai, wait!"

He jabbed the button for the elevator over and over. I almost rolled my eyes. Could he be more obvious about trying to escape from me? I caught up to him just as the elevator opened. He took a step toward the open doors, but I darted in front of him, blocking his entrance.

"Kai! Will you please just stop for a minute and talk to me?"

Rem appeared, his steps slowing as he approached Kai and I standing off in front of each other. "Hey, Frost," he said awkwardly.

Kai's response was barely more than a grunt, and he never once looked away from me. He and Rem worked together at every rodeo, and Kai was being completely rude.

"Uh. Okay then. I'm just gonna..." Rem jerked a thumb in the direction of the elevator, and I stepped aside letting him pass. Behind my back, I heard Rem jab a button, and then the doors closed.

Kai sighed and took a step back, obviously realizing I wasn't letting him go that easily. He moved away from me until his back hit the wall.

"Look, I'm sorry." I inched forward. I should have been giving him the space he obviously wanted, but my feet seemed to have a mind of their own.

"For what?"

"For not telling you why I was here."

Kai raised an eyebrow as he folded his arms across his chest.

"Can you not?" I sighed. "I already feel bad enough."

Kai snorted.

Asshole. "I do!"

He said nothing.

God, he was infuriating with his stupid silent act. "Can you just yell at me or something, please? I get it. I'm the Wicked Witch of the West, tagging along on your tour, writing about things I have no business having my nose in."

"That's not how I see you."

I paused. "It's not?"

He shook his head. "I know this is a big break for you."

"So you don't think I'm exploiting Sunny's death?"

He blanched at the mention of Sunny's name. Or maybe it was at the mention of Sunny and death in one sentence. His throat bobbed before he spoke again. "Out of everyone on this tour, Sunny enjoyed publicity the most. He'd be loving the fact he's getting so much attention." The corner of his mouth lifted slightly, but then it fell. His voice dropped a notch. "He'd be happy it's you writing the stories. He loved you. He would have wanted you to succeed."

I stared at him. Sunny loved me? Sunny and I had never said anything like that to each other. Guilt swirled in my gut. I'd loved Sunny as a person. But I'd never been in love with him. And I didn't think his feelings had run that deep either.

I opened my mouth to reply, but Kai shook his head and moved past me. "I just need to get my things and then I'll be out of your hair."

I let him walk a few steps, then I called out again. "What about you?"

He stopped and turned around. "What about me?"

"What do you want?"

Kai lowered his eyes, the brim of his hat shadowing his handsome face. "I just want to ride."

"Then have dinner with me, and let's talk about riding."

"Dinner?"

"Yeah, you know, when you sit down in the evening to eat food? Preferably food that someone else has cooked? I'm on my way out. Come with me."

He glanced back toward my room, like he was considering escape.

"I just want to talk. That's it." My stomach growled. "And eat."

With jerky steps, he came back toward me and hit the button for the elevator. Just once this time. "Fine. I'll come. But don't think I'm going to start sharing my deepest darkest secrets with you just because you buy me a meal."

"Oh, I'm buying, am I?" I teased.

The tiniest of smiles flittered across his face. "You asked me out, not the other way round. Isn't that how it works?"

My heart flickered. I hadn't meant this to be a date. But he knew that, surely. He was just joking.

So why did the thought of it not being a date leave me a little disappointed?

The elevator pinged open before I could analyze that any further.

*a*ddie chose a pizza and pasta place with an Italian flag in the window. I followed her through the doors, taking my hat off as I went, and watched in silence while she spoke to the maître d'. I was still on edge about the whole publicity thing, but it was a lot easier to be mad at her when she wasn't right in front of me. I'd spent all day riling myself up in my head over why she was here and what she was trying to do. Eventually, I'd found a gym and taken my frustration out on a treadmill, running until my screaming muscles drowned out the constant questions in my head.

I wasn't one for confrontation, so I'd deliberately waited as long as possible to go up to her room to get my things.

That had worked out real well. Somehow, I'd gone from seething mad to having dinner with her. Even now, as we were seated at a little wooden table with a red-and-white-checked cloth, I wasn't quite sure how that had happened. "Can I get a whiskey on ice, please?" I asked before the waiter who had shown us to our table disappeared. Because, fucking hell, if I was going to make it through an entire meal just Addie and me, I was going to need alcohol.

"Drinking on a school night?" Addie teased. "Don't you have a rodeo tomorrow?" She picked up a pitcher of water from the table and poured two glasses, pushing one toward me. She nodded at it. "Just in case you want to alternate."

"Thanks." I took a sip, because looking at her across a table, with nowhere for my gaze to escape to, made my mouth dry. She'd taken her bandages off, and I guessed she wouldn't want me staring at her scars. So I didn't, even though I wanted to examine each one and make sure the doctors had taken care of her properly. But that wasn't my place.

I swallowed hard, grateful for the cool liquid that dislodged some of the tightness in my throat. But I eyed the waiter because that whiskey couldn't come quick enough. "Madison Square Garden tomorrow night. Opening rodeo of the season."

She rested her elbows on the table and propped her chin on her hands. "Big night. How you feeling about that?"

I narrowed my eyes. "You going to put that in your story?"

"How you feel about the opening night of the rodeo? Yes, probably. Is that really such a big deal?"

I shrugged.

She sighed. "You're what? Twenty-three? Yet you have no social media accounts. And the public barely knows a thing about you because you refuse all interviews."

"Not all," I mumbled. I lifted my head and motioned around the room. "I'm here right now."

"But you don't want to be."

"That isn't true." The words tumbled from my lips too quickly for me to catch. Fucking hell.

Addie looked confused. I couldn't blame her. So was I. I didn't want to do interviews. I avoided them like the plague. But I was here with Addie because she'd asked. And I couldn't say no to her. But Sunny was the only person who I'd ever truly let in. Though my attraction to Addie made me want to give her more, loyalty to Sunny would never allow it. He was the only one who had known all my secrets and never judged me for them. Not even when I judged myself. And I wasn't going to betray him. Not then. Not now. Not ever.

The waiter finally appeared with my drink, and I swallowed it in one gulp before asking for another. Addie frowned but didn't comment. Instead, she sat back in her chair and studied me.

"Were you happy with the way you rode in Australia?"

I shrugged.

"You came second."

"Second isn't first."

"You set high standards for yourself then."

I nodded. That much was true. "Very."

"I admire that."

"Most don't."

"What makes you say that?"

I ran my finger around the rim of my empty glass. "You've seen how they get after a rodeo. Everyone goes out partying. I go back to the hotel and study my rides. And then they call me Frost because of it."

"You don't like that name?"

"Don't much care one way or the other. I know I'm not exactly a ray of sunshine like Sunny was."

She smiled while she fiddled with the straw in her glass. "Not many people are like Sunny. It's hard to always be on an 'up' like he was."

I sloshed the ice in my drink around, wishing it was full of alcohol again. The first drink hadn't even taken the edge off.

"So what's your goal for the US season then?"

I raised an eyebrow. "Isn't that obvious? To win."

"You like winning?"

"Doesn't everyone?"

She lifted one shoulder. "I don't think everyone needs it. But I think maybe you do."

"Probably right there."

"You're a perfectionist. Losing bothers you because it means you didn't get something right."

I snorted on a laugh. "Interesting theory. But if I'm a perfectionist, I'm not a good one. I get a lot wrong. Too much."

Like the accident. I'd gotten so much wrong that night, and it had cost my best friend his life. If I'd taken a different route. If I'd driven a little slower in the rain. If I'd spun the wheel in the opposite direction...

"I don't know about that," Addie said quietly. She gazed up at me through lowered lashes.

I froze. Fuck. She looked so damn sexy when she did that. I quickly turned away.

"From where I'm sitting, you get a lot right. How long have you been riding for? Everyone keeps calling you the hotshot rookie who came out of nowhere, but nobody gets as good as you are that quickly."

"I can't remember a time where I didn't ride. Grew up with it."

"Yeah? You did lessons somewhere?"

I laughed and shook my head. "No, no. Nothing like that. Not 'til I was older anyway. My family has a ranch. Dad rode bulls in his youth. He had me out riding the sheep as soon as I was old enough to hang on to one of them."

The corners of her lips turned up. "I bet that was cute."

My cheeks warmed, but I couldn't help but give her a small smile back. Her smiles were contagious. "Yeah, real cute, falling off into a pile of sheep shit. Always a good time."

She laughed. "Your parents must be really proud of you. Seeing how far you've come."

My second glass of whiskey arrived, and I swallowed it down.

"I guess they're proud of me."

The skin between her eyebrows pinched together. "You guess?"

I'd already told her more than I'd told any other reporter. I couldn't even blame the alcohol for loosening my tongue. Her smiles made me want to keep talking just to see if she would smile some more. She was easy to talk to. Just like Sunny had been.

Fucking hell. Sunny. Whenever she was around, he was never far from my thoughts.

"They're proud."

"Will they be in the crowd tomorrow night? I'd love to meet them."

"No." The word came out sharp, and I knew Addie noticed when she visibly recoiled.

"Uh, okay. Sorry. I don't have to meet them."

"No, it's not that," I lied, because it *was* that. It was exactly that. Addie could never meet my parents. Never. If she did, she wouldn't speak to me again. She'd cut me right out of her life, and I was barely hanging in there as it was. "They aren't coming tomorrow, is what I mean. It's too far from our place. They'll come to the rodeo in Georgia, and there's one later in the year in Alabama that they might show up for." And when that happened, I would do absolutely everything in my power to make sure they were never near her. Not for a single second.

12

ADDIE

*T*he house lights were still on as I picked my way through the crowd trickling into Madison Square Garden. It was wall-to-wall denim, and I'd obviously missed the memo about wearing a cowboy hat. I checked the tickets Brad Pruitt had given me, mumbling my seat number and row while I searched the grandstand.

"Addie!" a familiar voice called.

I looked up and happiness spread through me. "Isabel!" I rushed toward the older woman who I'd gotten to know a little during the time I'd been dating Sunny.

Isabel and her husband, Johnny, were veterans of the circuit, and I was glad to see her. The only other woman I knew well was Paisley, but Bowen had announced his retirement from the pro circuit so I knew I wouldn't be seeing her in the friends and family section.

Isabel stood as I approached and gave me a warm hug before pulling me down to sit next to her. "I have to tell you something!" She clutched my hand, excitement spilling from her petite frame.

Her enthusiasm was infectious, and I perched on the edge of my seat. "What! Tell me!"

"Johnny and I got a call from an adoption agency today."

"Wait, what? What adoption agency?"

She grinned. "We've been keeping it pretty quiet, because we didn't want to get our hopes up. We've been disappointed a lot in the past, you know. When we couldn't get pregnant ourselves."

I hadn't realized they'd had problems conceiving. But I could imagine her heartache. I wanted kids. That was for sure. It wasn't in my immediate plans, since I didn't have anyone to have a baby with, but I'd never had a family. And it was something I wanted with all of my heart. That thought reminded me of the phone number Rem had given me. It was still burning a hole in my purse. The thought of using it to perhaps find my birth family was intriguing.

"So, they called today, and they might have a match for us. We're leaving straight after the rodeo tonight to fly home and meet with them."

I grabbed her for another hug, and she held me so tight I was surprised that bones didn't crack. "I'm really happy for you both," I said into her hair. "You're going to be great parents."

"Ah! Don't jinx it. Nothing is confirmed yet," she warned. But then she winked. "Who am I kidding, I'm already imagining painting the spare room of our cabin and buying baby cowboy boots."

Baby cowboy boots sounded freaking adorable. "I bet you are."

She waved a hand around in the air. "But enough about me. How are you? When Johnny told me you were on tour, I didn't believe him at first, considering you only just got out of the hospital."

"I'm a lot better now that I've had some decent sleep. I don't feel so weak and dizzy anymore."

She squeezed my hand. "That's really great. You seem so much better." Her shoulders fell an inch. "What about... everything else? Sunny..."

I gave her a tight smile. "I'm okay."

"You must miss him."

"I do," I said truthfully, even though her sympathetic eyes were making me uncomfortable. She was giving me that, 'Oh, you poor grieving widow' look. The one I didn't deserve. "I think everyone does."

She nodded. "For sure. Johnny has been in a funk all day. How's Kai?"

My cheeks went warm. "Uh, I don't know."

"He must be struggling today. First rodeo without Sunny."

After dinner last night, Kai had walked me back to the hotel, and we'd said a very polite farewell as he'd picked up his bags from my room. And I hadn't seen him since. I'd been trying to respect his boundaries. But I wanted to talk to him some more, because we'd barely scratched the surface. We hadn't even spoken about the accident yet. It was like a hot-button topic that was just easier to ignore.

"I really don't know."

Isabel quirked an eyebrow. "I thought you two would have grown even closer in the last few weeks, after all the time he spent with you in the hospital."

"What do you mean?" I twisted in my seat so I was facing her. "We weren't there long. I just got a bit woozy and passed out. We were only at the hospital for a few hours. I wasn't sure if I had healthcare here, so I checked out as quickly as I could."

Isabel shook her head, her long dark hair floating

around her face. Big hoop earrings dangled from her lobes and her dark eye makeup brightened her green eyes. "What? You were in the hospital here? I meant, when you were in the hospital in Sydney."

I dug my fingers into the plastic of the seat. "Kai wasn't with me then."

Isabel tilted her head to one side and frowned. "He was there every day. Every time we checked in on you, he was slouched in the chair beside your bed."

My eyes grew wide. "You're joking."

"You don't remember?"

I strained my brain, but the doctors had said I'd been unconscious for some time, and the days after I woke up were foggy. But I did remember seeing Kai's face—in my dreams. And hearing his voice, letting it wrap around me, making me feel safe when everything else was hazy and confusing. I'd assumed I'd dreamt it.

"Why would he have done that?" I mumbled to myself.

But Isabel heard and answered for me with a laugh. "That's what friends do."

"We aren't friends, though. He doesn't like me."

Isabel squinted at me, her smile sobering. "Then perhaps you need to ask him why he was there."

Perhaps I did.

---

*I*sabel and I chatted until a young couple with their two pre-teen sons approached, and I realized I was in one of their designated seats. With a quick wave to Isabel, I moved down a few rows so I was sitting in the correct place. I smiled tentatively at the older man beside me, but there was an aisle on the other side, and I was grateful for the extra space to put my gear. The New York office had sent over a camera that was a lot fancier than the one I'd been trained on. I'd also brought a notepad and pen so I could jot down any memorable moments I might want to expand into a story later.

"Ladies and gentlemen, please take your seats. The show begins in two minutes."

The lights flickered a few times in warning, and the stragglers sat down. A man two rows in front of me looked over his shoulder, holding up a phone to take photos of the stadium and the big screen. He was middle-aged, with pale white skin and startling blue eyes. I smiled. I'd bet he was a tourist, too. His gaze caught with mine, and I gave a polite nod.

The man's lip curled up in a sneer.

I blanched at the pure hatred on his face, then glanced behind me, wondering what had changed his mood so suddenly. But there was nothing out of the ordinary, and when I turned back to face the front, he'd done the same thing. I studied the back of his head for a moment before shrugging off the incident. No point concerning myself with somebody else's bad day. Especially when mine had been pretty decent. Kai and I had actually sort of had a good time last night. We'd managed to be alone anyway. And now, with what Isabel had told me... I had a lot to think about.

Kai was still on my mind as the lights went down and pyrotechnics lit up the ring. The riders ran out onto the dirt of the arena floor, waving their hats and stepping over the fire trails the rodeo was known for. I spotted Kai right away. He pulled his wide-brimmed hat off and waved it at the cheering crowd, but it was so quick you could have blinked and missed it. He didn't grin or whoop it up like some of the other guys did, his stony expression firmly in place even though the crowd cheered louder for him than anyone else. I'd noticed he was never one to smile much during these entrances. I'd only been to two rodeos as Sunny's girlfriend, but I'd watched a lot of them on the TV in my apartment. The commentators always talked about 'Frost' and his sober expressions. They'd discussed how focused and driven he was, and how by the time he made it onto that arena floor, he was already picturing how his ride would turn out.

I didn't really know where they got all this information. Kai's interviews were few and far between, with barely anything more than a yes or no on his behalf. I assumed they'd gleaned these facts from other riders. Like Sunny, who loved to run his mouth to anyone who'd listen and even to those who wouldn't. He'd talked Kai up anytime he could.

My heart gave a little squeeze when Kai stopped farther away from the next rider in the line than usual. He was leaving the space that Sunny normally occupied.

In a rush, I felt like such a jerk. Isabel was right. He had to be struggling tonight. And I hadn't even checked in on him. Everybody kept checking on me, but I'd been Sunny's girlfriend for two minutes. Kai had lost his best friend. Perhaps his *only* true friend. And their relationship had been long and full. The gap in Kai's life had to be whale-sized.

The announcers called for a minute of silence to remember Sunny, and I bit my lip watching Kai drop his gaze to his feet. His chest rose sharply, and I ached for him. And for Sunny. For a life lost too soon. For two best friends who should have never been separated so early.

"All right, let's get this party started. First rider of the night—Jesse Hardin!"

The crowd clapped and cheered before settling down as Jesse strode to the bucking chutes to get ready for his ride.

He lifted his hat and smoothed his hand over his bald, dark-brown head three times then put the hat back on. I made a quick scribble on my notepad that said: pre-ride ritual?

"Goddamn nigger."

The disgusting racial slur shocked me so much I pressed my pencil too hard into my notepad and snapped the tip. I jerked my head in the direction of the voice. The man who'd sneered at me earlier being shushed by his wife.

"You can't say that here!" she hissed beneath her breath.

I was frozen to the seat. I glanced around at the other people in the crowd, but nobody seemed to have noticed.

Or nobody had the guts to say anything and were deliberately pretending they hadn't heard.

Bile rose in my stomach. On the arena floor, Jesse's bull burst out of the gates, spinning and bucking wildly. His free arm waved, and he dug his legs into the beast's sides, but within two seconds he was listing hard to the right. Well before the buzzer sounded, he was lying in the dirt.

I sucked in a sharp breath. The bullfighters rushed in to distract the bull, but they weren't quick enough, and Jesse took a heavy hit to the shoulder. I winced as he fought to get out from beneath deadly hooves.

In front of me, the man laughed. He leaned into his wife and said loudly, "That bull knows what's what. He don't want no black on his back."

I blinked hard, my blood pounding through my veins. My fists clenched into balls. Fuck this guy. Cheering when a man went down and was injured? What kind of animal was he? I opened my mouth to give the man a piece of my mind but then I abruptly shut it. I closed my eyes and counted to ten in my head, saying each number deliberately, and slowly. Then counted backward. When I opened my eyes again, one by one, I unfurled each of my fingers and flexed them. I was here in a professional capacity. And not only that, I was the only person of color in the immediate area. This wasn't the first time I'd heard a racial slur. And throughout the years, I'd learned to pick my battles. Sometimes I spoke my mind. And sometimes, speaking your mind was dangerous. Weighing up the odds right now, I decided this situation fell into the latter. Not only was I in a large, mostly white crowd, but there was a very real chance any scene I made here tonight could spell the end of my career.

And small-minded assholes like him weren't worth losing my future over.

That didn't mean I had to like it, though. The cowboys kept riding, but I found it increasingly difficult to concentrate on them. My gaze kept drifting back to the man, and my muscles were all locked up, tense and stressed, just waiting for him to make another barb.

It was a relief when Kai's name was eventually called. The racist in front of me cheered loudly. How fucking typical. Kai with his blue eyes and light-colored hair would be this guy's favorite.

I shook my head, reminding myself to just ignore him. I wanted to concentrate on Kai. My gaze flicked over to the big screen. Kai's eyes were laser focused as he settled on the back of the bull. His fingers moved swiftly, twisting the rope around his hand and shifting his weight forward, getting comfortable. This was Kai in full 'Frost mode.' The tiny smiles I'd managed to get out of him last night were gone, replaced by lips pressed firmly together.

Butterflies rioted around my belly. I was nervous for him. I knew he wanted to make a splash tonight and I wanted it for him. Starting the year off right was important. Showing everyone that his second place in Australia wasn't just a fluke was crucial. For his mindset, and for his ranking.

"You got this," I whispered.

The chute flew open, and the bull bucked his way out. A smile curved the corner of my lips, as I took in Kai's form. He was amazing. There was no doubt about that. Instinctively, he moved with the bull, anticipating its turns and kicks and shifting his weight to compensate. His body stayed taut, his ass planted to that bull's back until the eight-second buzzer sounded.

He dismounted, landing easily on his feet and ran for the rails as Abel and Rem distracted the bull. My smile morphed into a grin, and I pushed to my feet with the crowd around me to cheer for him.

"Yes! That's my boy! That's my boy!" a deep voice in front of me yelled.

My arm fell mid fist-pump.

The racist turned to the man sitting next to him. "You see that ride? That's my son!"

13

KAI

*I*t was dark and cold outside of Madison Square Garden, but a large crowd gathered while we waited for the team buses that would take us back to the hotel. Some guys traveled with their young families in tow, so there were plenty of kids running around between the adults who tugged their jackets closed against the chilly January air.

"Good job tonight, Frost."

I nodded my thanks as the praise kept coming. My cheeks heated. I got slaps on the shoulder from the guys, and arm squeezes from their wives, and I forced myself to keep saying thank you. But with each compliment, I grew more and more anxious. I hated all the attention. Yeah, I wanted to win. But it sure as hell wasn't for the glory. I loved bull riding. I loved the rush. And yeah, I loved the money. The money was what drove me to win. I needed it if I wanted to set myself up and get a ranch of my own. One day, I wouldn't have to do all this. I wouldn't have to do the press and the crowds. The dreams of sitting on my own piece of land, overlooking a quiet sunset with a woman I loved by my side and a ton of our kids running around in the dirt—that was what drove me.

I pushed through the crowd, searching for the woman whose face too often appeared in those dreams. I scanned each person I crossed, looking for Addie's long dark hair, her flawless skin, her shining eyes. I knew she was here somewhere, and I just wanted to see her. I'd been thinking about her all day.

"Kai!"

I froze.

"Kai!" The call came again. No mistaking it that time.

I whipped my head around, my gaze colliding with my father's. He jogged the last few steps to where I stood, my mother grinning at me from behind him. He reached my side and gathered me into a hug. I didn't respond. Every muscle in my body went stiff, though the older man didn't seem to notice. His icy blue eyes, so like mine, gleamed at me.

"So proud of you, kid. You nailed it out there."

Mom caught up and wrapped her arms around me. "Sorry for not calling," she whispered into my ear, mid hug. "Your father wanted to surprise you." She looked worried when she pulled back.

I smiled stiffly at her. I loved my parents, and we'd always been close. But they couldn't be here right now. Not tonight. "What are you both doing here?"

"I told them I was coming," a voice said from behind my mother. "And they decided to come with me."

I stifled a groan. Jesus fucking Christ. Could this get any worse? Della Flannery sidled up to me and wrapped her arms around my middle, resting her head on my chest and squeezing me like she owned me. Her body pressed against me was familiar—we'd dated all through high school, and for a while there, I'd thought we'd be like this forever.

But things changed. And now, even though her touch reminded me of good times we'd had in the past, it didn't bring me any comfort. Quite the opposite, in fact. I peeled her arms off me and took a step back, but she didn't get the hint.

She laced her fingers through mine. "Aren't you happy to see us?"

No.

No, I wasn't fucking happy to see them. Well, Mom maybe. But I certainly didn't want to see my old man here. Or Della.

A flash of bright pink caught my eye through the crowd. Addie was watching me from beneath a knitted hat. Panic coursed through my system. *"I'd love to meet them,"* Addie had said as we'd discussed my parents last night. Fuck! She couldn't come over here. I tugged Della's hand and motioned for Mom and Dad to follow me to the edge of the crowd—the farthest point I could get from Addie before I hit the barricades.

I dropped Della's hand like it was hot. She pouted up at me, giving me that big-eyed, puppy-dog stare that had worked every time when we were dating. But now just reminded me how manipulative she was. And why we'd broken up in the first place.

She didn't seem to notice how standoffish I was being. She grabbed her phone from the ass pocket of her too-tight jeans and held it up, sliding in close to me. "Smile, baby," she purred.

I didn't, but she snapped the photo anyway. "I'm going to Instagram this. I'll tag you."

I didn't even know what that meant, and I didn't care.

Especially if it meant she left me alone for a minute. I focused on Mom and Dad.

"You rode like a champion today, Son." Dad slapped me on the arm again.

I had to fight the urge to cringe away. What were they doing here? It was bad enough I'd have to see them at the rodeo in Georgia later in the tour. I was prepared for that. I had weeks to figure out a way to keep them away from Addie. But this? Turning up unannounced and with my ex-girlfriend, of all people, in tow? It was too much.

Mom patted my arm. "Congratulations, sweetheart."

I softened as I looked down on her. "Thank you." She'd always been my number-one supporter. Both my parents were. Despite my father's misgivings, and our disagreements, he'd always supported my career. "Did you have to bring Della, though?" I whispered. "What is she doing here?"

Mom shrugged and gave me a small, knowing smile. "It was her idea. I think she misses you."

I rolled my eyes, and Mom tapped me on the shoulder. "Don't be like that."

But it *was* like that. Della and I had a very public, very messy breakup a long time ago, and I didn't care to repeat it.

Della, apparently finished with her phone, tucked her arm through mine. "It's so good to see you. I was saying to your mom and dad that we should all go get some food. Late dinner? I'm starving."

Dad was nodding enthusiastically, and although I would have liked to see my mother a bit more, I just couldn't do that right now.

"I can't." The engine on one of the buses behind me rumbled to life, and I glanced over my shoulder, relief pouring through me when I saw the rest of the team boarding. "Buses are leaving, and I need to get back to the hotel to study my rides for the next round."

Della pouted, her glossy bottom lip sticking out like a cranky toddler's. Once upon a time, I'd loved her lips. And I'd spent hours kissing them, stoked with how lucky I was that she wanted to be with me. A dumb kid who related better to bulls than he did to people. But now, I just wanted to get away from her.

And find Addie.

"We fly out early tomorrow morning. Can't you just spare one night?" she whined.

I shook my head. "Sorry." I bent to kiss my mother's cheek. "See you at home in a few weeks, okay?"

She looked disappointed, but I could also see she understood. When I pulled away, my father was glaring at me. I sighed and held my hand out for him to shake. He took it, though it seemed grudging. He was mumbling something about a lack of respect when I strode to the doors of the bus.

I couldn't bring myself to care.

14

ADDIE

From a window seat at the very back of the bus, I watched Kai's family reunion. I was cold to the bone, as he shook the hand of the man who'd made such horrible, downright racist remarks throughout the rodeo. My eyes tracked Kai's every move as he hugged his mother, then turned to a cute blonde. She cuddled into him in a way that immediately told me they were a couple. She was overly familiar with him, too familiar to just be a friend.

Anger made my heart pulse faster. He'd never mentioned a girlfriend. But it wasn't just that. It was her. With her bouncy blonde hair and pale white skin...I'd bet Kai's dad wholeheartedly approved of the two of them. I doubted he'd sneer at her, or cheer if she was injured. Not like the way he had with me, and with Jesse when he'd come off the bull.

With shaking fingers, I stabbed the Instagram icon on my phone. In the search bar, I typed in Kai's name and waited, forcing my eyes to remain on the little screen in my hands. I couldn't look outside at him anymore. It was too much. But like a woman obsessed, I just couldn't let it go either. I could blame that on my journalistic influences...but that would just be lying to myself. I wasn't searching his name as an interested reporter. I was searching his name as a jealous woman with a full-blown crush.

Shit. How was that even possible? Kai and I hated each other. Him sitting by my bed in the hospital, and one semi-nice dinner, didn't change that. My brain battled back and forth with myself, but one half was a liar. The plain truth was, there'd always been something more between Kai and me. Some sort of spark had been there, even in Australia. It was easy to ignore when Sunny was occupying my thoughts but had multiplied tenfold in the last few days.

Or at least I thought it had.

Which was why realizing it was all one-sided cut like a knife.

As the bus rumbled to life, I looked up and noticed Kai and his family had disappeared. I scanned the bus, spotting him right at the very front. I sank lower in my seat, grateful for the distance between us.

The bus pulled into the traffic, and the lights of New York City flashed by. And I didn't see any of it. I scrolled through the photos on the Kai Hunt hashtag. There were a handful from tonight. A few short clips enthusiastic fans had posted of his ride; a few blurry photographs as he'd left the stadium without stopping to pose with fans.

And one, with a cute blonde pressing her perky tits into his side, smiling up at the camera while she took a selfie. *Always #1 to me. #kaihunt #wbra #champion.*

I couldn't help it. I tapped through to her profile. Her name was Della. The first few images were mostly just of Della by herself. Della in some fall leaves. Della posing in a bikini during the summer. I scrolled down. And immediately wished I hadn't. Scrolling through her public account was like watching Kai date another woman. The two of them smiling over burgers and fries. The two of them ice skating at a local rink. Football games, with Della in a cheerleader's uniform. His rodeos with photos of them both smiling, him holding a trophy almost bigger than her petite frame. Them dressed to the nines, him kissing her like he hadn't even realized someone was watching.

Photo after photo of their happy high school and college photos. And I looked through them all. Photos of them with friends and family. Photos that spanned years.

And not a black person in any of them.

15

KAI

*T*he quiet of my hotel room was soothing after being surrounded by people and noise for the past few hours.

I rolled my right shoulder, wincing at the tug in the muscle that told me I'd strained something during one of my rides, and kicked off my boots. I stripped off layers as I went, dumping my coat over the back of the couch before sinking into it gratefully. I closed my eyes, resting my head back against the cushions and tried to analyze my performance tonight. Sure, I'd made the eight seconds both times, but that didn't mean they'd been perfect. No ride ever was, but one day, I wanted to be close. I wanted to be the man to beat the all-time high score. So just like I did after every rodeo, I visualized how I could do better next time.

Only this time, I couldn't conjure up the right memories. All I saw was Addie staring at me across a checkered tablecloth in that little Italian restaurant. I saw her long dark hair cascading down her back, and her graceful fingers wrapping around the stem of her wine glass. If I breathed deep enough, I could almost remember the scent of her perfume, and I sure as hell remembered the sound of her laughter. My heart beat faster. That laughter had normally been directed at Sunny. But last night, it had been me who had made her laugh. Who'd made her smile. It had been me on the receiving end of her attention.

Loud thumping on the door broke my concentration. I groaned, slinging an arm over my eyes. I wasn't in the mood for the guys. They always did this. They liked to party after rodeos and they always tried dragging me along. Sunny had succeeded more often than not. But my heart ached at the knowledge it wasn't Sunny out there, pounding on my door tonight.

"Go away!" I yelled.

The banging stopped for a moment, but then there was a "No!" yelled back through the door, and the banging started up again.

That hadn't been the voice of one of the guys.

"Addie?" I said. I scrambled to my feet and rushed to the door, yanking it open so quickly she stumbled over the threshold.

On autopilot, I caught her, wrapping an arm around her waist to keep her steady. She blinked up at me in surprise. For a moment, neither of us said anything.

Then something cold and hard came down over her eyes, and she shoved me away, advancing past me and into the darkened room.

I shut the door quietly before turning to face her. I'd seen a lot of expressions on Addie's face over the past few months. But I'd never seen her look like this.

Her eyes were piercing, burning a hole right through me. Her fingers balled into fists, and her breath came in short, sharp pants.

But she didn't say anything. And second by second, I

grew more and more uncomfortable. Me. The man, who loved silence, and spent more time watching and listening than I did participating. But this silence bothered me. A lot. Addie was never silent like this. Silent, and mad as hell.

I hated it. "What?"

Her words exploded from her lips. "Don't 'what' me!" she snapped.

I recoiled at the tone in her voice. I'd known she could be fiery but I'd never heard her speak to anyone with such sharpness.

"Is that why you freaked out when I mentioned meeting your parents last night?"

I screwed up my face. "What are you talking about?" But a sinking feeling spread through my chest. Before I had time to fully catch on to what she was insinuating, she spelled it out for me.

"Your parents were at the rodeo tonight, Kai. You forgot to mention that your family is a bunch of racists!" She paced away from me, her steps jerky, like she was barely able to control her feet. She spun back around when I didn't say anything. But this time, there was hurt mixed in with the anger. "That's why, isn't it? That's why you've always hated me? I never understood it. I thought it was maybe because I'd stolen your best friend, but Sunny and I were always so careful to include you in everything. So much so it sometimes felt like I was dating the both of you. We never wanted you to feel left out. But it didn't matter, did it? You hated me anyway, and now I feel like a fucking idiot! I laid awake at night sometimes, you know? Wondering what the hell I'd done to make you hate me so much. And I could never come up with anything. But now I know. Now I know it was the color of my skin." She gave a laugh that had no joy in it. "You were never going to like me, no matter what I did."

I opened my mouth, but words jumbled in my brain. And all that came out was a pathetic sounding, "What?"

That only seemed to piss her off more. "Don't play dumb with me, Kai! You've never liked me. Everybody knows it!"

Her yelling shocked me into action. I narrowed my eyes and took two steps forward. Then two more when she retreated. I crowded in until her back hit the wall. She inhaled sharply, and I kept moving until I was well into her space. "Fuck everybody." My words came out laced with gravel. "All I care is what you think."

She tilted her head back, her angry gaze meeting mine, all fire and determination. "Well, your dad certainly doesn't like me. At the rodeo, he used the most offensive term to describe Jesse. I was right behind him, and you should've seen the look on his face when he saw me."

Her words were like a punch in the face, but every inch of my body was responding to her nearness. My blood thrummed in my veins. "You think I'm like my old man?" My gaze strayed to her lips, and when they parted, my heart stopped. I stared back up into her eyes, and this time, I saw something different behind the fire.

Want.

Need.

Lust.

Everything I'd ever wanted to see in her eyes was right there, begging for me to take. "I'm *nothing* like him."

She cocked her head to one side. "You sure about that?"

I slammed my lips down on hers.

She didn't hesitate. Not for even a second. Her arms snaked around my neck, and she tugged me close. I pressed my body against hers, pushing her into the wall and feeling every delicious inch of her in a way I never should have wanted. She molded to me, her breasts flush with my chest, and I ran my hands over her arms, pulling them away from my neck, linking my fingers through hers and pinning them to the wall. Our lips moved in perfect unison, and when her soft mouth parted, I stroked into her with my tongue, lapping up the moan that escaped her lips.

"Fuck, Addie," I whispered over her lips.

And immediately wished I hadn't.

Her eyes flew open, and she forced me back, yanking her hands from mine. I breathed hard, hating we were no longer kissing. But the heat had gone from her eyes, and all that was left was anger. She pushed me again, the heels of her hands hitting my pecs.

"How dare you?" she seethed. "You can't just kiss me to try to prove something to yourself, Kai!"

What? I took another step back, shaking my head. "I wasn't!"

She shoved her hands on her hips. "Then what the hell was that?"

It's what I've wanted to do since the moment I laid eyes on you. It's what I've dreamed about every night and every day since.

It was wrong.

Sunny's laughing face flashed into my mind. Him slinging an arm across my shoulders and ribbing me about being shy. Sitting with him at bars and in hotel rooms, and hanging off fences, watching him ride. It all flashed through my head, swirling and storming around until every good feeling I'd had was obliterated.

I'd just kissed my best friend's girl.

Addie stood, waiting for an explanation I couldn't give. I knew what she wanted. She wanted me to say that kiss had been more than what it seemed on the surface.

But I couldn't give her that. Because admitting I'd had

feelings for her the entire time she'd been with Sunny made me the lowest sort of cockroach there was.

So I said nothing. And I let her walk out the door. I let her think the kiss had been nothing more than me trying to prove I wasn't as racist as the man who'd raised me. I let her think that kiss hadn't been the most earth-shattering moment of my entire damn life.

16

ADDIE

"It's been four weeks, Addison."

No hello. No how's it going? How are you settling in? I squeezed my fingers a little tighter around my phone. "I know. I'm sorry."

Sally, my US editor, sighed down the phone line. "What happened to the piece on Kai Hunt? This story on the bull-fighting brothers..."

I slunk down in the plush hotel armchair, wishing I hadn't answered this call in public. A steady stream of people trickled in and out of the large glass doors of the hotel lobby, bringing the sounds and smells of the cool, dark evening. Although logically I knew none of them could hear my boss giving me a lecture, it was still somehow embarrassing.

Like a glutton for punishment, I prompted Sally to finish her sentence. "The piece on the brothers is..." I waited, though I had a feeling I knew what she was going to say.

"It's fine. Good even. But it's a fluff piece. And that's not what you're there to write. Well, not entirely anyway."

"What does that mean?"

"It means we were never particularly interested in anything outside of the accident. The rest of the stories are basically nothing more than paid advertising. The WBRA pay, and we provide. But the story we want is Kai Hunt. After the accident, and his success in Australia, people want to know about him. He's the WBRA's hottest star right now."

I tried not to snort over her calling Kai a star. I mean, he was, but the funny part was how Kai would have reacted if he'd heard her say that. He would have been horrified.

I stared at the blank screen of the laptop sitting on a low table in front of me. I'd been trying to write down ideas for Kai's story for the past hour. And all I had was a blinking cursor and a whole lot of white page. I stifled a groan of frustration. "He's not exactly forthcoming with information." That was the understatement of the century. He hadn't spoken a word to me in weeks.

I could practically hear the disapproval in Sally's breathing. "You're the journalist. If he won't tell you, there's probably more of a story there than we even realized. Dig for it."

I knew she was right. If this had been anyone else, I would have already at least Googled him. But I'd done nothing, not wanting to pry into Kai's private life when he obviously didn't want me there.

If I was honest with myself, it had been easier to just pretend the piece on Rem and Abel was going to be enough to buy me some time. It was easier to sit and talk with Rem, who was an open book, than to even think about Kai. Because thinking about Kai meant thinking about that kiss... I closed my eyes. That kiss had been weeks ago, but it was never far from my mind. The way his mouth had crashed down on mine, and the way it had stolen my breath had played over in my dreams every night since it had happened. It didn't matter how much I tried to avoid him during the day, and how much I tried to keep myself busy with writing and interviewing and running all around whatever town we'd stopped in, playing tourist. When I closed my eyes each night, that kiss and the way it made me feel, rushed straight back in and gutted me all over again.

"Addison? Are you still there? Is there going to be a problem getting the story?"

I shook my head, even though I knew she couldn't see it. "No, no problem. I'll get it."

"Good. Be sure you do, or there's no point you being on that tour. Understood?"

"Got it."

She didn't even bother saying goodbye. I stared at the dead phone for a moment before placing it down on the table. Shit. I was royally screwed. There was no way around it. I was going to have to talk to Kai.

"How's my story going?"

I glanced up and smiled when Rem was heading in my direction. He plonked himself onto the couch beside me and leaned in, his arm brushing against mine. He nodded his head toward my blank laptop screen. "Ouch. That bad, huh?"

I cracked a half smile. "That's not your story. Yours is done. It's actually going to be the first one that goes out."

Rem's brow furrowed. "I thought you were doing a piece on Kai first."

"Don't ask."

He chuckled. "Fair enough. Come have a drink with me tonight, then?"

I shot him a peek from the corner of my eye. "A drink?"

"Yeah, you know, those things that come in glasses? Usually contain alcohol and coincide with having a good time?"

I couldn't help but smile at him.

"Beats sitting around staring at a blank screen, doesn't it?"

He had that right. I really should have stayed in to work, but I'd been trying to write for the past hour, and look how far that had gotten me. But I wasn't sure what Rem's motivations were, and I really didn't want to give him the wrong idea.

Rem read into my hesitations correctly. "I just wanna go hang out. That's it."

I elbowed him, and he elbowed me back. Then he reached across me and closed the laptop.

"Hey!"

"Is what horses eat." In one slick move, he pushed to his feet, gathering my laptop as he went, and strode across the lobby to the reception desk. "I'm checking this in with reception," he called over his shoulder. "Then we're going to get drinks. You're too damn serious."

I couldn't argue with that. And I did want to get out. Staring at a blank screen wasn't exactly bringing me any story motivation. I scrambled to shove my notepad and pens into my bag and was ready and waiting when Rem held out an arm for me to take.

I linked my arm through his with a wide grin, and we headed for the wall of glass doors.

We'd taken exactly three steps before Kai walked in from the outside.

"Oh. Hey, Frost." Rem said.

The two of us stopped awkwardly in front of Kai, and even though I knew I wasn't doing anything wrong, I pulled my arm from Rem's on instinct.

Kai barely took note of Rem. His gaze moved straight to

me, and I knew he hadn't missed I'd had my arm linked through Rem's.

"Where are you off to?" Kai asked.

I hadn't spoken a word to Kai in the weeks since that disaster of a night at Madison Square Garden and our kiss at the hotel afterward. But now my body reacted like the weeks apart had never happened. A flutter of butterflies rioted around in my belly, and I sucked in a deep breath to settle them. But that was a mistake, too, because all I got was a lungful of Kai's masculine scent. Funny. I hadn't noticed Rem's, even though I was standing closer to him. But Kai's I recognized instantly. I took an involuntary half step forward. Kai's eyes flared just a fraction, but I saw it.

"We're going out drinking."

Kai didn't respond. His gaze flicked over my face and down my body, warming me as it went, and then scorching me on the way back up. I was still angry as hell at him, and I hated the way my body reacted to his attention. I'd been craving it for four weeks, my hormones not seeming to care he hadn't explained himself at all.

The silence was drawing out, Rem's gaze flicking back and forth between us. I hated we were putting him in an awkward situation. Again.

"We should go," I said, at the same time, Rem asked, "Do you want to come with us?"

"What?" I squeaked, my head whipping in Rem's direction. He shrugged.

"No, he doesn't." I answered for Kai.

Kai cocked his head to the side, and finally, turned to Rem. "Actually, yeah, I do."

Rem shook his head, his expression wary. "Are you two going to play nice?"

I shot him a death look. I assumed Kai did something similar because Rem rolled his eyes.

"Well, this will be interesting," Rem said. "Come on." He didn't wait for either of us.

I turned to Kai. "You're seriously coming out?"

"Yeah, so?"

I shook my head. Great. Just great.

---

*R*em kept up a constant stream of chatter, while the three of us walked the streets of Sacramento, searching for a good spot to hang out for the evening. Kai was quiet as usual, and I was so distracted by his presence that I didn't say much either. After vetoing a handful of places that appeared too dead or uninteresting for Rem's liking, he picked a bar that had people spilling out the door and music thumping from inside. I followed him through the doors, into the crowd. The lights were dim, the bar long, stretching almost the entire length of the room. I was relieved to see the people inside were all casually dressed, like I was. Most stood in small groups, holding drinks while they yelled at each other over the DJ dropping beats from the corner of the room.

Without saying anything, Kai stalked off in the direction of the bar. I followed him with my eyes until Rem held out a hand to me. "Come dance?"

I nodded. I needed to do something to ease the tension in my muscles, and putting some space between me and Kai seemed like a good idea.

Rem led me out onto the dance floor, and I grinned as he spun me around. But when he began to dance, he left some space between us. I rolled my hips and let my body find the natural beat of the song. I loved to dance, so it was second nature to allow the song to pulse through me and just move my body in time.

It was lucky dancing required no thought, because my brain was occupied by sneaking looks at Kai. He sat perched on a barstool, his elbow resting on the bar top, his legs spread wide.

He was watching me.

I tried to focus on Rem. I really did. But my gaze kept straying over his shoulder. Kai's gaze grew more heated with every passing moment.

Shit. I liked the way he stared at me. Heat bloomed between my legs, an ache starting up that slowly spread through the rest of me. Why did he have to be so attractive? Why did he have to watch me with that piercing gaze all the time? It was too much. And it wasn't fair. He'd had his chance. After he'd kissed me, I'd wanted him to say there was something more between us. And that he hadn't just been kissing me to prove a point to himself. But he hadn't said a word. He'd just let me walk out.

He'd let me walk out of his room, and until tonight, hadn't made any effort to find me. So fuck him. I was here with Rem. And I was determined to have a good time. From the corner of my eye, I watched a pretty blonde approach Kai. She was so similar to his high school girlfriend that I did a double take. She smiled at him, and that was all I needed to see for a stab of jealousy to catch me in the gut. I turned away.

"You two are hilarious," Rem yelled over the music.

"Huh?"

He jerked his head in Kai's direction. "Just go screw already, will you? The sexual tension is so thick, even I'm turned on."

He grinned, and I swatted him with the back of my hand. But then I sobered. "He hates me."

Rem snorted. "That man does not hate you. That man wants to get in your pants. I can practically feel the heat from the death looks he's shooting in my direction."

I glanced back at Kai. Sure enough, the blonde was gone, and he was alone again.

"When are you two going to get your act together and just admit it?"

I shook my head. "It's not that easy. There's more to it."

Rem nodded. "The Sunny thing."

It startled me to realize Sunny hadn't even been on my mind. Not since the night in New York and Kai's kiss. There was more than just Sunny's ghost causing problems between Kai and me now. Despite how angry I still was over that night, I didn't want to out Kai as some sort of racist, just because of who his father was. Without anger coursing through me, I'd realized I'd had no proof Kai was like his dad. And then there was the kiss. Maybe it was just me, but that kiss had felt like there was more behind it.

Which had only made his rejection hurt all the more.

I hadn't been able to make sense of anything in the last four weeks, so there was no way I was going to make Rem understand while trying to relay the story over the pounding music. So, I just nodded. "Yeah, the Sunny thing."

But Rem rolled his eyes. "That's stupid. You and Sunny were together, what? Two months? You were hardly his wife. And damn. Even if you were, you're allowed to move on. You're both young and hot, and from what I can see, there's definitely a spark between the two of you. I think Sunny would be happy for you."

I gave a small, sad smile. "I think he would, too."

Rem stopped dancing and squeezed my arm. "Okay,

enough about that then, 'cause I'm supposed to be showing you a good time, and now you look like you're going to cry."

"I'm fine." Though I really kind of wasn't. I was so confused, and hurt and angry, and...lonely. Everything was out of my comfort zone, and nothing felt easy. Gah.

"I need a drink," I announced.

"Definitely."

I followed Rem to the bar, almost dreading being in Kai's presence again, but to my surprise, he wasn't where I'd last seen him. I cast my gaze around the room but couldn't see him anywhere.

"So, did you call that investigator yet?" Rem asked, while we waited in line to be served.

I cringed. "No?"

"Why not? Still not sure about finding your birth family?"

I shuffled forward a few steps and edged closer so it would be easier to hear each other. "No, I definitely want to do it. I'm just..."

"Scared?"

"Maybe."

We reached the front of the line, and Rem leaned across the bar and asked the bartender for two shots of tequila.

He waved away my protests and pressed one of the little glasses into my hand. "Drink that. Then go call the investigator."

"It's nearly midnight!"

"So? Investigators work weird hours. Maybe he's still awake."

"Or maybe he's asleep at home with his family and doesn't want some random woman calling in the middle of the night?"

Rem's wide smile was devilishly handsome. "Won't know until you try, will you?"

He tapped the tequila glass then downed his own shot. I rolled my eyes then followed suit. The liquid burned, but the warmth it left in its wake was pleasant. Rem nodded to the bartender, and when he placed a second shot in my hand, I didn't protest.

"Now go make that call."

With two shots of tequila swirling through my system, making a call to a private investigator about digging up some dirt on my birth family didn't seem like a big a deal. "It's too loud in here." I jerked my head in the direction of the exit sign. "I'm going outside to find somewhere quiet."

"You want me to come?"

But I could already see Rem's gaze focusing in on a pretty redhead who was giving him the eye from across the room. And I didn't want an audience when I called anyway. This was something I needed to do by myself.

So I shook my head and left Rem stalking across the dance floor in the redhead's direction. I pushed through the rear doors of the bar, finding myself in an outdoor area that probably would have been full of people in summertime. But we were still in the grips of winter, and the frigid night air was like a slap in the face. The music muted as soon as the door shut behind me, and I wandered to a vacant table and perched on the edge. White fairy lights were strung in the courtyard trees and around the guttering of the building. The quiet was soothing after the noise of the bar. I pulled my phone out from my bag and then riffled around for the slip of paper with the investigator's number. It was tattered around the edges from how many times I'd picked it up over the last few weeks, debating whether or not to use it. I didn't give myself time to think. I dialed in the numbers and hit the 'call' button without hesitation. Butterflies flapped around my belly, and I told myself not to be ridiculous while the phone rang and rang.

"You've reached Mathew Radcliffe, private investigator. I'm not able to come to the phone right now…"

I groaned at the pre-recorded message. "Should have waited until Monday," I mumbled. But when the message finished, I didn't hang up. "My name is Addison St. Clair," I said to his voicemail. "I was abandoned at a month old, in a small country town in rural Australia. I know it's a long shot, but a friend of mine said you might be able to help me find my family. If so, could you call me back on this number?" I went to hang up and then quickly added, "And sorry about the midnight phone call!"

I squeezed my eyes shut tight and took a deep breath. It was done. I'd taken the first step, and maybe the whole thing would end in tears, who knew, but at least I could stop wondering. The wheels were in motion, and I felt lighter than ever.

"You're looking for your birth family?"

I jumped, the voice startling me. I thought I'd been alone. But my shock subsided quickly, and I didn't even need to turn around to know who it was. My entire body sparked to life at just the sound of his voice.

"What are you doing out here, Kai? Following me?"

He rounded the table so we stood face-to-face. He hadn't grabbed his jacket either, but suddenly, I wasn't noticing the cold. Heat burned in Kai's blue eyes, like laser beams in the darkness.

"Yes," he said simply, without a hint of apology in his voice. "Your date isn't exactly doing a good job of taking care of you."

I bristled. "I don't need anyone watching out for me, thank you very much."

He took a step closer. "Are you dating Rem?"

He kept moving forward, until I had to tilt my head to keep my gaze pinned to his. Turning away wasn't an option. Not when I needed to show him I wasn't going to back down from his challenge...and not when he was gazing at me with eyes that made my knees fall apart. He stepped in closer between my legs, and I stared up at him from my seat on the outdoor table.

"That's none of your business," I challenged.

"What if I want it to be my business?"

A mix of emotions swirled through me, all heightened by the alcohol and the natural rush of endorphins from making the call. Or maybe those endorphins were from how close Kai was standing to me. He dipped his head, his eyes searching mine, and my resolve weakened. His eyes were so beautiful, so blue, yet haunted. A slight glassiness told me he'd been drinking, too.

"You're drunk," I accused.

"Have you ever seen me drunk?"

I thought about it for a second, then shook my head. I hadn't.

"I don't lose control like that."

I shivered.

His gaze dipped to my mouth. "Even if I was, I'd still want to do this."

He lowered his head, and my heart stopped.

"Do what?" I whispered.

His lips brushed over mine. The touch was featherlight. A question, more than a demand. A chance for me to back out, and I knew I should. I knew nothing had been resolved between us since the last time we'd kissed, but God. I edged forward on the table, my hands landing on his shirt-covered abs. I fisted my fingers in the fabric, telling myself to send him away. But the pulse between my legs ached for me to pull him close. A neediness in my chest screamed to be crushed against his pecs. And my mouth craved to taste him again.

I let my body win out over my head. I tugged him down, and he fused his mouth to mine. The world around us faded away. There was no cold air. No bar. No Sunny. No father who would never accept me. There was just me and him and an aching need that was only fulfilled by touch.

His fingers gripped the sides of my face, tilting it up to meet his lips, and we both opened, our tongues searching for each other, urgent and strong as we sank deep into the kiss. Every nerve ending in my body came alive and I fought to get closer to him. I pushed to my feet, and he wrapped one strong arm around me, hauling me tight against his hard body while his other hand moved to the back of my head, pinning me to him. And we kissed like we needed each other to breathe. His kiss stole the air from my lungs, but I would have happily died there, because no kiss had ever felt so right.

Until it felt so wrong.

Slowly, my brain won the war over my heart. It shouted accusations, until I jerked away, gasping for air.

"What's wrong?" he murmured, his warm breath misting over my face.

My body screamed at me, demanding I go back to kissing him. But my brain. Goddammit. Once the thoughts were there, I couldn't turn them off.

"We can't, Kai. You can't just kiss me without any explanation and think that this is all okay. It isn't!"

Kai blinked hard, but he didn't say anything.

"Talk to me. Tell me what you're thinking. I never know what's going on inside your head."

Still, he remained silent.

I laughed, but the sound was cold and bitter. And this time when my head said to shove him away, I listened. He stepped back, and I straightened my shirt. The cold night air suddenly made itself known, and I shivered again, but this time it was from nothing more than the frost. The one in the air. Not the one standing in front of me, wearing his usual stony, silent mask. I pushed past him, not giving him the chance to come up with a bullshit excuse.

"You owe me an explanation, Kai. When you're ready to give it, come see me."

With that, I left a little piece of my soul with a man whose kisses made my heart beat. But right now, that wasn't enough. I needed his words, too.

17

KAI

I was an idiot, a weak one at that. That much was clear, because twice now, I'd let myself kiss Addie. And even worse, twice I'd let her walk away.

I paced the area behind the bull pens while I waited for the announcers to call my name. I had a pre-ride ritual that needed to happen, but I couldn't concentrate. All I could think about was her staring up at me in the dark as I tried my luck by moving in on her. Memories of her lips on mine, fingers twisted around my shirt, dragging me closer, urging me on, made concentrating impossible.

The air felt thick and hot around me. I linked my hands behind my head, opening my chest to let in as much oxygen as possible. But it did little to ease the choking sensation. Probably because it was all in my head, and all to do with Addie. I was so stupid. Every time I was around her, I screwed things up even more. I'd be lucky if she ever spoke to me again. The thought of her hating me only brought a headache.

My name echoing around the large indoor arena snapped me from my daze, taking me by surprise. Shit! It couldn't already be my turn. Before every ride, I took the time to get in the zone. I blanked out the crowd and any problems I had. Anything that was on my mind was wiped, and I envisioned how the ride would go. I recalled the bull I would be riding and thought back through the hours of footage I'd watched for this sole purpose. I studied each of my rides until I knew that animal better than I knew my own name. All I had to do was block everything else, and my body would know what to do.

Easier said than done when all I could think about was a woman I couldn't have.

A hand slapped me on the back.

"You okay?" Rem asked, pausing on his way to the arena floor.

I nodded. "Fine." Total lie, but I'd never been one to share my problems. I definitely wasn't about to start thirty seconds before I was supposed to compete for a fifty thousand dollar paycheck.

Rem seemed like he wanted to argue, but we both knew he didn't have time. I was the first rider, and Rem, Abel, and another bullfighter, Eric, needed to be in the ring, ready to go when I was.

"See you out there. Good luck." Rem tipped his hat at me and ran out onto the arena floor, waving to the crowd as he went.

I shook out my arms and bounced on the balls of my feet a few times, then strode toward the bucking chutes. I attempted to look confident, because the last thing I needed was anyone else asking me if I was okay. Because I wasn't. I was rattled, and unprepared, and I hated the way it felt.

But the crowd didn't care my head and my heart were floating around outside my body. And the thousand pound bull didn't give a shit either. I sucked in a lungful of air, nodded to the team waiting to assist me, and climbed over the fence.

The bull lunged sharply to the right as I put my foot on his back, and my spotter tightened his grip on my vest. If the bull decided he wasn't putting up with me today, the spotter was the only one making sure I didn't end up at the bottom of the chute before it even opened. He'd keep ahold of me until the last second possible.

I settled into position, wrapping my hand with the rope and shifting forward. My body felt awkward and disconnected, but it was too late to do anything about it now.

Out of the corner of my eye, I saw Rem, Abel, and Eric move into a triangle formation, ready to distract the bull when I came off. The crowd in the stands went quiet, waiting for me to give the nod to pull the gates.

I didn't nod. I wasn't ready. I shouldn't have been noticing all these things. I shouldn't have smelled the tobacco smoke on my spotter's shirt. I shouldn't have noticed one of the stadium lights flickered every few seconds. I didn't normally notice anything but my body and the way the bull was reacting beneath me.

This was all fucking wrong. I wanted to get off, walk away, go find Addie and sort this whole thing out with her once and for all. But I didn't have any choice in the matter. I still needed this ride. I still needed to win this round, as much as I'd needed to win any other. It didn't matter my gaze kept straying to the friends and family section where I knew Addie would be sitting. I groaned, desperate to release some of my frustration.

And then I nodded. Because otherwise we'd just be sitting here all day.

The gates flew open, and the bull burst out of them, bucking and kicking out. Muscle memory switched on, and

I dug my heels in, gripping his back while I tried to keep my balance by waving my free hand. I kept it well clear from the animal to avoid disqualification.

None of it mattered. Within a second, I knew I was in trouble. I was jolting too high off the bull's back, and there was no rhythm to my movements. I was uncomfortable in a way I'd never been before, trying to find my center but missing the mark with every jerk of the massive beast beneath me. At four seconds, the bull changed directions, spinning to the left. Caught unprepared, my body slid off his side.

Knowing there was no saving my ride, I yanked the rope, freeing my hand, and hit the dirt on my hands and knees.

The impact thudded up through my limbs, making me slow to get moving again.

Too slow.

Rem and Abel rushed in, running in a circle around the bull, but it was too late. His hoof caught me in the thigh.

Pain speared through my leg, but I didn't have time to just lie there and whine about it or I'd have a lot more than a busted leg to worry about. I limped to the nearest fence, and using mostly my upper body strength, hauled myself up.

My breaths came in short, sharp pants as I clung to the metal frames, watching while Abel and Eric chased the bull back to the pens. Once he was behind the safety gate, I gingerly climbed down, testing my weight on my bad leg. Pain ricocheted through me, and my head spun. My stomach churned, and I fought to keep the pain from taking control.

Rem appeared at my side. "Shit, you all right?"

Rem's concerned gaze narrowed in on my leg, and he held an arm out toward me.

I ignored it, my pain turning into anger. "No, I'm not

fucking all right, Rem! Fucking bull just damn near put his hoof through my thigh! Where were you guys?"

Rem blinked, and his hand dropped to his side. "Come again?"

Irritation rolled through me, a mixture of frustration over my ride and pain from my injury. "Forget it," I snapped.

I limped toward the tunnels that would take me back to the changing rooms, but Rem rounded on me, blocking my path. His normally friendly expression had morphed into something harder. He held his hand up in a 'stop' motion.

"No. You don't get to walk off like that. You've always been good to us. You're not like some of those other assholes who think what we do out in the ring is a joke. What the fuck was that about?"

I instantly felt a rush of remorse. He was right. I had nothing but respect for the bullfighters. They put their lives on the line to keep us safe every time we competed. Some of the other guys on the tour laughed behind their backs, calling them the talentless hacks who could only run away from a bull instead of ride one. But I'd never felt like that. They were a hell of a lot braver than I was.

"It's nothing. I'm sorry."

"No, bullshit. That wasn't you out there. What's going on?" He followed me to the very far edge of the ring so we were just inside the tunnels. I knew nobody could see us, because we stood in the shadows, but we could still see out into the crowd. My gaze immediately went to the friends and family area, searching out the woman I couldn't get out of my head.

"Ah," Rem said, crossing his arms over his broad chest. "This ain't about getting stomped. It's about her."

I shook my head. "Look, it's not my business if you two have something going on. I want her to be happy."

Rem let out a laugh. "We're friends. I'm helping her with something. That's it." He paused. "Not saying I wouldn't have tried, but she's interested in someone else."

"What?" I roared.

Rem raised one eyebrow. "Oh yeah, sure. You're not bothered about her dating someone else at all. Chill out. It's you." He rolled his eyes.

I shoved my hands in my pockets. "Oh." A flicker of hope ignited in my chest. I knew Addie and Rem were friends. I'd seen them talking a few times. And now all I wanted to do was corner Rem and question him about everything Addie had ever said about me.

Like I was back in fucking high school. Hell. When had I become such a loser?

Rem eyed the ring. The next rider was beginning his preparation, and Abel was looking in our direction, his mouth pulled into a pissed-off grimace.

Rem elbowed me as he walked back toward his brother. "Just tell her, would you? You obviously can't concentrate while things are unsaid between the two of you. Just rip the fucking Band-Aid off already."

I nodded, but the problem was, what if I ripped off the Band-Aid and the wound beneath it was still bleeding? I could lay it all out on the line, everything I'd ever felt for her. But was it going to make any difference when there was still that one giant hurdle I wasn't sure I'd ever be able to get over?

I realized with a start I wanted it to make a difference. I wanted to get over that hurdle. The thoughts that taunted me, blamed me for Sunny's death, and accused me of stealing his girl—I wanted to silence them.

I wanted her to be mine.

18

ADDIE

$\mathcal{F}$or a man who'd competed in a professional sport for the past two years, there was very little online information about Kai. I scrolled through a few pages of YouTube videos, all of them just footage of his rides. Some other sites had brief paragraphs that were nothing more than his name and scores. The man's Wikipedia page only consisted of his date of birth, his parents' names, and the awards he'd won.

Not exactly the information I wanted.

I sat back in the chair and sighed. I wasn't sure whether I was relieved or frustrated by the results of my Google search. On one hand, I already felt wrong hunting down information Kai clearly didn't want to share with the public. If there was nothing online to find, there was nothing to tell, and my editor at the website would just have to make do with what I already knew about him.

On the other hand, what I knew made for a pretty boring story. And my editor wouldn't be impressed with me. My fingers hovered over the keys. I hated this. I wanted to do a good job. I was a journalist, and though the paper back home was small, I still took pride in my work. And this assignment was a big opportunity for me. I didn't want to blow it.

"Argh!" I groaned to the empty room. "Why does he have to be so difficult!"

The empty room didn't answer.

I brushed my fingers over the keyboard, debating over what I was supposed to do now. My editor was expecting this story tomorrow, and right now, all I was handing in was a fluff piece that merely stated the facts. Kai was a good bull rider, who'd been the driver of a car accident that killed his best friend. Despite being in that same accident, I knew nothing more than those simple facts everybody already knew anyway.

I wanted to bang my head on the table. Instead, I went back to Kai's miserable- looking Wikipedia page and reminded myself of his parents' names. Cora and Cyrus-Lee Hunt. My nose wrinkled involuntarily as I typed Kai's father's name into the search engine.

I was hoping to find something about Kai's childhood— maybe there was something about the farm he grew up on, or a story on his family from before the time he'd ridden professionally.

The screen filled with results, and my fingers shook while I took in story after story featuring the name Cyrus-Lee Hunt. With dread rising in my gut, and feeling suddenly dirty, I clicked the first link. I scrolled through the website's photo gallery, my skin crawling and each image making me feel sicker than the last. Until one caught my eye.

"Oh my God," I whispered, clapping a hand over my mouth. I shoved the laptop away, not wanting it anywhere near me.

Because there in the galleries of a white supremacy

website, was a photo of Kai's dad. And beside him, a little boy, whose piercing blue eyes burned me even from within an image that had to be ten years old.

I got to my feet and stumbled toward the bathroom, fearing I'd be sick. I caught myself on the wall, just in time for the hotel door to rattle slightly beneath the weight of a heavy knock.

Somehow, before I even staggered over to the door and opened it, I knew it was him.

Kai's face was paler than normal, which only made those startling eyes bluer. My hand fell from the door handle, and I just stood there, staring at the older version of the little boy in the photo.

"Can we talk?" he said without saying hello, which was so typically Kai I could barely stand it. I didn't have the energy to speak. I just felt...drained.

I stepped aside, and Kai followed me into the room. I went to close the door, but he ducked his head, so his eyes were level with mine. He reached out and gripped my chin between gentle fingers, tilting my head up. "Whoa, hey. What's the matter?"

I just shook my head helplessly. "Nothing? Everything? I don't know, Kai. I don't know anything."

His thumb stroked along my jawline, and damn if I didn't just want to close my eyes and press into his touch. My skin prickled with awareness, sensing how close he was. His pale white skin. Mine dark brown. A color his father hated.

Like father, like son.

I pulled away. "Why are you here?"

He dropped his hand to his side, suddenly appearing stiff and uncomfortable. "I came to ask if we could do that interview."

"Now?"

He nodded.

I choked on a humorless laugh. "I wish you'd come about an hour earlier."

His eyebrows furrowed in. "Why?"

I shrugged and pointed to the open laptop on the small coffee table. "See for yourself."

He gave me a look that clearly said he didn't understand what was going on, but I didn't have the energy to explain it to him. That photo would tell him everything he needed to know without a single word from me.

He moved to sit at the seat I'd been occupying just moments earlier and brought the laptop closer.

His face paled. "What is this?" he whispered, shooting a horrified glance in my direction.

I walked slowly, as if the air was made of molasses. I took the seat beside Kai. "You honestly don't know?"

He shook his head. "I mean, I can see what it is. White Unite. It's a hate group website. But how...?"

"I think we both know how." I sucked in a breath, trying to steady myself, but only succeeded in getting a noseful of Kai's fresh, clean scent. My mouth watered. I'd always liked the cologne he wore. Not that I'd ever told him, because why would I? He'd been my boyfriend's best friend, and that would have been weird. And now I still couldn't tell him. Because his freaking photo was on a white supremacy website, and I was anything but white. How was I supposed to tell him anything ever again?

His big hand covered mine on the table. I moved to pull away, but he only gripped me tighter. "Look at me."

I couldn't. All I could do was stare at our differing skin colors.

"Addie," he growled. "Look at me."

I lifted my head, hating that tears glistened in my eyes.

But his were clear and bright. "I didn't know about that photo, Addie. I swear it."

"But you knew what you were doing when it was taken."

He shook his head vigorously. "No. I mean, yes. I knew what it was. But I was a kid. I had no choice in where I went or what I did."

"Or what you thought?"

"No," he said with conviction lacing every syllable. "I always knew what I thought. And I never believed in anything those men preach. My father included."

He inched closer, and my brain said to move away. But my damn traitorous body just wanted to lean into him. I shrugged again, because the whole thing felt impossible. Who he was. Who *I* was. How I felt about him.

"How am I supposed to believe that?" I whispered.

He turned and yanked my chair, maneuvering it so it was between his widespread legs, forcing us to face each other. He leaned forward, and I found myself mirroring his actions. When he spoke, his warm breath misted over my tingling lips.

"Because I could never hate you, Addie." His gaze broke from mine, dipping to my lips. "Not when all I do is think about you."

My breath caught. "What are you saying?"

His gaze locked firmly on my mouth.

"I'm saying that all I think about is kissing you. Being with you. Wrapping you in my arms and holding you, because I feel like that's the only way I'm ever going to be whole."

My mouth parted, and he ran his thumb across my lower lip.

"I know I've been an asshole. And I've screwed this thing up so many times..."

My head reeled, and I struggled to keep up with his words. "What thing, Kai? The thing where you hate me, but then you kiss me and then you ignore me? I'm really sick of that thing." My tone was sharp and sarcastic, and I knew I was coming across as a bitch, but frankly, he deserved it. "What do you want? Sex? To take it to the next level, just to have you walk out on me the next day? Maybe that's what you mean by 'thing'? Because I'm not interested in fucking you, just to have you screw me over when the sun comes up and you realize I'm not good enough."

He winced, and I braced myself for his inevitable walk-out. Because that's what he'd done the last two times. Things got serious between us, and he bailed. I was so sick of people walking out on me.

But this time, he didn't move. His heated stare pinned me to the spot. "I meant that thing where I like you more than I should. More than any friend should." His lips were mere inches from mine, and they hypnotized me until I was powerless to stop him moving in. "I don't just want sex, Addie," he whispered. "It's more than that. I want you. All of you. I always have. From the very first day I met you."

His mouth connected with mine in a kiss that was so soft and sweet my heart ached. Suddenly, so many things made sense. His moodiness around me. His refusal to look at me when Sunny was in the room. Isabel insisting he'd sat by my bedside night and day. And yet, I'd been so quick to put his kiss down to him trying to prove something.

I'd been wrong. So very wrong.

Because there in Kai's kiss—our first true kiss that wasn't all pent-up passion and fiery desire—I sensed the truth. And it was more reassurance than any words could ever be.

I let my walls fall. I wrapped my arms around his neck and kissed him back, my mouth opening, allowing him in when his tongue moved over my lips. My heart pounded and he dragged me closer, cupping my face between his big hands. We kissed long and slow, sweet, drugging kisses that had the power to undo me.

One by one, his kisses evaporated my fears, replacing them with the knowledge that in his arms, in his embrace, I was cared for.

"Addie," he whispered between kisses. "I want to show you."

It took me too long to drag my mouth away from his. "Show me what?"

His eyes flared. "How I feel about you."

His voice was a deep rumble, full of promise and longing. Without clarifying, I knew what he meant. A shiver of anticipation rolled down my spine.

He held out a hand, and I placed mine in his, this time not noticing our skin, but how our hands fit perfectly together. I linked my fingers through his as he led me to the bedroom.

I eyed the bed, nerves fluttering about in my belly, anticipation of what was to come quickening my breath. But Kai was completely in control. I reached for him, but he caught my wrists, pinning them to my sides. He leaned in close, so his lips brushed my neck. "I said I wanted to show *you*. Not the other way around. Hold still."

My stomach flipped. I would never have picked loner Kai and his quiet, mild-mannered ways to have this dominant side. But without a doubt, it was the hottest I'd seen him yet. My underwear grew damp, and my core throbbed with need, anticipation making me eager for what was to come.

Slowly, his fingers came to rest on my hips. I raised my arms again to place them on his shoulders, but he cut me off with a look. "I said, hold still."

I dropped them back down. Only then did his fingers move. He slid them beneath my long-sleeved sweater, brushing the bare skin of my sides as he lifted it up. This time when I raised my arms, he didn't reprimand me, only pulled the knitted fabric over my head. I let my arms drop to my sides once more, my bra the only thing covering my breasts from his gaze.

It should have been awkward, standing there in front of him in so little clothing. Only a scrap of lace covered my nipples. I wasn't drunk. It wasn't dark. And it was *Kai* with his hot gaze running all over my body. But I'd be lying if I said I hadn't been thinking of this for weeks.

He stepped in close again, pressing his lips to the side of my neck, just higher than my shoulder. I shivered at his touch and tried to control the rapid rise and fall of my chest. His lips trailed down across my shoulder, takin my bra strap with him. Without missing a beat, he did the same thing on the other side then kissed his way over my collarbone. My head dropped back, and I moaned at his deft fingers undoing the clasp of my bra, setting my breasts free.

I wanted him to touch me. And he didn't make me wait long. The palm of his hand traced the path his lips had taken earlier before dragging south over the swells of my breasts. My nipples hardened even though he hadn't gone near them yet. His fingertips slid down my stomach, stopping at the waistband of my leggings.

I hissed out a breath, his fingers running beneath the elastic waistband, just barely glancing over the top of my mound through my underwear. I rubbed my thighs together, trying to find relief for the throbbing between my legs.

Kai's mouth lifted at the corner then he leaned in, his mouth landing on my nipple.

"Oh!" I cried out at the sudden warmth of his mouth.

His tongue swirled around my nipple, drawing it between his teeth and sucking it until my fingers speared through his short blond hair.

A light slap on my ass caught my attention. "Hold still," he demanded.

His hand cupped my other breast, pinching the nipple with two fingers and rolling it. My blood pulsed with desire.

He kissed his way down the underside of my breast and along the flat planes of my stomach. I whimpered when he got to my waistband again.

"You want me to touch you, Addie?" he murmured, kneeling at my feet. "Or do you want me to taste you?"

Heat rushed through me, and my knees wobbled. He tucked his fingers beneath the elastic of my leggings and underwear, dragging both down in one movement. I stepped out of my clothes and waited, staring down at the beautiful man kneeling before me like I was his queen.

My heart skipped a beat as our gazes connected, and when he broke it, it was to place an open-mouthed kiss on my bare skin, just above my slit.

"Oh God," I whispered.

His tongue trailed lazy circles around my mound and down, over the outside of my lips. My thighs shook, wetness pooling at my entrance, just waiting for his fingers or tongue to slide through it.

"Lie down, Addie," he commanded.

I sure as hell wasn't going to argue. The authoritative tone only made me want him more.

I sat on the bottom end of the neatly made bed, then slid backward toward the headboard. My mouth dried as Kai prowled after me. His hands ran up my shins and then my thighs, dipping between them and pushing them wide open so he could settle himself in the gap. With a look that scorched me, he dipped his mouth to my center.

My hips bucked off the bed, and I pressed into the pile of soft pillows, eyes rolling back. "Kai!" I yelled.

He stopped, waiting for me to settle. "Look at me."

Our gazes collided. He lowered his head again, and this time I was more prepared for the sensation of his tongue sliding through my pussy. I held his gaze, watching his tongue lazily glide over my clit, while his fingers gripped my thighs, keeping me open to him.

I didn't turn away and he slid one hand closer to where his mouth was driving me wild. He nudged at my entrance. I moaned my need to have some part of him inside me—I wanted it to be his cock. My mouth watered at the thought of how big and thick he might be. I wanted to know what it would be like, to have him plunge inside me, stretching me, dominating me like he seemed to enjoy. But he was running this little show, and I'd take his fingers if that was what he was offering. The need inside me was building, mounting, and I needed more.

Kai's eyes were scorching when he pushed two fingers up inside me. I couldn't hold his gaze a second longer. I moaned loudly, closing my eyes, and giving in to the sensation. He sucked my clit, while his fingers slid in and out, taking me higher and higher with each stroke. I rolled my hips against his hand, and he moved faster, matching the pace he finally let me set.

"I want to watch you come, Addie," he said, voice gruff.

That wasn't going to be a problem.

He hooked his fingers, brushing that spot inside, the one that heightened every feeling. "Oh God, Kai!" I yelled. Sensation exploded inside me, spreading out through my torso, then my limbs, my blood rushing to take the warmth through my entire body. I rode his hand, shifting my hips while he sucked my clit, until sensation overwhelmed me. I grasped his head, pulling him away from my oversensitive flesh.

My eyes fluttered open.

"You're so fucking beautiful," he whispered.

Emotion laced his every syllable, and I dragged him up the bed while I simultaneously slid lower, needing his mouth on mine *now*. Our lips met in a bruising, claiming kiss that I felt right down to my soul.

He was still fully clothed, and I was still very naked, but in that moment, the physical didn't matter. That kiss was more than just two bodies seeking pleasure. Though he might not be a man of many words, that kiss said more than anything he could have spoken aloud.

*I*t was late, but I wasn't tired. The mind-blowing orgasm had me relaxed but not sleepy. I watched with interest as Kai pulled away from our kiss and shifted to the side of the bed. He took off his boots and socks before he stood, and I giggled at the thought he'd been going down on me without even taking off his shoes. He reached behind his head, grabbing a handful of his long-sleeved T-shirt and tugged it off. My gaze strayed to his muscled chest, then to his abs, a light trail of hair leading from his belly button and disappearing beneath the waistband of his jeans.

"Enjoying the view?" he asked, with a smug grin that was so unlike him it surprised me.

But it looked good on him. Everything looked good on him...and off him. "Very much so. Take off your jeans."

He raised an eyebrow.

I mirrored the action. "What? You think you're the only one who likes to be in control in the bedroom?"

His grin widened. "Wild cat."

I winked. "Might be."

He groaned, and I laughed, but I got my way. He undid

the button on his jeans and lowered the fly. His boxer briefs were plain black cotton, and I eyed them once he was crawling back into bed with me.

"Roll over," he said. "I'm the big spoon."

I didn't. The thought of Kai being either sized spoon was bizarre. "I wouldn't have picked you for a cuddler."

He shifted over in the bed so we were face-to-face. "I'm about to blow your mind then."

"Again?"

He chuckled. "I'm a grade A snuggler. Professional level, even."

We were so close our noses were practically touching. Kai laid on his biceps, and I had the white hotel sheet tucked up beneath my arms. I trailed my fingers over the planes of his bare chest and wriggled closer. "We can snuggle later. I want to do something first."

I explored his abs and felt the change in his skin as it pebbled into goose bumps. He caught my hand when it reached his underwear.

I pouted. "What's wrong? You don't want me to?"

He swallowed, his Adam's apple bobbing. "I do. Trust me, I *really* do. But not yet. We need to talk first."

I kissed his lips. "Talk later." I reached for him again, but he pulled away.

"Addie, don't. I just can't let you do anything like that without explaining myself."

I blew out a long breath. I knew he was right, but with my body still singing, talking about what was going on with us wasn't appealing. Because I knew that conversation wasn't going to be an easy one. For either of us. But it did have to be done. "Okay," I said, slowly moving my hand back to my side of the bed. "Normally dragging words out of you is like beating a dead horse."

He grimaced. "I know. I've been a dick."

"Yeah," I agreed. "You sort of have."

He didn't seem hurt by my words, just resigned. "You wanted to talk to me weeks ago, but I just wasn't ready."

I fingered the edge of the cotton sheet. "Are you truly ready now?"

He hesitated for a moment. "Am I on the record?"

"Only if you want to be."

He bit his plump bottom lip, worrying it between his teeth. "I never started any of this to become famous, you know?"

I knew. Kai was the last person anyone would accuse of being fame hungry.

"When I was about thirteen, I started winning a few local rodeos. Beating out grown men who'd been bull riding twice as long as I had. Turned out, I was kind of good at it."

I smiled. "I noticed."

He found my fingers and laced his in between, then brought my hand to his lips. He brushed his mouth over my knuckles. The gesture was so sweet my heart ached.

"Bull riding was really the best thing that ever happened to me. It was where I met Sunny." His voice wavered on Sunny's name, and his entire body went stiff. He rolled onto his back, flinging one arm over his eyes. "Shit."

I could imagine what he was feeling. Every time we'd come together, we'd gotten lost in ourselves, in a little world where it was only him and me. As soon as Sunny's name came up, Kai froze. The fact he'd just made me come, and we were lying naked in bed together hadn't changed that.

But it had changed me.

I sat up and pulled his arm away from his face. "Stop it," I demanded. "If you're going to Guilt Town in your head, you need to stop and back up right now. Tell me how you met Sunny."

Kai inhaled a shaky breath, but he didn't try to fight me. I snuggled in against him, fitting myself into the crook of his arm and resting my head on his chest.

"We met at a training camp," he said eventually.

"How old were you?"

"Seventeen." A rumble of laughter rippled up his chest. "You should have seen Sunny back then. He was so tall and gangly with these ears that stuck out just a bit too far for him to not be teased about it."

I giggled. "So not much changed in the years afterward?" He'd still been tall and gangly at twenty-two, right before he'd died. And his ears had stuck out a little, but I'd thought it adorable.

Kai pressed his lips to my forehead. "He walked over to me on the very first day of camp, thrust his hand out for me to shake, declared we were roommates, and therefore, best friends."

I smiled into his chest. "I can imagine him doing that."

"We went up through the levels together. He wasn't as naturally good as I was, but fuck. He was the most determined kid I'd ever met. He knew, even back then at seventeen, he was going to make it big. And really, I just went along for the ride. Sunny trained harder and longer than anyone else. And because he was the only one who spoke to me, I trained right alongside him."

I turned my head and kissed Kai's biceps, the warmth of his skin beneath my lips. "How did it feel when you made the pros together?"

"Amazing. It just made us closer. Because then we were traveling everywhere with the team. He became more like my brother than my best friend."

I could feel the unspoken "but then" in the air, and I knew he was struggling with his memories. I hated that. I just wanted to make it easier for him.

"What's this from?" I asked, tracing a scar down the middle of his chest. The scar was faded, but it was thick, like he'd suffered a major trauma. "Did you have a heart surgery?"

"No. The doctors in the hospital told me it was near identical to a heart surgery scar, though."

"What's the scar from then?"

"Had a run-in with a bull horn."

"Ouch."

"You're telling me. I had more stitches than I could count. But we weren't talking about my scars. You're letting me off the hook." He tucked a strand of hair behind my ear.

"I know it's hard for you to talk about. I don't want to push you."

He lifted his head to brush his lips over mine, but then he dropped it back down to the pillow and stared at the ceiling. "There it is again. You're too damn nice for me. You're always so...nice."

"Um, thanks? Though it kind of sounds like a back-handed compliment."

He shook his head. "No, it's not. It's one of the first things that really attracted me to you." He closed his eyes, and his voice lowered an octave. "I was *too* attracted to you. I still am."

I bit my lip.

"That's why I couldn't talk to you. Or if I did, it just came out all stiff and wrong. I had to bury it all." He pulled his arm from beneath my head and sat up suddenly.

I followed, not caring the sheet pooled around my waist, exposing my bare breasts. Kai didn't seem to notice either.

He was too wrapped up in his own head. He ran his hands through his hair, and I shifted so I was in front of him, my knees digging into the mattress.

"Kai..."

When he looked up at me, my heart nearly broke.

His gaze was so filled with pain. "You were his, and I wanted you anyway."

"I never knew," I reassured him. "*He* never knew."

"Does it matter? I still wanted what wasn't mine to take. And now he's gone, and I just swoop in and take it anyway. Fuck!"

He edged away from me, but heat still burned behind the pain. "I want you so damn much, Addie, but I don't know how."

My heart clenched. I crawled into his lap, wrapping my legs around his narrow waist and my arms behind his neck. My breasts pressed into his chest, and I gathered him to me, trying to absorb some of his pain. His lips touched my neck, and he trembled, his breaths ragged as he tried to keep himself together. And I held him tighter, wishing there was more I could do.

A gasp escaped me as he twisted, and I found myself on my back again, the springs in the mattress squeaking at the sudden change of position. Kai's mouth fused to mine, his tongue diving deep. His cock—still covered by his underwear—ground against my center, and I squeezed my legs tighter, trying to increase the friction. Holding his weight on one arm, he slid the other down between us, and I groaned, his fingers finding my clit.

"Want to make you feel good," he mumbled into my lips. I didn't dare point out he'd already done that. I was ready to do it all again. Wetness pooled between my thighs, and I ached for more. We kissed with such urgency that every thought, except his hands and lips on mine, was obliterated from my head. This time when I reached for his boxer briefs, he didn't stop me. I pulled his underwear over his ass and shoved it down his thighs, setting his impressive cock free. The tip of him slicked between my legs, seeking an entrance. I was ready for it, moaning my approval and lifting my hips to meet his. His cock notched and pushed inside the tiniest fraction of an inch. Just enough for me to feel how big he was. And for me to crave the full length of him.

But then his eyes flew open.

He jerked away. "Shit, Addie. No. I can't." His breath heaved, and his cock jutted out, long and thick and proud as he sat back on his knees.

I lifted onto my elbows and drank in my fill of him, my core aching, his hot, needy gaze raking my heated flesh.

"It's okay," I soothed. I realized what was going on. "I get it."

He could touch me. I couldn't touch him.

But I could work with that. I slowly trailed one hand up, sweeping it beneath my breast. I cupped it, finding the nipple, squeezing it hard. Pleasure jolted through me, and Kai's eyes flared.

I moved my right hand low, to my bikini line and then between my legs, finding my clit. I rubbed a small, tight circle over my nub, letting my legs fall wide so he could see exactly what I was doing.

Moisture beaded on the tip of his cock, and I eyed it, wishing he would let me lick it off. But if he wasn't ready for me to touch him, I could at least show him what he was missing. And watching him watch me, turned me on like never before.

"Now you," I whispered, slicking my fingers through my

lower lips, teasing my entrance then slowly returning to my clit.

I wasn't sure whether he'd do it, and disappointment ricocheted through me when he paused. But then I dipped one finger into my aching slit and let out a moan.

His answering groan of want filled the room. His thick fingers circled the base of his cock, and he stroked his length, moving up over the head before returning to the base.

"Again," I commanded.

He did. His right hand stroked his cock, and I dipped two fingers inside myself, matching the rhythm he set.

It was too good. Too much. Watching this beautiful man touch himself, his abs contracting and releasing as he fisted his thick length. One hand dipped to cup and squeeze heavy balls, while moisture leaked from the head of his dick. My own orgasm was building, my hips rolling in time with my fingers, and I tried to keep the waves of pleasure at bay, not wanting to come before he did.

With an expression of pure desire, he worked his hand faster, pumping himself, until he dropped his head back on his shoulders.

"Are you close?" I breathed through my own pants of pleasure. I prayed he was, because I was so ready to tumble over the ledge with him.

"Fuck, yes," he bit out. "I need to come. Come with me."

I wasn't even sure if I responded with words, but his demand was all it took for my inner walls to clamp down around my fingers and for a cry of pleasure to rip from my throat. Kai groaned my name again, his seed spilling hot onto my thighs and belly. I let myself fully fall into my orgasm, knowing he was doing the same.

Waves of sensation washed over me, my muscles tensing, then loosening, one by one. I sank deeper into the mattress; boneless, sated, and...sticky.

The mattress dipped, and I cracked open an eye to admire Kai's perfect naked ass as he disappeared into the bathroom. The sound of running water floated back, and then he reappeared with a wet cloth and pink cheeks.

He leaned over and kissed me softly, his eyes tender, his smile a little embarrassed. "Sorry about the mess."

I shook my head, reaching for the cloth, but he moved his hand and took care of it for me. I shivered as the warm, wet cloth wiped over my still sensitive flesh. My skin was rapidly cooling now without the heat of a building orgasm keeping me warm, and Kai pulled the blankets over me.

A wave of exhaustion threatened to drag me down, my eyelids suddenly too heavy now that I was relaxed and sated. Kai lifted the blankets and tucked himself in behind me, his warmth like a drug to my system, dragging me even farther down into the clutches of sleep.

"We still need to finish our talk," he murmured.

But I was too far gone to respond.

20

ADDIE

*K*ai wasn't wrong about being a grade A snuggler. I woke up early the next morning, his thick arm was still bounded around me so tightly I could barely breathe. His face was buried in a cloud of my hair, but he didn't seem to notice or care. His breaths were deep and even, and when I managed to gently extract myself from his embrace, he didn't even twitch. I couldn't help but run the backs of my fingers down the side of his stubbled jaw. It would have been all too easy to climb back into bed with him, then start working over his naked, muscled body, waking him up in the best way possible. But after his reluctance to let me touch him last night, I didn't dare.

Instead I wrapped myself in a spare blanket and padded over to where my laptop lay discarded on the table. I plonked down on the chair, tucking my feet in beneath me.

The photo of Kai and his father was still on the screen, and I pondered it for a long minute, hating I'd even found it. My heart pounded for more than just the fact Kai had been involved in such a group. If I was honest, my heart raced because a story like that? A public figure being outed as a

white supremacist, was big news. And the journalist in me
—the one who died a little every time I had to report on a
funeral of some elderly resident, or a flower show in a tiny
town no one had ever heard of—she got excited over the
idea of such a big story landing in my lap.

I closed the internet browser and brought up my notes
on Kai. I added in details from our talk the night before,
surprising myself when I included all the personal stuff
about how he felt about me. *"I don't just want sex, Addie. It's
more than that. I want you. All of you. I always have. From the
very first day I met you."*

Even as I wrote the words, I couldn't believe I'd heard
them with my own ears. And the more I wrote down and
relived the conversation from last night, the more I found it
hard to believe he could have been serious. I didn't doubt he
had feelings for me. I'd seen that in the way he'd struggled
to keep control of himself, and the guilt he felt because of it.
But last night, I'd let myself think those feelings ran deeper
than his words really admitted. That was stupid.

I glanced over at his sleeping form. We might have taken
one step forward last night, but in some ways, it was just
another step back. There were still things left unsaid
between us. I wanted my stupid brain to just switch off.
What was wrong with me? Why wasn't I in bed, just
enjoying being wrapped in the arms of a man I was clearly
incredibly attracted to? Why did I have to overanalyze everything, searching for hidden stories and deeper meanings
within every word he'd said, and every move he'd made?

Nope. I shut my laptop. I *was* going to be that girl who
spent the morning wrapped in his arms. Because with how
skittish Kai had been in the past, I didn't want to lose my
opportunity to know what it felt like. Something had
changed between us last night, but what if it wasn't enough?

What if he woke up and was firmly back in charge as the mayor of Guilt Town, and didn't want anything to do with me? I padded back to bed, ready to slip in beside him when my phone vibrated on the nightstand.

I snatched it up quickly, not wanting its buzzing to disturb Kai, and glanced at the unknown number on the screen. Frowning at it, I hit the green 'answer' button but waited until I was safely in the bathroom before speaking.

"Addison St. Clair?" The voice was male, deep. Unfamiliar. Possibly someone from the New York office? Maybe my editor was on vacation.

"Speaking."

"It's Mathew Radcliffe."

It took me a moment to realize why that name was familiar. "The investigator!"

"That's me." He sounded like he was smiling, but I was suddenly filled with nerves. Since I hadn't immediately heard back from him after my drunken call at the bar, I'd just assumed he wasn't interested in my case. It had been easy to forget about when Kai, and my dramas with him, were taking up all my thoughts. But now my heart thumped so hard I was surprised the man couldn't hear it down the phone line.

"You got my message?"

"I did. And like I do for all potential clients, I've done a quick background check using the information you provided in your message. I believe I can help you, Miss St. Clair. I might already have a lead on your birth mother."

"Oh." I sat so hard on the floor, I was sure my ass would ache later.

"Should I continue with my investigations? There'll be a fee."

"Yes. Please." I blurted out the words before I could

really think them through. I had a small amount of money saved, and enough cash to live on while I was here...as long as I managed to hang on to my job. If I delivered a piece on Kai, the job wouldn't be a problem. And Kai was finally starting to open up to me.

"Okay then. Text me your email address, and I'll send you over the bill. I'll be in touch soon with a list of information I'll need from you."

He hung up abruptly, and I was left staring at the phone while my stomach churned with a mixture of excitement and terror.

"Addie?" Kai's quiet voice called from outside the bathroom.

I pushed to my feet, and on wobbly legs, opened the door and slipped out.

He cast an anxious eye over me, gripping one of my bare arms. "Are you okay?"

I nodded, holding up the phone as if it held all the answers. "The investigator has a lead on my mother." My voice cracked on the word mother; stupid, hot, hopeful tears suddenly filling my eyes. A sob rose in my throat so quickly it took me by surprise.

"Oh, baby. Come here." He pulled me into his arms while I added a clenching heart to my mix of bodily responses. Him calling me baby was so simple, and yet it made my emotions flip-flop. They were already so scrambled it was hard to keep up.

I clutched his chest, letting a fat tear roll down my cheek. "I'm so sorry," I mumbled over and over. "This is terrible."

Eventually he cupped my face between his palms and tilted it up. "Stop. It's not terrible. It's important to you."

I nodded, trying to fight back a fresh round of tears that

threatened to spill over. "I've never had a family. And I know my parents gave me up, but..."

"But you don't know why. Maybe they were young and scared and thought they were doing the right thing by you."

I nodded. "Exactly. I know it's unlikely, but what if they still think about me? What if they've just been waiting for me to contact them all these years?"

He brushed a gentle kiss over my lips. "I bet that's the case."

I let out a laugh. "You're biased."

He grinned as he shook his head. "Hey, you thought I hated you until yesterday, remember? I'm not biased at all. I'm just saying you don't know, until you're actually told."

"You told me you had feelings for me yesterday."

The words fell and died on my lips, and I closed my eyes, wishing like hell I could take them back. Words muttered in the heat of passion weren't the same as words said in the cold hard light of day.

"Addie, I—"

I pressed a finger to his lips. "No, don't. Just...don't. It's too much right now. You. My job. The possibility of a family. I know we still need to sort things out, but can we just take a pause and have five minutes where there isn't a drama?"

He looked like he wanted to argue, but the expression on my face must have convinced him otherwise. Instead he kissed the top of my head. "Okay. But later..."

I nodded, breathing in the scent of his skin. "Later."

"Fine. Then do you want to go on a date with me tonight?"

I took half a step back and smiled up at his eager face. "A date? Like a proper one?"

"Yep."

Something clicked into place in my head. "We're flying

to Georgia this morning for next weekend's rodeo. Back on your home soil."

His grin got a little wider. "Just so happens, I know all the best date places in town."

"That so?"

"I've got the whole night planned. You just have to say yes."

As if I was going to say no.

21

KAI

*T*he wheels of the plane touched the tarmac, bumping and hopping over the smooth blacktop, then rolled to a complete stop. Before the light even switched off, I had my seat belt undone, letting the metal clips clank off the sides of the seat. I was pulling my carry-on luggage out of the overhead compartments as most of the others on the plane got to their feet. My footsteps ate up the aisle, and I arrived at Addie's side right as she was taking off her airline-issued headphones.

She started, dropping the little white earbuds. They hung off the back of her neck while she gaped up at me. "How did you get over here so quickly?" She peered around me to the flight attendant section, her lips turning up in amusement. "You're in trouble."

I glanced over my shoulder, and sure enough, one of the flight attendants was giving me the stink eye. I wasn't normally the type of guy who broke the rules, but Addie and I hadn't been able to swap our tickets for seats together, and the flight to Georgia had been too long. All I'd done was think about the show she'd put on last night—her long dark fingers stroking between her thighs, her head thrown back in pleasure, tiny moans escaping through her pillowy lips... I'd had to force myself to push the memory from my mind to avoid an embarrassing tent in my jeans. I didn't think the middle-aged businessman in the seat beside me would have appreciated me sporting a hard-on while he tried to read a boring-looking report on his laptop.

"Which bag was yours? I wasn't paying attention on the way in." I opened the overhead compartment and studied the gray bags while Addie gathered her iPad, pens, and a notebook into her purse.

She pushed to her feet and nudged me playfully aside. "That's because you were too busy paying attention to my lips."

Ha. She was right. I hadn't been able to take my eyes off her. Addie giggled, grabbing a small suitcase and pulling it down. I caught it midair and took it from her, despite her protests that she was perfectly capable of doing it herself.

"Don't argue with me. I'm trying to be a gentleman here. We're in the South. My mom will tan my hide if I don't use my manners."

She raised an eyebrow. "And if I do argue?"

We shuffled down the aisle that was rapidly filling with people. I leaned in closer so my words wouldn't be overheard. "Then I'll have to tan your hide, I guess."

Heat flashed in Addie's eyes, and there was no stopping the tightening in my pants this time. Fuck. I let my hand drift over her ass, sneaking a squeeze of her perfectly pert behind as I went. Her sharp intake of breath told me she was just as horny as I was. Impatient, I shuffled forward again, so close to the older man in front of me that he turned around tutted.

"Sorry," I muttered.

Addie snorted her amusement.

By the time we got off the plane, and into the terminal, I was so damn hot for her I was ready to take Addie into the nearest restroom and bend her over a sink. But before I could even look around for a bathroom sign, Addie was pulling me out of the line of people making their way to baggage claim and tugging my lips down to meet hers.

Fuck. Yes. I wrapped my arms around her, my fingertips brushing her lower back. She reached for my neck, linking her hands behind my head and holding me to her in a way that made the possessive male in me growl in approval. Our lips moved in unison, and not caring who saw—be it the guys on the tour or the waiting area full of perfect strangers —I delved my tongue inside her open mouth. The hot, needy stroke did nothing to help my erection, thankfully hidden by Addie's body. I'd never been one for public displays of affection, but I couldn't keep my hands off her. That flight had been too long.

An exaggerated cough barked in my ear. I jerked away from Addie, my irritation with whoever had interrupted us instantly sky-high. I knew we weren't exactly keeping things G-rated but I was sure these airport walls had seen more risqué homecoming reunions than the clinch Addie and I were in right now.

"Kai."

The heat swirling through my blood went cold at the familiar, disapproving tone. I lost my erection quicker than I would have thought possible. I swiveled slowly, pulling Addie slightly behind me as if she needed protecting from the five foot two, one hundred and ten pound ex-cheerleader.

"What are you doing here, Della?"

She held up a familiar looking set of keys while peering

around me at Addie. "Your mama said you were getting in today. She was going to come pick you up, but I convinced her to let me come instead." Her eyes narrowed. "I thought it would give us some alone time to talk, but I see now that's not the case. You want to introduce me to your...friend?"

Shit. Addie was still standing behind me. I stepped aside and took her hand. I squeezed it, but she didn't squeeze back. Her jaw was tight, as if she might have been grinding her molars together.

Shit. I'd never seen that expression on her face before. Not when she was with Sunny. With Sunny all she did was smile and laugh. But right now, she looked...well, as frosty as I normally did.

She was pissed. Fuck.

"Addie," I said slowly. "This is Della. She's uh—"

"His girlfriend," Della said snootily, crossing her arms beneath her breasts.

I rolled my eyes. "*Not* my girlfriend. My ex-girlfriend," I said firmly, shooting Della a look of annoyance.

She was trying to mark her territory. She used to do it when we were in high school, too. One time when we'd been seniors, Lacey Davis had been assigned as my partner for an after-school assignment. Della had practically cocked her hind leg and pissed all over me before she would let me be alone with the poor girl. Lacey had told me quietly she didn't even like men, so Della's little show of badly veiled aggression had all been for nothing anyway.

Obviously, nothing had changed. Except now, I wasn't hers to piss all over.

I grabbed the keys for my truck from her hand. "Thank you," I said stiffly. "For picking us up. You didn't need to."

And I really wished she hadn't. Though the thought of getting in my old truck and driving it along the open roads with Addie beside me, wind blowing in her hair, did sound real appealing. If I ignored the fact Della would be sitting in the back.

The three of us walked to the baggage claim area and watched bags go around the conveyer belts, the silence mounting and becoming more uncomfortable with each bag that wasn't ours. By the time we made it out to my truck, the silence was downright awkward. I ushered Addie to the front and let Della fend for herself while I threw our bags in the truck bed.

Shooting a worried glance in Addie's direction, I hoisted myself into the driver's seat, smacking my knees on the steering wheel shaft in the process. "Ow! Fuck!" I yelped.

Della sniggered from the back seat, and I shot her a glare in the rearview mirror before shoving my seat back.

"Sorry," Della said so sweetly, it was actually anything but. "I'm short."

The engine rumbled to life, and I settled back into the familiar position. I'd owned this car since I was sixteen and kept it for the rare occasions I came home. I'd gotten pretty good at living out of a suitcase over the past few years, but there was nothing quite like getting behind the wheel and back on the roads I'd grown up on.

"I think maybe you should just drop me back at the hotel," Addie said quietly from the passenger side.

"Great idea!" Della chirped.

I ignored her, focusing on Addie. "Hey, no." I squeezed her thigh through the flowy fabric of her skirt. "I want to take you on that date."

Addie finally twisted to look at me. "Maybe another night would be better."

"Please, Addie? I really want to show you something."

Her gaze lifted to meet mine, and though I could see she

wasn't particularly happy about it, she nodded. Behind me, Della clapped her hands. "Great, because I've organized a bonfire. Everyone is coming."

"What?" I spluttered.

Addie's eyes went wide, but Della carried on without paying either of us any attention. "It's perfect timing. The sun will just be going down when we get back to Milper River, and all the crew will be waiting in the field. Just like the old days."

I dug my fingers into the leather of the steering wheel. "What crew would that be, Della?"

Her laugh tinkled around the cab of the truck. I got us out on the road, heading toward my hometown while Della recited a list of names of people we went to high school with. People who had been *her* friends. They'd tolerated me as her boyfriend, but I would never in a million years have even called them acquaintances. Let alone my 'crew.'

Addie didn't say a word as my truck's tires ate up the miles of country roads. She just curled up on her seat and twisted her body away from me, staring out the window while Della rattled on about our high school antics. By the time the sun was starting to sink, my nerves were so on edge from Della's constant chatter that I wanted to push her out the window. I tried to block all that out as we rolled into town.

Nothing had changed, even though it had been over twelve months since I'd last been home. The buildings on the main street were all bathed in late afternoon sunlight, and the residents still wandered between stores or made their way to their cars, laden down with shopping bags. A few store owners were closing up their businesses for the night, shutting off lights and locking doors.

I accelerated past the turnoff to my parent's place

without a word, but Della, of course, couldn't let it go. "You aren't going to stop and say hello to your parents?"

Addie glanced at me sharply. It was the first time all trip she'd turned my way, and I took the opportunity to grasp her hand.

"No," I said, answering Della's question while looking into Addie's eyes. "I'm not."

Addie frowned, but I also saw the flicker of relief in her expression.

"I wouldn't do that to you," I said quietly. "I don't want you anywhere near him."

Della's eyes burned a hole in my back, and I just knew she was eavesdropping. I jerked the car down a side street.

"We're going on that date," I promised Addie. "Just you and me. I need to drop Della home first, though."

"You could at least take me to the field." Della's voice had turned annoyingly whiny. "People are expecting us, and even if you're going to be a no-show, some of us have friendships to maintain."

I ground my teeth together. The field was only a few minutes outside town. It wouldn't kill me to take her. "Fine."

I didn't miss her smug smile.

When we got to the field, I pulled off the road and bumped over the dirt and grass to stop my truck beside a row of similar-looking vehicles. They were parked in a semicircle around a small fire a few of the guys were tending to, feeding it little sticks and coaxing it into life.

A small group had gathered, red Solo cups in hands already. It was a scene straight out of my high school years. I let the engine idle, while Della let herself out.

"Kai's here, everyone!" she yelled.

I let out a groan as they all cheered. Della slammed the door behind her and trotted over to the people we'd gone to high school with. They swarmed my side of the car, banging on the hood and hollering at me to get out and join them.

"I'm so sorry," I said to Addie. "I don't even like these people."

The tiniest of smiles pulled at her mouth. "You don't?"

I shook my head. "They didn't bother talking to me in high school. I was just *that guy* who hung around Della."

A tiny laugh escaped from her, and I relaxed a smidgen. Without Della in the car, some of Addie's stiffness seemed to be wearing off.

I leaned in and tilted her chin up so her gaze met mine. "Hey."

"They're all waiting for you," she said, shifting her eyes to the left, as if facing me directly was too hard.

"Yeah, but I want to know that you're okay before I get out of this truck. If you're not, I'm going to throw this thing in reverse and get the hell out of here. This is not what I planned for our date, you know. And those people aren't my friends. They only want to talk to me now because of what I do for a job."

She finally turned her gaze back to me. "I'll be fine."

She was lying. I could tell. And I knew exactly whose fault it was she was nervous to meet my friends, even if I did use the term loosely.

"They're not going to treat you the way my dad did, Addie." The muscles across my back went tight, and my anger at my father for the way he'd spoken to her that night at Madison Square Garden rushed back. "Not everyone from around here is like him."

She nodded. "I know. And I know it's stupid to get upset when I've been dealing with this my entire life—"

I cut her off with a kiss, because I hated there was distance between us right now. If I could have, I would have lifted her across the stick shift and onto my lap. When we broke apart, I said firmly, "Your feelings are never stupid. You hear? They're always valid. You get uncomfortable, just say the word, and we're out of here."

She shook her head and put her fingers on the door handle. "I want to meet your friends."

"Not my friends," I mumbled again, making her laugh, and we both pulled open the doors.

"Frost!" one of the guys yelled, coming over to slap me on the back.

I smiled tightly at him and circled the car to take hold of Addie's hand. The fact he was calling me Frost told me he watched the WBRA, because it had been Sunny who'd given me that nickname, and it was the guys on the tour who had run with it. None of the people I'd grown up with would know it if they weren't following my career. Finally, I turned back to him. "Alec, this is Addie," I said, introducing her.

I tugged her around the group of people, accepting their congratulations on my recent rides, and shooting the shit about bull riding in general. A few of the women struck up a conversation with Addie, but before I was pulled away to watch a replay of one of my rides, I shot her a look that clearly said, "You okay?" She nodded and smiled, shooing me away as she went back to the group of women, who included Della. I narrowed my eyes when I caught her staring at me.

She threw her hands up in the air. "What?"

I shook my head. She was up to something. That was for sure. I had no idea why she was trying to get me out here. But it had trouble spelled out all over it.

22

ADDIE

I couldn't work out Kai's ex-girlfriend. She was the exact opposite of me. I was tall, she was short. I was willowy, she was curvy. She was white blonde to my dark black. Physically, we didn't share a single quality.

On paper, she was everything he should have wanted. His high school sweetheart. I'd put money on it that she'd been the homecoming queen, who would bake fresh cookies for their babies before sending them off to school each morning, just like her mama had done for her.

A pang of regret ached in my chest. One day, I wanted to be that mother who baked in the mornings. But I'd never had anyone like that in my life. If good mothering skills were genetic, I was screwed.

I shook my head. It wasn't the time to dwell on my lack of family role models. The group had lost interest in interrogating me and had settled around the bonfire. Someone had brought a guitar, and they were actually pretty good. Music, singing, and laughter filled the night air. Nobody, bar Della, had made me feel weird. I was the only person of color in the group, but there had been no racial slurs, no whispers behind my back. Unlike Della, the rest of the group had all just accepted me as Kai's new girlfriend.

Girlfriend. The word echoed around my head. Was that what I was? No, that was stupid. One hot night of oral sex and mutual masturbation and I was wondering if we were in a relationship. I pushed my finger against a splinter in the log beneath my butt. *Stupid, Addie. Stupid.* The logical side of my brain recognized sex, or rather, almost sex, didn't equal a relationship. But the words he'd said before we'd got naked... Ugh. I was so confused.

I just had to keep an open mind when it came to Kai. Take it one day at a time and keep myself on a short leash. I wanted him. There was no doubt about that. And for the last twenty-four hours, he'd run so hot. But I didn't trust him. I knew at any moment, that hot tap could run cold.

He caught my eye from across the bonfire, and I took in his relaxed posture and his easy smile. He leaned on the rusting side of an old Ford pickup, his fingers wrapped loosely around the neck of a beer bottle. The two guys he was talking to—I'd been introduced to them but had promptly forgotten their names—were telling stories about a prank they'd pulled in high school. Kai seemed...happy. Warmth curled around me that had nothing to do with the heat from the bonfire, sending up orange sparks into the dark night. I liked seeing him smile. 'Frost' might have been the persona he showed the rodeo world, but out here, he was just Kai. A kid from a small town, who had friends excited to see him again after a long absence.

A stab of jealousy took me by surprise. Not because I wanted less for him. But because I wanted more for myself. I'd never really fit in anywhere like he did. Despite his protests that they weren't really his friends, they obviously were. They were all interested in hearing his stories and sharing their own. Even if he didn't keep up with them regularly, he had a history with these people. While I'd moved around from foster home to foster home, changing schools practically as often as I changed my underwear. By the time I'd ended up in Lorrington in my last year of high school, it had really been too late to make long-lasting friendships.

I'd been trying to rectify that since meeting Sunny. He and I had been friends. I'd truly liked the man. He was sunshine personified, hence his nickname. So when he'd asked me out, I'd agreed. I didn't get that rush of feelings as I looked at him. But I'd told myself an initial spark wasn't necessary. A great relationship could be built on friendship.

I still believed that. But I also knew a spark—that chemistry that truly drew you to a person—well; relationships needed that, too. And Kai and I had sparks in droves. Maybe all we were was sparks that would ignite, then fizzle out to nothing once they were set free into the dark night. But I wanted to know if there was more. Because maybe we were more like that bonfire. Maybe whatever this thing between us was, once it truly caught fire, maybe it would light up the night.

Kai caught my eye and jerked his head, motioning for me to come to him. I pushed to my feet, dusting log dirt and debris from the back of my skirt and picked my way around the fire, weaving between couples making out and old friends catching up.

He didn't move from leaning against the old truck, but he held one hand out as I approached. I took it, threading my fingers through his, my skin tingling when it met his. He pulled me against him, his arm over my shoulders, and I bent my elbow so I didn't have to let go of his hand. His warmth engulfed the whole left side of my body, and his lips brushed my cheek.

"Hey," he murmured. "You having fun?"

I smiled. "Yes." I wasn't sure I was actually having fun, but I wasn't having a bad time either. And seeing him smile? That was fun for me.

I turned my attention to the two guys Kai had been talking to, racking my brain for their names, but came up blank.

The taller of the two glanced between Kai and me, then gave Kai a meaningful look. He chuckled. "We're going to get another beer. You guys want anything?"

"No thanks," I answered.

Kai held up his mostly full beer bottle, and the two guys nodded, stalking off.

I watched them go. "Was it something I said?" I asked, self-conscious suddenly.

By then Kai was dragging me around to stand in the space made by his widespread legs. He tugged me forward until our bodies were pressed flush together. His icy blue eyes were a little glazed, and I realized he'd probably had more to drink than I'd thought.

"Not something you said," he whispered, leaning in and running his nose up the side of my neck until he brushed my earlobe. "I gave them the sign."

I pulled back, studying the smug expression on Kai's handsome face. "What sign might that be, Kai Hunt?" My tone was playful, and I relaxed again, enjoying this different side to him.

One side of his mouth turned up, and heat built low in my belly. Gosh, he looked good when he smiled like that. How was it that teenage girls all over America didn't have posters of him hanging over their beds? It was a blessing he so rarely smiled in public. Even as Frost, he was stunningly beautiful, with his all-American looks and muscles sculpted by the physical training he did for his job. He was the complete package, all wrapped up in a body made for sin. Luckily for me, it was his smile that took him from, hey, he's a handsome dude to, holy shit, my panties just disintegrated. And he seemed to save his smiles for those who knew him best.

And right now, I was one of those people.

His free hand snaked around the small of my back, his fingertips brushing the top of my ass before his palm slid down to cup one cheek.

I raised one eyebrow. "Is that the sign?"

His half smile spread across his face. "No, the sign is an eyebrow wriggle and a 'get the fuck out of here' head jerk. "

"Subtle."

"Hey, you didn't notice."

He had a point there. "And what does the sign actually mean, apart from scram?"

He put his beer bottle down in the bed of the truck. "It means there's a beautiful girl in my arms, and I want to be alone with her."

His free hand reached around to grab my other ass cheek, and he squeezed them both, making me giggle.

"Kai," I warned, but it was half-hearted.

He leaned in and kissed me, tasting mildly of beer, but it wasn't unpleasant. Our tongues swirled together, and if he was drunk, he was good at hiding it, because there was nothing sloppy about his kiss. His lips moved over mine, slow and teasing, his tongue plunging in just enough that heat wormed its way through my body. He retreated before I'd really had enough, leaving me wanting more. When he pushed off the truck and walked me backward, away from the circle of light created by car headlights and the bonfire, the heat that had been coursing through my body all pooled between my legs.

"Where are we going?" I whispered, never letting him go for a minute.

The ground beneath my feet was rocky and uneven. I clutched at the fabric of his shirt, my fingers pressing into his strong biceps. But I never for a second thought I'd fall. I was vulnerable, walking backward through the dark, but his strength and size and the way he devoured my mouth with such intense certainty, left no doubt in my mind. He'd catch me if I stumbled.

"Want to be alone with you," he whispered back. "I've wanted to be alone with you all day. You know I was going to fuck you in the bathroom at the airport?"

My clit throbbed at the thought. And at the crassness of his words. "You wanted that to be our first time?"

He shook his head. "No, I want our first time to be special. But hell, Addie. I spent that entire plane ride thinking about the things we did last night...."

"Oh." The words fell from my lips sounding breathy and feminine. I'd blocked out the night before, because I'd needed to finish a story for the paper and I couldn't do that if I was thinking about Kai's enormous cock, or the way it looked when he'd stroked himself until he'd come.

But now...gah, now I was thinking about it. We were so far away from the fire that the music had become muted and we were almost in complete darkness. Plunging my tongue into his mouth, I took control of our embrace. I lifted his shirt, fisting the material in my fingers and exposing his lower abs. My fingers slid down over the hard planes of muscle, following the V lines either side of his hips. His muscles contracted beneath my touch, and his hands came up to cup the sides of my face as our kiss intensified. We both tussled to own it.

I grabbed his belt, tugging the stiff leather through the loops on his pants and undoing the buckle. I let both sides fall while our mouths warred, both of us hungry and demanding. The kiss stole my breath, until my body was so starved of oxygen, I felt lightheaded.

I pulled away, panting hard, and my gaze met his. His lips were slightly swollen in the pale moonlight, mixed with just the very edges of the glow from the fire. Slowly, giving him every opportunity to stop me if that was what he truly wanted, I dropped to my knees.

His eyes flared, and my heart stopped.

"Kai," I whispered. "Please let me."

Ignoring the not-so-soft blades of grass and the stones beneath my knees, I lowered the zipper on his fly, never taking my eyes off his for a second. He watched me with nothing but heat and desire burning in his gaze. Then, taking the chance he was giving in to what he really wanted, I pulled his jeans and underwear down his thickly muscled thighs.

His cock jutted out, bobbing just inches from my face. The thick, blunt head of him made me ache between my legs. My breath stuttered at just the thought of guiding him to my entrance, and getting him where I really wanted.

I gazed up at him, daring to swipe my tongue over his tip. He jerked, and I stopped. For a long moment, his expression turned tortured, but then I did it again, and I watched his resolve weaken. He reached down and brushed my hair back from my face.

"Fuck, you look beautiful like that," he gritted out hoarsely.

"Do you want this?" I whispered back. Though he was

responding in all the right ways, I needed to know he truly wanted me to do it. I knew I did, but I wouldn't have him feeling guilty about it afterward.

"I want it," he whispered back.

"Say it. Say what you want."

His eyes flared again. Something hotter, bolder, more... dangerous appeared in his expression. The wetness between my legs soaked through my panties.

He wrapped my long hair around his fist, and the tugging sensation only turned me on more.

"Suck me, Addie," he demanded.

I let out a moan that was probably too loud, considering a group of people were gathered not far from us. But holy hell. It was exactly what I'd wanted him to say. What I'd goaded him into saying.

"Open your mouth, beautiful. I want in."

I did as I was told, not because he'd said to, but because it turned me on. And because I wanted him to feel the same way I was feeling in that very moment. I opened my mouth, and he thrust his dick inside without any further preamble. Shallowly at first, just the head, giving me a moment to adjust to exactly how big he was. I tongued off his precum, moaning again at the new wave of pleasure washing over me as I took him inside my mouth.

His next thrust was deeper, his hot length sliding over my tongue, and on the third stroke, he let out a guttural groan. I wanted to come without him even touching me.

"Fuck, Addie. Your mouth..."

I peeked a look up at him. He had his head thrown back, his eyes turned to the skies. I took over. I gripped the base of his cock with one hand, his balls with my other. Moving my hands in time with my mouth, I worked him in and out. I ran my tongue up the underside of his dick, feeling the

sensitive vein, circling the head, alternating between licking
and blowing. I sucked him until his dick was slick and shining, and then I gripped his balls, squeezing them gently,
watching his face for cues to how he liked to be touched. His
hips rolled, and I took more and more of him into my mouth
with each stroke. My own orgasm built, encouraged by the
noises he made and the fact we were in public. Anyone who
wandered in our direction could have caught us. I ached to
push him back on the grass, yank my skirt up, and ride my
cowboy, right there in the dirt. But I didn't want to push him
too far all at once. I didn't want him to stop me, and so I put
all my efforts into making sure he got off right then and
there.

"Addie..." he groaned, and I knew he was going to come.
His grip on my hair tightened, and I welcomed the tiny sting
because it took my focus away from how wet and needy I
was. I worked him harder, faster, until his balls tightened
and his legs buckled.

His cock pulsed, and then his orgasm roared. His abs
contracted, and he bit out my name, the guttural word
ringing in my ears and sounding oh so fucking sexy. I swallowed him down, taking everything he had and not even
caring it wasn't something I normally did. I'd never wanted
to do that with a man before, but something about Kai made
me want everything.

Everything.

I licked and sucked at him until he pulled away, dropping to his knees in front of me. I probably tasted of his
cum, but he smashed his lips down on mine, claiming my
mouth as his once again. Needy little mewling noises came
from the back of my throat as we clawed at each other,
desperately trying to get closer. I needed him. I needed
relief. I was so close to my own orgasm, I wasn't sure how I'd

get up and walk back to the fire without it overpowering me, sending me into a fit of breathy cries.

"Get on your hands and knees."

"What?" I asked through my lust-filled fog.

"You heard me."

I had, I was just trying to reconcile this Kai with the one from last night who wouldn't let me touch him.

I liked this Kai a whole lot better.

I got on my hands and knees, my legs trembling at the thought of him filling the ache inside me. I knew I wouldn't last more than a stroke, but I wanted him so badly I'd self-combust if he didn't touch me soon.

The tremble turned into a full-body shake as he lifted my skirt and let it settle around my waist. His bare palm stroked up my thigh and over my naked ass cheek before moving to the thong in the middle. I stifled a moan, his finger slipping beneath my underwear, pulling the soaking material out of the way, exposing my center. I readied myself for the thick head of his cock to get inside.

But it was his mouth that slicked through my folds and his fingers that pushed into me, immediately seeking my G-spot. Two quick thrusts of his fingers, timed perfectly with his tongue on my clit, and I was freefalling over the edge. My arms wobbled, sensation crashing over me as I dropped down onto my forearms in the grass. Kai's fingers dug into my hips, holding my ass up in the air. He continued to go down on me, sucking and licking me, my pussy pulsating and bliss rocketing through every muscle in my body. I would have collapsed face-first in the dirt if he hadn't held me up, and he worked my body until he'd drained every inch of pleasure.

I slowly came back to earth, and he hooked his strong arm around my middle while putting my thong back in place. The wet material rubbed on the sensitive parts of me, and I groaned as he smoothed my skirt and sat me on his lap. Somewhere along the way, he'd managed to get his jeans and underwear back up.

I curled up on his lap, and his arms locked tight around me. Silence settled. The distant sounds of the party wrapping up filtered back again, but I couldn't bring myself to move. I just wanted to stay there in his arms, in this perfect moment beneath the stars. Well, almost perfect moment.

"Why won't you have sex with me?" I asked quietly.

He stilled, but then he went back to stroking the bare skin of my thigh where my skirt was still hitched up and crooked.

"It's hard to explain."

"Try me."

He let out a slow sigh. "You...you don't feel like mine yet."

The breath in my lungs turned icy, and my heart sank. "I don't?"

He shook his head. "I'm getting there, Addie. I swear, I am. You're so damn beautiful, but I promised myself I wouldn't until..."

I waited.

"I don't deserve you yet."

I pulled a face. "What are you talking about?"

His expression became tortured again. "Fuck, I don't know. I just...this is all moving so damn fast. Yesterday you were barely speaking to me, and now we're..."

"Making each other come?"

"Yeah." He grinned at me. "Not that I'm complaining, because you blew my mind tonight."

A little thrill of pride shot through me at that thought.

"It's not you, Addie, you know that, right? It's me. And

I'm not just saying that, otherwise I would have just screwed you then left."

Just the thought of that made me feel hollow inside.

He gripped my chin and forced me to look at him. "I'm going to have sex with you, Addie. I'm going to fuck you, and I'm going to make love with you. I want them both. But I don't want to be doing that while my head is a mess of confusion. When I make love to you, I want it to be just you and me in the room. No ghosts."

His eyes pleaded for me to understand, and finally, I did. I didn't want Sunny's ghost between us any more than he did. And though I could close him out, if Kai wasn't there yet, then I could respect that.

"No ghosts," I echoed. "Okay."

23

ADDIE

*K*ai and I stumbled back to the party, my arm tucked around his waist, his over my shoulder. He dropped a kiss on my upturned face, and a round of catcalls broke out from the now, much smaller group left around the dwindling fire.

"Still got it, Kai," one of the guys yelled good-naturedly.

Kai stepped away to punch his friend in the biceps. They tussled, mock fighting, and I edged away, not wanting to cop one of their wayward elbows in the face.

"You two have a good time?" Della asked, appearing by my side.

I cast her a sidelong look, my orgasm-relaxed body suddenly tensing again. I'd forgotten about her when Kai and I had been alone.

"He's good in bed, isn't he?"

I wasn't even going to dignify that with a response, and Della seemed to realize that when I walked away from her.

She grabbed my arm. "Addie, wait. I'm sorry."

Reluctantly, I turned back. "I don't want drama. You have a history with him, I get that. I'm not trying to compete with you. I don't even know if the two of us are a couple or what, but he's with me tonight."

To my surprise, Della nodded. "I know, I agree." She gazed across the fire at him, and I followed her line of sight. Kai was standing quietly, watching the two of us talk. His eyes flitted from Della's to mine, and he tilted his head ever so slightly, a questioning eyebrow raised. It was a clear, are you okay, or do you need saving from my crazy ex-girlfriend?

If he'd asked me a few minutes earlier, I might have waved a flag for help. But for the first time all night, Della actually seemed sincere. I gave Kai a tiny nod, and he turned back to his friends.

"You make him happy," Della said eventually.

"What makes you say that?"

She shrugged. "He might have been on tour the last two years, but I still know him. He was my best friend all through high school. He's more relaxed here tonight with you than I've ever seen him."

I didn't respond, because what was I supposed to say? Hey, he likes me more than he liked you, so suck it? I was bigger than that.

Della twisted a lock of hair absently around her finger. "I like seeing him happy. I want that for him. I'm proud of him for getting out of here and going after his dreams. And if you're who he wants now, then I wish the both of you the best."

I softened a little toward her. I understood what it was like to come from a small town. Her options were limited, and maybe she'd been holding on to the memory of her and Kai, expecting he'd come back for her some-day. But life had taught me people didn't always come back and you had to make your own way in the world.

Because in the end; you could really only count on yourself.

"I like seeing him happy, too." My heart kicked up a notch as we both watched him.

His short blond hair was still mussed up, his eyes still sparkling with the very last effects of the alcohol we'd consumed. Three-day stubble coated his normally smooth jawline, and his perfectly kissable lips turned up in a grin. He was devastating, but it was the strength and compassion he had inside that completed the package. And now that he was talking to me, *really* talking to me, I planned to peel back every single one of his layers. I wanted to know who he really was beneath his Frost persona.

If we did that naked, then all the better.

"You've got your work cut out for you, though," Della mused.

I dragged my attention off Kai. "What do you mean?"

"His family. They'll never accept you."

My gaze narrowed, unwanted heat flooding my cheeks. She didn't have to say why. I knew.

Della turned to me, her expression full of fake innocence. "I don't agree with them, of course!"

Of course, my ass. I suddenly realized the nice girl act had been a farce.

"His daddy will disown him, you know. His granddaddy, too. They'll never stand for it."

Never stand for me, was what she meant.

"But I'm sure if you two are really in love, none of that will be a problem. He was always so tight with his parents—after all, he's their only child. But that doesn't matter in the face of true love, does it?" Her voice dripped with fake sugar. "I'm catching a ride home with some of the others, but it was really lovely meeting you, Addie. I'm sure we'll see each other again soon."

I didn't respond, because I was too busy grinding my teeth. If I'd let myself talk, it would have likely ended in a scene, and I didn't want to ruin what had mostly been a nice night.

But I was done with this. I moved away from the fire, walking stiffly back to Kai's truck, mumbling goodbyes to the few people I passed. In the shadows, away from the people, I sucked in a deep lungful of breath and let it travel around my body. It wasn't Della who I was angry with, really. She'd only pointed out what I already knew. Racists didn't change. Especially not men like Kai's dad, who took his naïve hatred to extremes.

Soft footsteps crunched on the grass behind me. I jerked, my body going stiff when his arms wrapped around me. He paused, then spun me around, ducking his head to search out my face. "Hey, what happened? Last I saw, you and Della seemed to be getting along…"

I forced my lips to curl into a smile, but I knew it wouldn't meet my eyes. "That didn't last long."

The relaxed, smiling, happy Kai—who'd been around most of the night—was shut back in his box. "What did she do?" he seethed. "I could strangle her. She's got no business—"

"Stop. It's not worth it."

"What did she say?"

I shook my head again. I could tell him, but it was nothing he didn't already know. Nothing we *both* already didn't know. We'd just been ignoring it. And even though I'd been dragged back down to reality, that didn't mean I had to do the same thing to him. I didn't want to lose him. Not yet.

Instead, I pushed up onto my toes and brushed my lips over his. "It doesn't matter. Can we go? I'm tired."

His brow still furrowed in concern, but he gripped my face hard and pressed his lips against mine in a bruising kiss. When he pulled away, he dug his keys from his pocket, unlocked the car, and held my door open for me. I climbed inside gratefully, settling back on the seat. It had to be late. I fished my phone from my purse on the floor and checked the time. 2:00 a.m. Shit.

Kai slid into the driver's seat, and I glanced over at him, suddenly exhausted. "Are you okay to drive? It's late, and you've been drinking."

He paused. "I stopped drinking hours ago. But shit, I had no idea how late it was."

"It's a long way back to our hotel. Is there one here we can stay at?"

He shook his head. "Not one that will give us a room at two in the morning."

I bit my lip. The simple solution was for him to stay at his parents' house. But with me in tow, that wasn't an option. My spirit deflated further. It was starting already. The things we couldn't do because other people wouldn't accept us. I swallowed hard, fighting back emotion that threatened to spill over in the form of embarrassing tears.

Kai turned the car on and squeezed my knee. "I know where we can stay. It might be a bit rough, though."

I nodded, not daring to look at him, and trusted he wouldn't put me in a position where I was unsafe. If I knew anything about Kai, I knew he would never do that. Memories of the night of the accident flashed through my head. Kai reaching for me as the other car collided with ours. Spinning out of control, and his voice yelling my name...

Goose bumps pricked up on my skin, and I rubbed my arms. The truck bumped out of the field and onto the road. We traveled the back roads in the darkness. There were no streetlights out this far, and the headlights didn't do much but illuminate the dirt. But Kai drove with the confidence of a man who knew these roads well, and it was only minutes before we were slowing down again and turning into a driveway.

The headlights lit up a rusted mailbox, and Kai got out to open a gate but didn't bother closing it behind us after we drove through.

I watched the gate swing in the side mirror. "I think you just broke small-town rule number one. If you open a gate, you close it."

Kai chuckled. "Nothing on this property can escape."

"How do you know?"

"Because it's Sunny's."

I peered out through the darkened windows. "Really?"

"He bought it last year."

Hell. Kai pulled the truck up when the headlights illuminated a small cabin that was so run-down it was practically decrepit. "Uh, Kai? We aren't sleeping in there...are we?"

He faked insult. "You don't like it?"

"It was you who said we needed to escape from ghosts... that place looks full of them."

I wasn't joking. There were ratty curtains hanging from blackened windows, wood panels missing in the front steps. The doorway was boarded up, and what had perhaps once been a garden was now nothing more than a mass of tangled, waist-high grass. I wasn't a girly girl, and I could kill a spider with the best of them. It was a necessary skill in Australia, but I dreaded the thought of what was living in that run-down building. I wasn't going in there without boots and an extra-large can of bug spray.

Kai laughed and twisted, grabbing stuff out of the back seat. He came up with a thick blanket. "Might want to grab your headrest from your seat."

"What? Why?"

"To use as a pillow."

Too tired to argue, I shifted in my seat and pushed in the little button that released the headrest. I eyed it as I got out of the truck and followed Kai through the darkness to the truck bed.

He spread the blanket out and nodded to our bags. "Grab anything soft. Because this is not going to be the most comfortable night's sleep."

I studied his makeshift bed. It looked hard and lumpy. "Maybe you should just go to your parents' place? I can sleep in the car."

"No," he growled. "I'm not just going to leave you in the car by yourself. What kind of man do you think I am?"

"I'm a big girl. I'll manage."

"Just get in, would you? It's not that bad."

I was still doubtful as I pushed myself to sit on the truck bed. But then he held his hand out to me, and I couldn't help the tingly feeling that came over me. Our bed for the night might be rough and ready, but he was trying. And when I laid down next to him, it really wasn't so bad. The blanket helped a little, and Kai's arm around me helped a lot.

"See? What are you complaining about? This is like a five-star hotel," he said.

"Lucky it's dark so you can't see how hard I'm rolling my eyes right now."

Kai only responded by dragging me closer. I stopped

complaining. Though I did ditch the headrest in favor of Kai's chest. He put his jacket over me, and I snuggled in against him.

"Why did he buy this place? I assume it wasn't because he fell in love with that charming house?"

"Ha, no. He talked about bulldozing that. But the plan was after we were both too old, or too hurt from bull riding, we'd both come back here, to Georgia. I'd take over my old man's place. And he'd be here."

"Practically neighbors."

"Pretty much."

"You two were that close, huh?"

Kai let out a quiet breath. "We're both only children. I never even had any cousins. Sunny was the brother I never had. And I guess I was that for him, too."

"You guess?"

"I dunno. It's not like we actually discussed stuff like that. We used to talk about starting a bull riding school out here. Marrying beautiful women and having some kids running around."

I moved in closer, my eyes growing heavy. "That sounds nice."

"I used to dream of you out here."

That perked me up. "You did?"

Kai's voice got thick. "As soon as you met Sunny, my dreams about this place changed. Then you were here, with him, raising his babies."

"That wouldn't have happened."

"You don't know that."

"But I do. I liked Sunny. A lot. But he wasn't the one."

"You can't know that after two months of dating someone."

"Can't I? When you know, you know, Kai." His claims

were bullshit. Because I knew exactly how I'd felt about Sunny after two months of dating. Hell, Kai and I weren't even dating, and yet I knew how I felt about him, too. And the two feelings were not the same.

His lips brushed over my forehead. "Fuck. I'm sorry. I shouldn't have said anything. I told you, I've got ghosts."

He had, but maybe I hadn't realized exactly how tightly those ghosts clung to him.

24

KAI

*S*leeping in the bed of the truck was an awful idea. I woke as the sky was just beginning to lighten, with a back that felt like I'd slept on jagged rocks. Something dug painfully into my ribs, and my muscles cried out, begging to be popped and stretched.

But I didn't dare move. At some point during the night, Addie had pretty much ended up on top of me. Her hip still rested on the blanket covering the truck bed, her head laid out in the crook of my shoulder, but her thigh draped over mine, matching the way her arm was slung across my chest. My coat had slipped off her shoulders, and with my free arm, I tugged it back into place, trying not to disturb her.

The sun inched higher over the horizon, and I breathed in the scent of Addie's hair, mixed with the dewy freshness of early morning. The setting couldn't have been more peaceful, the only noises the morning chattering of birds and the rhythmic inhale and exhale of Addie's breath.

But inside my head was akin to something from a disaster movie. Storm clouds and strong winds swirled my thoughts, clouded my vision, and churned my gut.

I needed to go see my parents.

I'd avoided it last night, but I'd only been delaying the inevitable. I needed to confront my dad and demand he get that photo of me removed.

But there was more than that.

I knew how cruel my dad could be. I'd seen it growing up, passing people of color on the streets. How many times had he made a hateful remark as we'd encountered a family just out for the day, minding their own business? How many times had I been dragged to hate rallies and forced to hold signs that did nothing but display my father's ignorance? How many times had I wished the ground would open and swallow me whole when he went on a rant at a Sunday night dinner, about some perceived injustice he'd suffered because of someone who didn't share his pasty-white skin?

Bile rose in my throat as I remembered all the years I'd been too powerless to say anything in retaliation. And I remembered the stinging slap of his open palm across my face, when at fifteen, almost as tall, but thirty pounds lighter, I'd dared to call him on his redneck attitude. He'd been set off by the inclusion of a black football player in my high school team. Despite the fact Dwayne was twice the player I'd ever be, my dad had shown up at my practice and stormed the field, determined to tell my coach I wouldn't be replaced by 'some Negro.'

The word had fallen from his lips, and I'd exploded from the thick grass of the playing field, racing to where my coach was trying to placate a man who'd spent his entire life hating on people just because of their skin color. My grandfather had been the same, but I'd been determined to break the cycle. I was better educated than them both, and despite fifteen years of attempted brainwashing, I'd known what they were saying was wrong. I couldn't just sit there and listen to it. I didn't even like football, so hell, Dwayne was doing me a favor by taking my spot. All I'd ever wanted to do was ride bulls.

I'd intercepted my father and coach and got a backhand to the face for my trouble. Blood had filled my mouth from my split lip, but my father had turned around and stalked off. And when I'd sat beside Dwayne, he'd laughed and slapped my back. The fat lip and my father's scowls had been worth it.

But my father had never apologized. Not to Dwayne. Not to any of the people we'd passed on the streets. And that had never sat right with me. I hated the way I'd been raised, but I hated even more I hadn't done anything further about it since that day on the football field. Bull riding had taken me away from it all, and I'd been content to just let it remain a part of my past.

Not anymore.

"Addie, baby. Wake up." I smoothed her hair back from her face, noting the way the early morning sun bounced off her sweet nose. I kissed it, her eyelashes fluttering open, and she smiled up at me through groggy, unfocused eyes. She rolled off me and sat up, letting out a long groan as one of her joints cracked.

I grimaced. "Sorry about the uncomfortable night's sleep."

She pushed her arms up over her head, linking her long, delicate fingers together and stretching toward the rapidly lightening sky. "Your chest, while really good to look at, does not make for the softest of pillows. "

I grinned. "You like my chest?"

She nodded. "Very much. Take your shirt off, would you? I wouldn't mind another look at your abs either."

She chuckled, and I sat up, brushing my lips against hers.

"How long have you been awake for?" A yawn escaped her mouth.

"Long enough to do some thinking."

"Uh-oh. Want to expand?"

"I want to go see my parents this morning, before we head back into town."

Addie's smile faltered. "Oh."

"He owes you an apology."

A sigh fell from her lips. "Kai..."

I shook my head, indignation roaring to life in my gut. "No, dammit, Addie. He can't just treat people the way he treated you at the rodeo and get away with it. He owes you an apology."

She held the back of her neck and cocked her head to the side, rubbing at what had to be a stiff muscle. Guilt pricked at me, and I shuffled to sit behind her. I covered her fingers with mine.

"Let me do that," I whispered.

She dropped her hand, and I rubbed two fingers across the tight muscle at the base of her neck. I worked it until the knot started to break down, and Addie's head lolled back on her shoulders.

"Will you come with me?" I asked.

She twisted her head so we were facing each other. "Of course. I'd do anything for you."

I kissed the spot I'd just been massaging. "Thank you," I whispered against her skin.

I didn't know why it suddenly meant so much to me that my father apologize, but as I helped Addie down from the bed of the truck, I realized that was a lie. I did know why it meant something to me. It was because my feelings for

Addie ran so damn deep it felt as if they were connected to hers. Her hurts were my hurts. And I just wanted to make them better. *When you know, you know.* Addie's words from last night played back in my head, as I pulled myself into the driver's seat. She was right. Hadn't I known, practically from the very first day Sunny had brought her home? Hadn't I known I was going to spend the rest of my life mourning the fact he was the man who'd had the luck to meet her first?

We drove in silence to my parents' house. She chewed on a thumbnail, and I pulled it away from her mouth, bringing it to my own. I wrapped my lips around it, flicking my tongue over the pad of her thumb.

When I popped it out of my mouth, I gave her a wicked grin. "Let's go get this thing with my parents over and done with. I want to get back to the hotel."

She was still staring at my lips resting on her thumb. "Why's that?"

I kissed the tip of it. "Because your thumb isn't the only thing I want to suck."

I let her have her hand back, and she turned to face the front again. Trees and empty fields rushed by either side of us.

"I would never have picked this, you know?"

"What do you mean?"

The corner of her lips lifted. "I kind of thought you might have been a virgin."

I choked on a laugh. "I'm twenty-two!"

She shrugged. "But you could never really look at me, you know? You only spoke when spoken to. And even then, it was mostly one-word answers. You just always seemed so uncomfortable whenever I was around…"

"And you assumed that was because I was a virgin?"

She nodded. "Well, yeah. I guessed you didn't have

much experience with women. I didn't exactly think it was because..."

Because I was in love with her. I hadn't come right out and said it in the hotel room. I'd chickened out and down-played it to just having feelings for her. But I couldn't deny those feelings felt so much bigger. I'd loved Della. She was sweet and fun, and we'd lost our virginities in the back of my truck while we whispered about how we'd be together for ever. But had I ever been *in* love with her? If you'd asked me, pre-Australia, I probably would have said yes. But the way I felt about Addie...it was light-years away from anything I'd ever felt before. Whatever Della and I had all seemed like childish infatuation now. But Addie... I couldn't explain it. Something had clicked when I'd first met her and only grown in all the months since. It had been a nightmare trying to hide it around her. But I had, because Sunny was my best friend. And she was his.

But Sunny was gone. And I had to really start letting him go. I knew that.

We stopped in town at a little diner that opened early and closed late. Addie disap-peared into the bathroom after telling me to just order her whatever it was that smelled so good. I'd spent half my teen years hanging out here, with Della or with the guys from my football team, and I knew instantly that what she could smell was their signature pancakes and syrup. My mouth watered, and when our plates arrived, pancakes stacked ten high, Addie had raised an eyebrow.

"If I didn't know better, I'd have asked if you were compensating for something."

We chatted easily in between mouthfuls of gooey syrup and sugary pancakes, and it was easy to forget it had only been a few days that we'd really been together. My feelings were too damn big for my own body, and as I'd leaned across the table and kissed Addie's shining, syrup-slicked lips, I'd wanted to profess them all.

She deserved more. A bigger declaration. I stroked my finger over the back of her hand, familiarizing myself with every mark. She had a fresh-looking scar over her right forefinger, and I didn't have to ask to know it was from the crash. It had needed a single stitch to hold it closed. I knew because I'd stared at that bandage on her hand so many times when I'd been sitting by her bedside. I'd beaten myself up over that injury, and all the other ones I'd caused her. Deacon, Stacey, and I had all walked away from the crash with barely a scratch. But the passenger side of the car, where Addie and Sunny had been sitting, had borne the worst of the impact.

I stood abruptly and held my hand out to her. "Come on, let's just get this over with, huh?"

Addie was quiet on the drive over, and I grew more and more worried with every mile that passed beneath the truck's wheels. What was I doing, dragging this beautiful, kind soul into the dragon's lair? But then I was stopping outside my childhood home, and there was nothing to be done but get out of the car and get the job done.

"Wait," I said to Addie, motioning for her to stay in the truck until I could run around to the passenger side and open the door for her. I wanted her to know, that even though we were walking into enemy territory, we were walking in together. From the very first step. I jogged around the hood and gave Addie a huge smile I didn't truly feel, with unease churning through my gut. A screen door slammed back against the old farmhouse wall, and I spun around.

"Kai!" my mother called, rushing down the porch steps, closing a robe tightly around her. Her slippers thwacked on the short path that led to the driveway. "What are you doing here? I didn't expect to see you until the rodeo next weekend."

She rushed in, and I caught her in a hug, folding my arms around the smaller woman, still so familiar to me even two years after leaving her nest.

But the entire time I was hugging her, I was well aware that Addie was still sitting in the truck. I was extricating myself from my mother's embrace when Addie pulled the handle on the door, swinging it open with a squeak of the hinges. I was grateful my mother had come out alone. She was definitely the less intimidating parent.

I grabbed Addie's hand as she slid from the truck, linking my fingers through hers. I gave her a reassuring squeeze, and we turned to face my mother together. "Mom, this is Addie."

Mom's eyes went wide. They were as blue as mine were, but lined at the corners with age. One hand pulled her robe tighter, and the other fluttered around before landing over her heart. "Oh, I know you... You were at the rodeo in New York." Her gaze focused in on our entwined fingers. "Oh my," she muttered. Her gaze raked over Addie from head to toe. And while I was relieved to see no outward hate or disgust in her expression, I prickled when her mouth pulled tight with worry. "Kai, your father..."

I pulled my shoulders back. "Will apologize for his backward comments."

Mom took half a step back, her mouth turning into an O shape. Beside me, Addie shot me a similar look. I tried to hide my own surprise at the tone of voice I'd used. While I felt my words to my very soul, it wasn't like me to stand up to people. Normally, I just kept my head down and minded my own business. I'd never been one to make a scene or to yell or to even speak if I wasn't spoken to first. The backhand my father had dealt me at fifteen had taught me that lesson. But Addie stirred every alpha male tendency in my body. And the thought someone had hurt her, especially my own father, ate away at me like acid. I wasn't going to stand for it. He *would* apologize.

Mom wrung her hands together. "Kai, that's not a good idea."

Impatience rose. She might not have been openly racist like my father was, but she never said anything. Never called him on his bullshit. I hadn't done enough either. Until now. Now I was here, and I didn't care if I made a scene. I didn't care if I was no longer the dutiful son I'd always been. Somebody needed to speak up. And I wanted that person to be me.

"I love her, Mom," I said firmly. "So yes. It is a good idea."

Addie breathed in sharply. Hell. I shouldn't have said that. Not to my mother, before I'd even told Addie herself. But it was done now.

Mom gasped and covered her mouth as the screen door slammed again and my father came storming out. His long strides stiff and jerky until he stood beside my mother.

"What did you say, boy?" His voice was almost a snarl. He didn't spare Addie a glance, but I pulled her behind me anyway. Mom took a step back behind my father as he inched toward me.

This was nothing I hadn't seen before. The way he displayed his dominance with a show of aggression, puffing himself up, drawing to his full height and trying to intimidate me.

It had worked when I was a teen. Any argument I might have had, I'd given up in the face of his aggression. But not this time. This time, I stood my ground. I squared my shoulders and stared him dead in the eye. "This is Addie. My girlfriend. And I said, I love her."

Red heat filled my father's weathered cheeks. "You don't know what love is, you stupid fool." He looked past me to where Addie stood. "She's got you under some sort of spell. Some of her Negro magic."

I ground my teeth together. "Watch your mouth, old man."

He let out a laugh. "Or what?"

He took another step closer, until we were practically eye to eye. But I refused to budge. Refused to back down to his intimidation tactics.

"Kai, maybe we should go," Addie said quietly behind me.

"Not until he apologizes to you."

My father snorted. "Apologize? To her? For what? For saying exactly what she is? Some, black witch."

My blood boiled. I curled my fingers into fists, and my chest heaved with the force of my breath. He was goading me, I knew it. But I couldn't help the physical response. I wasn't a fighter. But I'd never wanted to punch someone so much in my life.

My father's eyes narrowed. "No son of mine sleeps with a black."

My tenuous hold on my patience snapped. My fist connected with his jaw before I even realized what was happening. Pain spawned in my knuckles, spreading out through my arm, and my dad's head whipped back.

"Kai!" both my mother and Addie yelled.

I shook my fist out, eyeing my father. He spat blood onto the ground before he straightened. His right hook caught me across the jaw. My mother screamed, but I welcomed the pain. I took the punch, knowing I deserved it. Not for standing up for Addie. But for all the times I hadn't stood up to my father. For all the times he'd made hateful comments. For all the times I'd stayed silent.

I stumbled after taking the punch, and Addie caught my arm, pulling me away until my back hit the metal side of my truck.

"Get in the car," she demanded.

I blinked through an already swelling eye. "He didn't apologize," I mumbled.

She looked furious. Her eyes burned with a fire and intensity I'd never seen.

"Get. In. The. Car," Addie demanded.

I glanced over her shoulder. Dad stood beside Mom, who had tears running down her face.

"Go," he growled. "Get off my property. Come back when you've come to your senses."

My jaw was tight—from anger or the punch I'd taken—I wasn't sure. I yanked open the door to my truck and slid behind the steering wheel. I waited for Addie to follow me. But she didn't. She spun and stalked back to face my parents alone.

"Addie!" I yelled through the open window.

But she simply held her hand up in a 'stop' motion.

I'd already royally fucked this up, it was obviously time to let her steer the ship. But I wasn't going to let her stand there, unprotected. I got back out of the car and stood at her side.

She glanced at me and nodded slightly then she faced

off with my parents. "I don't need your apologies," she said calmly. "Kai did. And that's the only reason I'm standing in front of you right now. I'm here because it was important to him. Don't think for a single second I'm losing sleep because you don't like someone based solely on the color of their skin."

Neither of my parents said a word.

Addie turned to my father. "There's a photo of Kai on a white supremacy website. He needs you to get it removed."

"Why would I do that?"

"Because that photo could destroy your son's career. And despite the fact you don't deserve a son like him, I don't think you truly want to destroy his dreams." She let out a long sigh. "I'll leave now."

Neither of my parents said a word when she turned on her heel and got back into the truck. In silence, I followed. I started up the engine and didn't look back. My parents disappeared in a cloud of exhaust fumes.

25

KAI

*M*y knuckles swelled, and once we got out of town where I didn't need to shift gears so often, I switched to driving with my left hand. Heat flushed my entire body as the silence in the cab of my truck drew out. My brain swirled with thoughts, some too complex to fully grasp hold of, but one thing that kept going through my mind was how Addie understood this whole thing so much better than I did. And I was a moron for going in all gung ho.

"That didn't go exactly how I planned."

She gave me a tight smile. "I figured as much."

"I just wanted him to apologize. I don't understand why he's like that, and I hate that he hurt you."

She sighed and rested her head back on the seat. But she reached her hand across the gearshift, and I gratefully took it. I was dying to touch her. To reconnect. I felt this horrible gap widening between us, one that was out of my control. I needed her touch to help bridge it.

She smoothed her thumb over the back of my hand.

"People like your father aren't ever going to change. I've been putting up with it my entire life."

"It's not right, though."

"I know. And I appreciate what you were trying to do."

"I shouldn't have taken you there."

"Probably not. But I'm a big girl. I can fight my own battles."

I groaned. "You did a better job than I did."

"Do you think he'll get it taken down?"

I shook my head slowly. "I honestly don't know."

"I think he will."

"What makes you say that?"

She finally glanced over at me. "Despite the fact he threw a punch at you today, I've seen how much he cares about you. He was so proud of you, that night at Madison Square Garden."

The throbbing in my jaw said otherwise. "I don't know about that."

"Yeah, you do. Who drove you to all your practices and competitions before you went pro?"

I stared stiffly out the front of the windshield. "He did."

"And if they'd allowed me to step foot inside that house, would I have found all your old trophies? How about newspaper clippings? Awards?"

I nodded. "Yes. It's like a shrine to my bull riding career in there."

She shook her head. "It's not just your bull riding career. It's you. I saw the excitement and love in your mother's eyes when she saw you today. I saw the way she ran into your arms and took too long to let go. She cried watching you and your father go at each other."

"Probably unhappy about having to clean blood out of

my father's shirts." The joke was feeble, and Addie's disapproving expression only cemented it.

"Don't do that. Don't downplay the love your parents have for you. You're lucky."

"But my father—"

"He has some backward ideas that were likely a result of the way he was raised. I feel sorry for him. And I hate he's so narrow-minded he believes that bullshit, because that makes him an unhappy person. But don't pretend he doesn't love you. He might have his flaws, but he's your dad. And I'd bet that photo of you will be down before we get back to the hotel in Atlanta."

When we finally made it back, we checked into our rooms. Hers was on the floor below mine, so we traveled up in the elevator together. Annoying jingling music softly played from tiny built-in speakers, but that was the only noise. Addie and I waited in silence, but when the doors pinged open, I grabbed her hand.

"I don't want you to go."

She turned to face me and cupped my cheeks between her hands. "Hey. Stop looking so worried. We're fine."

Were we, though? I wanted us to be. But I just didn't know how that was possible, after that horrible scene at my parents' house. Not to mention me saying I loved her, but not actually saying it *to* her. Fucking hell. Something deep inside me screamed if I let her out of my sight, the gap I'd felt open up between us would only get wider.

"Stay with me. In my room," I urged.

She bit her lip, and I immediately ran my thumb over it, popping it out from between her teeth.

Her big brown eyes stared up into mine. "That's kind of like living together. We're here all week."

I nodded. "I know." I held my breath, wanting her to say yes. Knowing I could show her I wasn't always a complete hothead, who went off with half-cocked ideas, if she just let me.

She glanced over her shoulders as the elevator doors grew impatient waiting for her to disembark and began to slide closed.

She didn't make a move to stop them. Instead, she brushed her lips over mine, a small smile forming. Then she tucked her fingers into my shirt. "I guess the elevator fates just decided for me."

"Remind me to thank them later." I'd said the words in a joking tone, hoping they covered the elation and the pure relief I felt on the inside. I pressed my lips hard against hers and the elevator began its ascent once more. The metaphorical gap between us narrowed just a tiny bit.

Outside my room, I waved the keycard in front of a scanner, but I put a hand out before she could enter. "Wait."

She raised an eyebrow.

"This seems like a momentous occasion. You moving in with me."

She laughed. "Well, moving in with you until the end of the week. I reserve the right to go back to separate rooms at the next stop if you snore or leave the toilet seat up."

My heart squeezed at the thought of mundane things like bathroom etiquette, and I realized I wanted those things with her. I wanted everyday conversations about coffee or where a missing sock was. I wanted dinners in the evenings and chats about our day. I wanted long Sunday mornings in bed with a couple of adorable kids bouncing all over us... I wanted that dream Sunny and I had talked about. Only this time, when I thought about us being neighbors and running a bull riding school, Addie was with *me*. It was me she watched with a sweet smile. Me who got to wrap his arms around her, kiss her, and take her to his bed each night.

Without letting myself think if that could really ever happen, I hoisted Addie up into my arms and carried her across the threshold.

She tipped her head back and laughed. "I think you're only supposed to do that if you're married."

The word stopped me in my tracks.

"You should see your face right now. Chill, Kai. We've been together a few days. Nobody is proposing."

Not yet, a voice whispered in my head. I blinked hard and placed Addie's feet on the floor. Not yet. But the thought of one day actually making her my wife stole my breath. How had I let this snowball so quickly? I hadn't even officially told her I loved her, and yet I needed her like I needed air to breathe. The thought of losing her now that I'd had a taste of what it felt like to be with her... Fuck. My throat constricted.

Oblivious to my inner turmoil, Addie shrugged out of her jacket and kicked the door shut behind us. I watched dumbly as she moved around the small kitchenette and waited until she wandered back over to me. I hadn't moved since I'd had this little revelation.

She gazed up at me curiously. "You okay?"

I nodded, not trusting myself to speak.

"I need a shower..."

She pulled off her sweater, leaving her in a lacy white bra. That got my attention. The white lace plunged between tight, high breasts, her dark-brown skin smooth and lickable. My dick stood to attention.

"Turn around and take your skirt off," I demanded.

Her eyes widened, and lust flared beneath the brown depths. She did as she was told, my dick hardening when she slid her skirt down over her perfect, peach-shaped ass. I groaned when I saw the white thong that dipped between her cheeks. I took a step in and palmed her ass, squeezing it hard. She let out a moan that only barely satisfied my sudden wild need to claim her. To prove to myself she was mine, and mine alone. I ran my fingers beneath the lace around her hips, dragging it down over her ass until the scrap fell around her feet.

"Put your hands on the countertop, Addie. And spread those legs. I want to see what you've got in between."

My dick hardened again, straining at the fly of my jeans, my own words turning me on. They seemed to work on Addie, too. I could already see how wet she was, the lips of her pussy peeking out as she bent her torso over the kitchenette counter. I palmed her ass again, then ran both hands between her legs, spreading them wide so I could see every inch of her. I'd had my face right there last night, but it had been so dark in the field and we'd been hurried. Now, I simply took in the beauty of her body. Her legs trembled in anticipation, and I ran one finger around her clit.

A small moan slipped from her mouth, but I wanted more. That need to pound into her, to fill her with my fingers, my tongue, and my cock, to make her mine in every way, coursed through me. Something primal in me wanted to erase all traces of Sunny from her body, even though I logically knew it was a caveman move.

I didn't care.

My finger rubbed over her nub. "Did he touch you here?" I whispered.

She stilled and glanced back over her shoulder. But something in my gaze must have reassured her there was no malice in my intent. This was just something I needed to know. Something I needed to do.

"Yes," she whispered.

I rubbed her clit, making tiny small circles until her breath changed to pants of need.

"Oh, Kai," she moaned.

Satisfaction rolled through me to see her on edge so quickly. But I backed off, not wanting her to come yet. I trailed a finger to her entrance, and ran it around the rim, nudging inside just a little.

Her knees buckled. "Kai, please!"

But I didn't relent.

"Did he touch you here?"

Her head dropped back. "Yes," she moaned. "Kai, please. Touch me there."

She didn't have to ask twice. I slid two fingers inside her slick pussy. When she was ready, I added a third and stroked in and out of her body, palming her ass, squeezing it with my other hand and watching her juices coat my fingers. I dragged them back another inch, and she yelped as I slid over the puckered star of her asshole.

"Here," I said, leaning over her and speaking gruffly into her ear. "Did he touch you here?'

She shook her head. "No," she said on a breathy exhale. "No one has."

I pushed against her back entrance experimentally, not entering her body, but just to see how she'd react. She let out a long, low sound of pleasure.

"Don't stop," she whispered. "That feels so good."

It was enough to nearly make me come in my pants like I was sixteen again. Fuck. An invitation like that was almost too good to turn down.

"Not yet. But soon. When you're ready, I'll take you right here." I pressed at her again, the very tip of my finger edging inside, and a fresh wave of wetness seeped from between her legs, coating her bare pussy lips.

"You're so fucking beautiful, Addie," I murmured. Precum leaked from the tip of my cock, and I ached to thrust it inside her. "I don't give a fuck about other men. I want to be the last. I want to be the one you remember when you're horny and touching yourself. I want to be the only man who touches you here or anywhere ever again. I want you to be mine."

"Yes," she moaned, her hips thrusting back to meet my fingers. "Yes, I'm yours, Kai. Please. Let me come!"

Keeping one finger on her ass, I slid two others inside her wet channel. Two quick thrusts, and she screamed, her internal walls clamping down, her ass taking a little more than she had moments earlier. I groaned my own pleasure at the sight, unable to take my eyes off the erotic sight of Addie all splayed out over a kitchen counter, coming hard.

"Fuck me," she whispered as she came down off her high. I continued to stroke in and out of her pussy.

She didn't stop me. "I want you, Kai. Your cock. Fuck me."

All reservations I'd had about letting myself feel too much around her fled. I suddenly wanted to feel it all. I wanted to plunge myself inside her and feel her come around my cock.

"I got you, baby." I grabbed my wallet from my back pocket, pulling out a condom. With haste, I shoved my jeans and underwear down my thighs and ripped the foil packet open with my teeth.

The sight of her wet, needy, and waiting spurred me on. I fumbled to get the condom over my dick.

My ringtone suddenly blared around the otherwise quiet room.

Addie jumped then groaned. "Ignore it."

But I made the mistake of glancing over at the phone on the countertop beside Addie's elbows. My erection shriveled.

"What's wrong?" Addie asked, looking over her shoulder. I couldn't stop staring at the phone. Her gaze followed mine, and she squinted at the screen. She straightened, picking it up. "Who's Jacqueline?"

I closed my eyes for a long second before taking the phone from Addie's hand. "She's Sunny's mom."

"Oh." Addie cast her eyes down at the floor. "I'm going to go take a shower. I'll give you some privacy."

I nodded stiffly and swiped the green 'answer' button as I pulled my underwear back up my legs.

"Jacqueline? Is everything okay?" I asked, my gaze trained on Addie as she collected her clothes from the floor and hurried into the bathroom.

She cast one last worried look back at me before she closed the door. I stifled a sigh so Jacqueline didn't think I was an asshole. Then I sank down onto the padded couch in the living area of the spacious room.

Jacqueline's voice sounded older and more tired than I remembered it being from all the times I'd visited Sunny at her house. The training camp we'd met at wasn't far from their place, and he'd dragged me back there for meals or to swim in their pool on countless occasions. Jacqueline had become somewhat of a mother figure to me while I was away from home. She was a single mom, Sunny's dad having died when Sunny was eleven. A lump rose in my throat, pushing away every good feeling I'd had just minutes before.

"Sunny's body was returned to me last week."

I ran my hand through my hair and fought back the urge

to swear. "That took a long time."

The older woman sighed, sounding so damn sad it near broke my heart. "Too long. I just want to lay him to rest."

"I understand. Can I be there?" The lump in my throat threatened to burst. I'd stood at the back of the memorial in Sydney and obsessed over Addie because I'd known I could. I hadn't had to think about Sunny's body being laid to rest because I'd known that would come later, when his body was returned to the US and he was buried in his family burial plot. Beside his dad, and his grandparents. Where he belonged, on the soil he grew up on.

"Of course!" Jacqueline said, relief in her voice. "I need you there, Kai. You were like a brother to him. It wouldn't be right to do it without you."

Moisture beaded behind my eyes at the thought of Sunny being my brother. He'd called me that on more occasions than I could recall. And it had always hit me in the feels because I'd never had a sibling to grow up with. I'd never even had cousins. Sunny was all those things rolled into one for me. My best friend. My brother.

"I know the tour comes through Texas next week, so we'll have the funeral then."

"Okay."

"Can you ask all the other men on the tour to come? Sunny spoke of them so highly, but I only met a few. I wouldn't know who to invite, so I thought it best to leave that to you."

I nodded even though she couldn't see me. I suddenly wished we were having this conversation in person. I knew how hard this had to be for her. And I just wanted to make it better.

"I'll tell them," I confirmed.

They'd all come. There was no doubt about that. Sunny

had been well loved by everyone who met him. All the guys and any family they had along with them would want to pay their respects.

"And his girlfriend? Addison?"

My heart stopped. "Addie," I corrected.

"Yes, yes. I know she was from Australia, but sweetheart, he talked about her all the time when we spoke on the phone. And he sent me a photo of them. She's so beautiful."

"She is." I choked on the words.

"Can you ask her to come? Please? I know it's so far for her to travel, all the way from Australia, but I want her to know that I want her with us when we lay his body to rest."

Jacqueline's voice cracked, and I realized how hard she must have been trying to keep herself together throughout this phone call.

The bathroom door opened, and a billow of steam poured into the main room. Addie's wide eyes, her lashes dark with water, wet hair hanging around her face, locked with mine. My heart squeezed.

"Actually, she's on tour with us at the moment, Jacqueline," I said, all the while staring into the eyes of the woman who made my heart thump so damn hard I'd committed the ultimate sin and betrayed my best friend. "I'm sure she'll come."

Addie watched me curiously, stepping from the bathroom wrapped in nothing but a fluffy white towel, and sat gingerly on the couch beside me. She gave me the same questioning look, but I let my head fall back on the couch and my eyes close.

Jacqueline continued telling me her plans for the funeral, but I barely heard them. All I knew was that I'd let myself get carried away. And I'd suddenly been brought back down to earth.

26

ADDIE

*S*unny's childhood home was the biggest house I'd ever seen. It couldn't even be called a house, because a residence of its size was nothing short of a mansion. Set out in what felt like the middle of nowhere Texas, surrounded by open fields and vast expanses of empty land, I'd expected a little farmhouse. But as Kai pulled our rental car up in front of what had to be a multi-million-dollar ranch, all I could do was blink in astonishment.

"This is where Sunny grew up?" I choked out.

Kai simply nodded.

I glanced over at him sharply, frustration rising in my gut. He'd gone into full Frost mode after Jacqueline had called him about the funeral. Any shell I'd managed to pry off him in the last few weeks had been firmly put back in place. Despite the fact I was sleeping in his room every night, I'd barely seen the man. He'd taken to staying up late, with his headphones on, watching his rides on his iPad. And when I woke in the mornings, his side of the bed was always cold. He left me notes, saying he was at training, or was running errands for Jacqueline, helping her with the funeral preparations. I'd kept myself busy, catching up on interviews with the other riders and writing stories for the newspaper. I still hadn't finished my piece on Kai, and I knew the newspaper was antsy about it. But I'd managed to hold them off so far, filling their column with behind-the-scenes gossip and commentary about the worst buck-offs and highest-scoring rides.

I let him be. When our paths did cross, he dropped a kiss on my head and kept going on his way. He didn't seem to want me to leave, but he didn't seem able to fully engage with me either. The closeness I'd felt to him just days earlier wavered in the awkward air between us, and I knew he was struggling with what we'd become to each other.

Today was going to be hard for him. It was hard for me, too, but not in the same way. I knew that, even if everyone else didn't. I just wanted to make it easier for him. The only way I knew how to do that was to follow his cues. So I let him be.

Movement at the front of the house caught my eye, and I pushed open the door of the rental car. An older woman flew down the steps, and Kai's strong arms caught her in a hug. She immediately burst into tears, her fingers bunching in the material of the black dress shirt he'd painstakingly ironed in the hotel this morning. His suit pants were equally wrinkle-free, and his boots were shined to within an inch of their life. I'd watched him knot a thin, black tie around his neck, his fingers shaking in the mirror.

"You made it," Jacqueline said in a wobbly voice.

"Of course." Kai glanced over at me as I rounded the car to stand beside him.

Sunny's mom was not exactly what I had expected. Where Sunny was tall and lanky, his mom was a little shorter than I was, and curvy beneath her demure mourning dress. But when she turned to me, her mouth spread into the most beautiful smile, one that lit her entire face, and that was when I saw the family resemblance. He'd had her smile. The smile that lit up every room and had earned him his nickname. He'd gotten it from her.

"Addison," the older woman breathed.

She opened her arms, and though I'd never met her before, I stepped into her embrace and held her tight. Suddenly a wave of emotion struck me hard. I'd spent so much time trying not to feel anything about Sunny's death. I'd thought I wasn't entitled to feel the pain of his loss because I hadn't been in love with him the way everyone seemed to think I was. I hadn't wanted to appear the grieving widow, because I felt as if I didn't deserve the title.

But with my arms around Sunny's mom, a tear dripped down my face for the loss of a great man. He may not have been the love of my life, but he'd been my friend. My lover for a little while. A good man who was taken entirely too soon. And I finally let myself feel that pain.

It stabbed through me like a knife, spearing my heart and taking a piece of it when it finally subsided. Jacqueline cried on my shoulder, and then almost in unison, we consoled the other.

"It's okay, sweetheart," she said at the same time I said, "He loved you so much."

We pulled apart and smiled, both of us with eyes wet from tears.

I wiped mine with the back of my hand and cleared my throat. "It's lovely to meet you, Jacqueline."

The older woman took me by the shoulders and looked me up and down in such a motherly gesture that it warmed me inside. "There's nothing of you, sweetheart. Let's get you inside and find you some food. It will be hours before everyone else gets here for the funeral service. And I want to get to know you."

I sniffed and wrapped my arm around her shoulders when hers tucked around my lower back. She led me up the stairs. Kai followed silently behind us.

Inside, I gaped around at the high ceilings and open floor plan. Shining wooden floors were covered in thick rugs. The beams in the ceiling were exposed, and a grand chandelier hung in the middle of a living area. The space was elegant, but perfectly aligned, overstuffed couches were cozy enough to sit on in your pajamas with a good book.

"Kai? Could you show Addie to the dining room, please? I'll go see about some lunch for us all." Jacqueline pressed a hand to Kai's cheek, and he gave a nod of agreement.

"It's really good to have you here," she said, her voice cracking again. "It's too quiet without you boys around."

"It's good to be here."

She left us, disappearing through an archway that I assumed led to the kitchen. We both watched her go, standing in silence until we were alone again. The silence drew out.

"Are you okay?" he asked quietly.

"Yes." I inched my hand closer to his until our pinkies brushed.

He jerked his hand away as if my touch had electrocuted him.

I tried not to get upset. I knew this wasn't the time or place for affection, but I hated that we were both hurting and couldn't comfort each other.

I followed him to a dining table that was longer than any I'd ever seen in a house, enough space for twelve to sit spaciously. I pulled out a seat and was surprised when Kai took the seat next to me. My skin prickled at his nearness, and I dared to try again. Beneath the table, I edged my leg over until it brushed against his.

He froze, but this time he didn't move away. "We can't, Addie. Not here."

I shook my head. "We're not doing anything."

"But just being near you..." He closed his eyes.

"Is that why you've been avoiding me the last few days?"

He didn't get to answer. Jacqueline returned, a uniformed servant in tow, both of them carrying dishes of delicious-smelling foods. My mouth watered, and Kai's stomach growled. Neither of us had eaten breakfast. We'd both chugged down coffee, but my gut had been rolling with nerves.

Jacqueline put plates of some sort of stew with dumplings in front of us, and we both went for the food like we hadn't eaten in months. Jacqueline watched us from across the table, pleasure in her expression. I ate ravenously, ignoring the older woman for a few minutes while I inhaled my food. When I looked up, her face was sad again.

"He should be here," she said softly. She eyed the empty seat to my right, and her eyes filled with tears. "He should be sitting right there next to you."

Kai's fork clinked onto his plate, but Jacqueline didn't seem to notice.

"It's not fair," she whispered, her eyes darting back to meet mine. "He loved you so much, sweetheart. He talked about you all the time." Her expression turned wistful. "I think he was real serious about you, you know?"

I choked on my food and darted a glance at Kai. "Oh, I'm not so sure about that."

But Jacqueline wouldn't hear of it. She shook her head firmly. Then she stood and dug her hands into the pocket of her dress. When she pulled them out, she held a red velvet box.

My fork fell from my fingers, and my mouth suddenly went dry. Jacqueline sat again and pushed the velvet box across the table. Her arms only reached halfway, but I didn't stretch forward to make up the distance. Instead, I just stared, wondering how a box turned into a ticking time bomb, right before my eyes.

"The last time I spoke to him, all he talked about was you, Addison. I think he would have asked for that at some point." She nodded to the box still sitting ominously on the table.

I didn't dare look at Kai. I couldn't even imagine how he was reacting to this.

"Go on, open it," Jacqueline said.

"What is it?" I asked instead.

The necklace I'd put on that morning suddenly felt so tight around my neck it may as well have been a noose.

Jacqueline grew tired of waiting and popped the box open. A large ruby sat in the middle of a gold band, smaller diamonds trailing either side of it.

"It's beautiful," I whispered. And it was. The rock shone like nothing I'd ever seen before.

"It was his grandmother's. On his daddy's side. She passed when Sunny was too young to even know what a girlfriend was, but I put it aside for him, knowing one day he'd want to give it to someone special." Jacqueline's eye shone. "I want you to have it."

"Me?" I squeaked, though she obviously didn't mean Kai. "Oh no, Jacqueline. Thank you. It's such a beautiful gesture, but I can't accept that. It's—"

"Pssh. You can and you will."

I shook my head, but Kai caught my attention. He

nodded ever so slightly, and I stopped. My gaze turned questioning.

"You should take it," he said stiffly. "Jacqueline is right. He would have wanted you to have it."

A ball of dread gathered in my gut. I didn't want the ring. But how could I say no, when it obviously meant so much to a woman who'd lost her only child? If it brought her some happiness, couldn't I give her that? But the stiffness in Kai's body was telling. He moved his leg away from mine, and I instantly missed his touch. I knew what accepting this ring was doing to him. Hell, just being here was undoing every step we'd made together. I could see the whole thing unravelling before my eyes and I felt powerless to stop it.

Jacqueline's eyes were big and pleading, and there was nothing to do but reach across the table and take the jewelry box. Happiness filled her expression. "Put it on, dear."

Maybe I'd done the right thing.

Though I knew if I looked at Kai, I'd see a whole lot of nothing. I already knew he was locking himself tight in his Frost persona. And as I pushed the ring onto my right hand, I wondered if I'd be able to pull him out of it this time.

The cars rolled in about an hour before sunset. First it was just one or two at a time, and Jacqueline stood on the porch, greeting each person as they arrived and thanking them for their condolences. But as the minutes ticked on, nearing the hour the burial was to take place, the slow trickle of cars became a flood. They filled the little dirt road, waiting in a line to turn into the property.

And Jacqueline introduced me to every single one of them. Every great aunt, every random townsperson, every old schoolteacher. Hundreds of people who'd known and had an impact on his life were introduced to Sunny's grieving girlfriend.

That invisible noose around my neck grew tighter with each and every hello I forced out of my mouth. The ring on my finger burned, and as discreetly as possible, I pulled it off, stowing it back in its box. I didn't want to hurt Jacqueline, but it didn't feel right.

The funeral itself was torturous. Jacqueline insisted I sit on her left. Kai on her right. She had no immediate family, and we could hardly leave the woman alone in the front row, so we both did as we were told.

I didn't hear a word of the service. The preacher seemed like a kind man, who had known Sunny since he was a boy, but I couldn't concentrate on his words. I kept darting glances at Kai, trying to catch his eye, but he stared steadfastly ahead, barely blinking. And when they lowered Sunny's coffin into the ground, my heart broke. Not only for the man we'd all lost, but for the man still left here in his shadow. I ached to reach out and take his hand, to put my arm around him. And I hated he didn't want me doing that.

After the funeral service, the congregation gathered back at the house for the wake. I was determined to get out of there as soon as humanly possible, but the minute I walked in the doors, a group of women grabbed me by the arm and brought me into their conversation. I'd been introduced to them earlier, but there was little hope of me remembering their names. Kai disappeared into the crowd, and I scanned it constantly, all while nodding and smiling at the women.

"You two would have made such beautiful babies!" one of the younger women cooed. "You with your beautiful brown skin, and him with his height and chiseled jaw. Those children would have been so darling."

I gripped my mug of coffee so tightly I was surprised it didn't shatter beneath my fingers. The women didn't seem to notice. They all nodded demurely, and a fresh round of "Such a great loss" started up.

I couldn't do it anymore. The giant mansion suddenly felt as tiny as a doll's house and shrinking by the minute. "Will you excuse me, please?" I asked the women as politely as possible. "I need to get some air."

Without waiting for a reply, I pushed my way through the crowd, zigzagging around people and ignoring the few who called out to me. I felt like everyone in the room was watching me, judging me. Could they tell I was a fake? A phony? That I didn't deserve their sympathy or the stunning ring that was burning a hole in my pocket? Sunny deserved all this fuss. But I didn't.

I made it back to our rental car and leaned hard against it, the cool metal at my back grounding me while I tried to catch my breath.

"Get in," a gruff voice said.

I whirled around, realizing instantly that it was Kai. He sat behind the steering wheel.

"What? But Jacqueline and all the people..."

"Exactly. Jacqueline has all those people. Who do you have right now?"

The overwhelming day crashed down over me like a tidal wave. "No one," I whispered.

"You have me."

"Do I?"

He nodded, then the gruff exterior dissolved, leaving me with the Kai I'd come to know. "You always did."

I slid into the car, closing the door behind me, and fused

my mouth to his. A sob erupted from my chest, and Kai reached across me, pulling on my seat belt. I curled into an exhausted ball on the passenger seat and let him drive me away from the wake. Night had fallen, and the roads were dark. Within moments, I was lulled to sleep by the rhythmic rocking of the car.

27

KAI

*O*ur hotel room was dark. With my fingers threaded through Addie's, I pulled her inside and closed the door softly behind her. Neither of us reached for the light. Instead, she reached for me. Her fingers untangled from mine and instead wrapped around the back of my neck. Slowly, she pulled my head down. Our faces hovered inches apart, our breath mingling in the blackness that surrounded us.

Like they had a mind of their own, my fingertips found the sides of her face and traced their way over her temples, across her high cheekbones and down to her jaw. They were featherlight touches, my skin barely drifting over hers, but a shiver coursing through her limbs told me I had an effect on her.

An effect I liked. I tilted her face upward, and our lips met in a heartbreakingly slow kiss. Our mouths moved in practiced unison, taking things steady, but at the same time making up for the lack of contact between us in the last week.

It had been me who had put that wall back up between us. And I still wasn't sure I was entirely ready to break it down.

But I already knew Addie wasn't going to take no for an answer. In the darkness, our lips never leaving the other's, she stripped me of my clothes. First the tie at my neck, then she undid the buttons of my shirt. She pushed it off my chest and arms, and finally broke away from my mouth to press slow, sweet kisses around my collarbone.

Her hands drifted to my belt, and we both stepped out of our shoes. She undid the button on my pants and lowered the fly.

Her mouth moved back to mine, and she plunged her tongue inside, taking control of the kiss and owning it. My dick stiffened in my boxer briefs. All rational thought evaporated.

She rubbed me through the fabric, stroking, getting me fully hard before she yanked off my underwear. Then she dropped to her knees, and I let her hot, wet mouth engulf me for the briefest of moments. I speared my fingers into her loose curls, and it would have been so easy to stay there for a lifetime, thrusting in and out of her wickedly talented mouth.

But I dropped to my knees in front of her. Despite the lack of light, I found the zipper on her dress and undid it, letting the straps fall down her slender arms, then pushed it farther down her torso until it lay in a heap on the floor. Her actions grew hurried, unclipping her bra, while I made short work of her panties, until we knelt before each other, completely naked and vulnerable.

I'd gone through more emotions than I'd thought possible today. Everything ranging from debilitating grief to keen realization that I couldn't have them both. I couldn't hang on to Sunny while I tried to make things work with Addie. I had to let one of them go.

I leaned in, brushing my lips over Addie's ear. "I'm sorry," I whispered.

"Why?" she breathed, not moving away from my touch.

The words were hard to get out, but I had to say them. "He could have given you so much more."

This time she pulled away. "What do you mean?"

I couldn't stop touching her. My fingers trailed down her bare back, over the bumps of her spine, memorizing each one as I went. "He could have given you that big house. Money."

"I don't care about that," she said.

I already knew. It was just a buildup to what I was really trying to say.

"He could have given you a family. One that accepted and loved you the way you deserved to be loved. Not..." My voice cut out, and I swallowed hard. "I can't give you that, Addie. My parents won't ever change their mind about you."

"Sssh," she soothed. "It doesn't matter."

But it did. "I took it all away from you. That night, in the car—"

"Was not your fault," she said firmly.

The sob in my throat threatened to choke me. "I killed my best friend," I whispered. "And I nearly killed you."

She grasped my hand and pushed it to the scar on her cheek. The one I always avoided when I touched her. The still-new scar was puckered and thick beneath my hand, and too smooth to be regular skin. "You didn't do this. The drunk driver who hit our car—he did it. You? Do you want to know what you did? You saved the lives of three people in the car with your quick reaction. You protected me when the car spun out of control. You sat at my bedside for weeks. Despite everything in your head telling you otherwise, you're a good man, Kai. You deserve good things. You deserve to be happy."

A tremble ran through Addie's lean body, and I chased it away with my palms.

"I want you," she whispered into the silent room. "Please don't reject me."

I shook my head. "Never."

A small whimper escaped her mouth, and I kissed it away.

"I love you," I whispered against her lips.

She paused, and my words hung in the air, thick and heavy, before she claimed my mouth as hers once more. "I love you, too," she whispered back between fumbling, hot kisses that seared my soul as much as my lips. My heart stopped. Then soared like it had grown wings and taken flight, straight out of my body.

"Say it again," I demanded.

"I love you, Kai."

I dug my fingers into her hips and lifted her onto my lap. She straddled me, her wet core pressing against my thigh, my erection prodding her belly. Her lips found mine once more, and this time, I took everything she had to give and fed it right back to her. *Mine*, a voice in my head roared. For the first time, I believed it. She was no longer Sunny's girl. With her whispered words of love, she'd cemented the fact.

"You're mine," I whispered.

"Always. Let me show you."

I groaned as she pushed me to the floor. I braced myself on one elbow, fisting my other hand into her hair. I tugged her roughly to me, and our lips collided in a kiss that set me on fire. Her body moved over mine until I was lying back on the floor. Her lips skated over my ear and jaw until she reached my neck. She bit and sucked, and I couldn't have cared less about the hickeys I'd likely have in the morning. I wanted them. I wanted her mark on me. Just like I wanted my mark on her. Mine. Only mine.

My cock strained toward her entrance, aching to fill her. I bit out the words, "I want you so fucking much."

She moved down my body, kissing and sucking and biting at my nipples, and I relished the quick stings, smoothed immediately by the flat plane of her tongue.

With every inch she covered, her pussy came closer and closer to my eagerly waiting dick, until my cock head was brushing her thighs, spreading precum over her and turning me on all the more. I knew how slick and beautiful she got between her legs. And I wanted nothing more than to sink my dick deep into her.

She took me in hand and gave me a hot, fast stroke that had my hips jerking off the floor.

"Fuck, Addie!" I roared, and when I came back down, her hot wet heat was surrounding me, my cock edging inside her.

My eyes rolled back, and all thoughts flew out the window. Nothing existed but Addie and me, our bodies and the places we were connected. Her lips on mine. Our hearts beating in unison. Her pussy taking my cock like we'd been built for each other all along.

She slid down my length, and I groaned hard. She braced herself against my abs, and there was just enough light in the room for me to watch her tits bounce as she rode me. She started slow, her hips rising and falling, a little rocking at the bottom giving her clit some friction. I palmed her gorgeous tits, squeezing the nipples until she increased in pace. I rolled my hips up to meet her, loving the sounds of her low moans each time my dick pressed to her G-spot.

"Baby," I whispered, the beginnings of my orgasm threatening. "You feel too good. I'm going to come."

She leaned down and silenced me with her lips. Her hips moved faster, and her breaths changed to pants. I wouldn't come before she did. I sat up, fusing my mouth to hers once more. I slipped two fingers between us to rub her clit and watched in pleasure as she bounced up and down on my dick, her head dropping back, her moans growing louder and louder the more I rubbed her.

"I'm going to come," she moaned.

Her inside walls clamped and spasmed around me, and she ground down harder. Her fingernails dug into the flesh of my shoulders, and she screamed her pleasure while I pounded up into her core. Her orgasm sent me barreling into my own. My balls tightened and I flipped her onto the floor, driving into her. Over and over until she'd taken everything I had, including my heart.

I collapsed down on her, and she wrapped her legs around my lower back, her fingernails leaving indents in my skin. Overcome with everything we'd just done, and how my body vibrated with the aftereffects of my orgasm, I buried my nose in the crook of her neck, inhaling her scent.

I was scared I was crushing her but when I tried to move, she wouldn't let me. She held me tight, and I gave in to the sensations flooding through me. Everything about this felt right. I'd been a fool to stop us each time we'd almost gotten to this point. The closeness I felt now, engulfed in her sweet body...it was everything. Everything I'd wanted. Everything I'd been missing.

"I love you," I said.

"Say it again," she demanded with a laugh in her voice, echoing my earlier words.

I shifted my hips against hers, making sure I pressed on her still-sensitive clit. She jerked and moaned, making me laugh. "I'll say it as many times as you want, Addie."

28

ADDIE

*M*y body still hummed with pleasure long after Kai and I stumbled into the shower, made love again, then fell into bed together. He'd stroked his fingers down my spine until his movements grew sluggish, and eventually he'd slept.

My internal muscles still clenched in memory of the mind-blowing orgasms I'd had, and my heart beat that little bit harder than it normally did. My head didn't want to switch off, though. It kept up a continual happy movie reel of every good memory Kai and I had shared over the last few weeks, conveniently fudging over the not so pleasant ones.

I realized abruptly, though, I didn't want to do that. I wanted to remember the harder things we'd been through in the short time we'd really known each other. Because they'd brought us to where we were right now. And right now was pretty damn amazing. For the first time, I felt like Kai had completely opened up to me and let me see who he really was.

I was ready to write the story on him. I'd been putting off

my editor for weeks, promising her what I delivered would be worth the wait.

Because *he* was worth the wait. In every way.

Not wanting to move Kai's thick arm that was banded around my waist, I grabbed his iPad from the nightstand and brought up Google Docs. And then I got to work. Typing while lying down and on an iPad screen wasn't the easiest way I'd ever written a piece, but my fingers flew deftly over the screen, not worrying about typos or poor grammar. I'd fix all of that later. The story fell from my fingertips. The way we'd met. The way I'd thought him a virgin who was scared of women. The way he'd protected me the night of the crash, and his loyalty in sitting by my bedside. His devastation over losing his best friend and the guilt he'd placed firmly on his own shoulders. I wrote about how skilled he was as a bull rider and how he'd followed in his father's footsteps, by becoming a pro. I wrote down all his technical stats I'd memorized in my research and talked about his odds of taking out the entire competition at the age of twenty-two. The whiz kid rookie who most knew as Frost. But who I knew as Kai. Kindhearted. Protective. Sweet. And talented as all hell.

It was a gush piece. There was no doubt about it. I had left out any hint of his father's racism, and checked that the photo of him was still missing from the White Unite website. It was. Like I'd thought, the photo had disappeared from the site within twenty-four hours of us confronting Kai's parents. But I'd been checking daily, just to be sure it stayed gone. Of course, once something was on the internet, it was never truly gone, but we both felt better knowing it was no longer out there in plain view for anyone to stumble across.

Kai stirred behind me, shifting closer to me, his half-erect dick pressing against my backside. My legs parted slightly, and we both groaned when his dick rubbed between them.

"How long have you been awake?" he mumbled, before pressing his lips to my shoulder. His dick slid leisurely between my legs, gathering my instant arousal as he went.

"I haven't slept. I was writing."

He peered over my shoulder at the tablet, but I put it facedown on the bed, suddenly shy about how I'd poured my feelings into the piece. "Stop! You can't see it yet. It's just a rough draft."

He flipped me to my back, and in one swift movement, pinned me to the mattress, enclosing my wrists with one hand. He plucked the iPad easily from my fingers.

"Hey! Cheater!" I wriggled beneath him, but without even looking at his iPad, he tossed it onto the soft carpet.

"No working in bed." His thick cock notched at my entrance. "Not when you're naked and so fucking sexy I don't know how you ever looked twice at me."

His dick nudged inside me ever so slightly.

"I'll never work again if this is my persuasion."

He laughed, sliding in a little more. Then it was an hour of kissing and slow, hot sex that curled my toes.

"I should put this in my story," I murmured. My mind was fuzzy with lust and tingly nerve endings.

"Hmmm?"

"I should put you fuck like a sex god."

He kissed me slow and deep. I lifted my hips and met his long thrusts. "That's knowledge only you need to know."

As the following weeks turned into months, it was more of the same. My private investigator kept searching for my birth family, while Kai and I lived in a bubble of travel, hotel rooms, and late nights, wrapped in each other's arms, our naked bodies coming together in the dark over and over again.

We traveled through state after state, Kai competing each weekend and steadily making his way up the leader board. We became the tour's most antisocial couple, always choosing to go back to our room and be alone, rather than go out drinking or dancing with the others. I wasn't even sure how many people knew we were truly a couple, since we'd never made a big announcement. But I didn't care. I loved what we'd found together. And I wasn't ready for the bubble to burst.

---

*T*he tour moved onto Alabama and into the final rounds that would determine who made the top twenty riders competing in the Las Vegas finals. The mood of each competitor grew more and more serious. The partying died right down, and the guys spent their days training and their nights going over past rides, studying their form or researching bulls they'd be riding that weekend. Basically, they all became a whole lot more like Frost. Like he used to be, anyway.

I sat on the edge of the bed in yet another hotel and opened my laptop while I waited for Kai to finish getting ready for that night's rodeo. I'd dressed in tight jeans, boots, and a low-cut top that showed off both my belly and my cleavage. I left my hair out, put in big hoop earrings, and placed a wide-brimmed hat on my head. The summer had well and truly spawned, and Alabama was hot and muggy as hell. Kai's eyes had bugged right out of his head when he'd seen my outfit choice, and I'd felt like the sexiest woman alive. A confidence I'd never felt before pumped me up, and I'd batted away his grabby hands, reminding him to go finish getting ready.

The springs of the mattress bouncing lightly beneath my ass, I moved my finger over the trackpad on my laptop and brought up the website I wrote for, navigating to the page that housed my weekly column.

Kai finished buckling his belt and glanced over my shoulder. "They still haven't run that story you wrote about me?"

I shook my head, closing the laptop again, the piece I'd written about Felix Irwin and his ninety-three-point ride last weekend disappearing from view.

"Have they said what the holdup is?"

I shrugged. "Nope."

He held out a hand and pulled me to my feet. "I still want to read it, you know."

Heat rose in my cheeks when I thought about the story I'd written for a man I loved. As the months flew by, my feelings only deepened. But the fact the website still hadn't run the story had begun to make me feel self-conscious. I'd read the piece over and over. It was personal, but at the time I'd submitted it, I thought it would make an amazing insight into the sport, as well as into Kai's character. One that really tugged on your heartstrings and made the public see the side of Kai he kept hidden. It would make them see him as a real person, one with strengths and weaknesses and triumphs and heartache. I'd thought it would help to increase his popularity, maybe even project him to a crowd favorite, which could do so much for his career. Crowd favorites got sponsorship deals that could mean more money than bull riding could ever bring in alone. But it had been months, and now every time I thought about the story, a swarm of butterflies took flight in my belly and my chest got tight. Maybe it had been too much. Maybe he would be embarrassed. Maybe the website wouldn't run it at all because it was complete garbage. My own insecurities got me hard in the gut, and every time Kai had asked to read the piece, I'd denied him, making it into a joke and saying he'd just have to wait and see.

Like he always did, he let it go. He never pushed me on it, and I was grateful.

"Ready to win?" I asked brightly, pushing my insecurities away.

He wrapped his arm around my waist and pulled me tight. "I already did, when I got you."

I fake groaned. "You're getting corny in your old age. By the way, are you planning on telling anyone it's your birthday?"

Kai rubbed his hands down the front of his jeans like his palms had suddenly gone sweaty. Alarm was written all over his expression. "No. And don't you tell anyone either. I don't want a fuss."

I linked my arms around his neck and brushed my mouth over his. "I know. My lips are sealed."

"Let's go then." He linked his fingers through mine, and we headed for the lobby. The buses would be waiting to take the entire team and their families to the arena. The elevator ride down was full of other riders, all doing the same thing we were, and I smiled and chatted with Kiera, one of the other girlfriends as the elevator descended.

"Kai," a deep voice called as soon as we stepped foot in the lobby.

Kai froze, his fingers squeezing mine. I stopped as well and glanced around to see who had called him. And then had to swallow down my shock.

Kai's parents stood by the reception desk. His dad's gaze

narrowed in on our joined fingers, and his lip curled ever so slightly.

I suddenly remembered Kai saying his parents would be at the Georgia and Alabama rodeos, but after the scene on their front lawn, I'd conveniently forgotten all about their planned trip.

"What are you doing here?" Kai asked without moving.

Keira gave me a questioning look.

"Go ahead," I murmured to her. "We'll catch up."

She seemed uncertain but she left. The rest of the team was forced to walk around us. I tugged Kai's hand to move him out of the flow of foot traffic, but he didn't budge. His entire body was locked up.

Ignoring his mother's big eyes and his father's rigid posture, I calmly extricated my fingers from Kai's. "I'm going to give you three a minute."

"No." His voice was like steel.

"Kai, look at me."

He turned his head stiffly. His eyes were hard.

I sighed. "I'm just going to sit over there. There's a lot you need to sort out. As a family. Me being there will just inflame the situation."

He seemed like he wanted to argue, but when I walked a few steps away to perch on the edge of a couch, he let me go. His mother rushed the space between them and threw her arms around him.

Despite the crappy way his family had treated me, my heart broke a little for her when he didn't hug her back. She stepped away to stand beside his father.

"What are you doing here?" Kai asked again.

"It's your birthday," his mother said quietly. "And we told you we'd come."

Kai glanced over at me. I tried to keep my face as impassive as possible.

"Is Dad ready to apologize?"

"For what?" the older man spat out.

I cringed. The pleasantries hadn't lasted longer than thirty seconds. It didn't bode well for the rest of the conversation.

Kai's fingers balled into fists at his sides. "You know very well for what. If you didn't come to apologize, I don't know why you came at all."

Kai's mother placed a hand on her son's chest, but he stepped back, and her arm dropped limply by her side.

"Please." Her gaze flitted between her son and husband, her eyes pleading. "Please don't fight."

Kai turned on his mother. "Then take a stand. Tell him he's wrong."

Unsurprisingly to me, his mother said nothing. And I was glad I couldn't see Kai's face clearly from this angle, because he was likely realizing something I'd learned as a little girl. Not to expect more from people who couldn't give it.

"I don't want to lose another child," she said, a tear slipping down her cheek.

Kai's father put his arm around her thin shoulders and shot Kai a dirty look. "You've upset your mother with this nonsense."

"Nonsense?" Kai choked out. "Dad, you're a racist. And you don't accept my girlfriend. That's not nonsense."

His father's eyebrows pulled together, and his face went bright red. His grip on his wife's shoulders tightened. "You watch your mouth, boy."

Kai ground his teeth. "I'm not your 'boy' anymore, Dad."

His dad's mouth flattened into a grim line. "No, you most

certainly are not." His voice became a hiss. "I won't stand for this. You're upsetting your mother when we've traveled to see you. You need to choose, *boy*."

The word was slung at him like a slur, and I dug my fingernails into the fabric of the couch cushions. "Her or us."

My stomach rolled with sudden fear and uncertainty. We'd spent every spare moment together for months, and I'd fallen so stupidly in love with him I barely even remembered who I was without that.

But they had a lifetime of memories. They were family. A true family, who had grown together, loved together, lost together. Despite his parent's misgivings, they loved their son, and he loved them, too. I knew that. I knew the argument we'd had with them back in Georgia had played on Kai's mind, even though he had denied it when I'd questioned if he was okay with it all. He'd buried it, just like I had, and now it was coming back to slap us both in the face.

"It's her." Kai's voice was calm and strong. "It's always *been* her. It *will always* be her."

Kai's mother let out a wail that drew the attention of several passersby. They shot concerned glances in the trio's direction, and I moved from my spot on the couch at the same time the hotel receptionist stepped toward Kai's mother.

"Is everything okay here?" the receptionist asked with a fake smile in place.

I put my hand on Kai's arm. He visibly relaxed beneath my touch, and ignored the receptionist, continuing to address his parents. "You've traveled to be here, and there's tickets in your name at the box office. You're welcome to use them. But don't bother waiting for me afterward, unless you're willing to accept Addie."

With that, he turned on his heel, walking toward the last of the buses that were waiting outside the fake gold-lined doors of the hotel. I trotted after him. But I couldn't help looking back over my shoulder. My gaze skimmed the anger in his father's expression. But his mother's was haunting. She was pale and drawn. Dark circles showed beneath hastily slapped-on makeup. And tears rolled down her face as she watched Kai take my side and walk out of her life.

I should have felt elated. The words he'd said. The way he'd stood up for me. He'd picked me over his own family.

But all I felt was bone-aching guilt.

29

KAI

*T*he sun was sinking as the bus rumbled along the streets to the arena. Bright oranges and reds crept across the sky, but I barely noticed. I was numb all over. From my head to my toes. I was so unaware of my own body that it took Addie three tries and a hard slap on the arm to get my attention.

"Sorry, what?"

Her delicate eyebrows were drawn together in a frown. She linked her arm through mine. "I'm worried about you."

I shook my head, but it did nothing to clear the fog surrounding my brain. "I'm fine."

"You're not. How could you be?"

"I'm fine," I repeated. Even to my own ears, my words were no more convincing than they had been the first time.

Addie bit her lip. "What was your mom talking about when she said she couldn't lose another child?"

The bus bumped over a pothole, jostling the two of us even closer, and I was grateful. I breathed in her scent—her mild perfume, mixed with the aroma of hotel soap and a fresh mint from the chewing gum she liked best. The smell had become so familiar. It reminded me, while one part of my life was falling apart, another was oh so right. *She* was right. I'd meant every word when I'd told my parents it had always been her. If Sunny had lived, and she'd gone on to marry him, it still would have been her. I would have gone to my grave, old and gray, still holding on to a secret crush I would have never done a thing about. And now that she was mine, I wasn't giving her up. Not even for my parents.

Though the look on my mother's face had nearly ripped me in two. "I had a sister. She was older by four years."

Addie's grip tightened around my biceps. "Was?"

"She died."

Addie clapped a hand over her mouth. "Oh my God. I'm so sorry. Was it recent?"

"No, no. She was five. I'd only just turned one. Truthfully? I don't remember her at all."

Addie nodded slowly. "Your poor parents."

I stared down at her in awe. "How do you do that?"

"Do what?"

"You always have compassion for people, even when they don't deserve it."

Her gaze narrowed. "You think your parents don't deserve compassion? They lost their child, Kai."

"But the way they've treated you..."

"Doesn't mean I'm going to treat them the same way."

I grasped her chin between two fingers and tilted her face up to meet mine. "You are the most kind, most compassionate, most caring woman I've ever met in my life, Addie. I hope you realize exactly how special you are."

I pressed my lips against hers, until the jostling bus jolted us apart. Then I just stared at the woman, who surprised and awed me in different ways every day, and felt grateful it was me sitting beside her.

Outside the arena, I kissed her goodbye, and she walked with the other family members through the high, wide doors and disappeared into the darkness. I followed the trail of riders into the employee area and then down into a holding area backstage. I dropped my bag on the floor and started going through my warm-up routine. I strapped fringed chaps over my jeans and swung my arms in wide circles, loosening my shoulders and shrugging out the tension in my back. I tried not to think about my mother's devastated face when I'd walked away from her, because I knew that wouldn't help my ride. Despite being in the top five of the leader board, I couldn't afford to screw up now. All I needed was a couple of bad rides and my ranking would slip right down. I'd be out of finals contention quicker than you could say yee-fucking-haw.

I pulled air deep into my lungs and tried to clear my thoughts. I needed to focus. But I found myself drifting to the edges of the tunnel that led into the arena. The crowd was rapidly filling. People dressed in jeans, boots, and cowboy hats all took their seats. I spotted Addie in the front row of the friends and family section, already getting busy with her notebook and pen. I knew from flipping through the pages, she always began by writing descriptions about the atmosphere around her. If the crowd was big or small. If they were loud and rowdy or quieter and more reserved. She liked to people-watch, and her notebook was full of details about various people she'd seen in the crowd at all the events I'd ridden in so far. Observing and writing down all those little moments was how she got in the zone. Much the same way concentrating on my next bull and remembering the way he moved and turned was mine. That zone of concentration was the sign of someone committed to their task. And I was proud, watching Addie get into hers. I realized with a start I hadn't actually told her that. Her writing was amazing, and I looked forward to reading it every week. I hadn't told her because I knew the attention would embarrass her, but life was too short not to tell people when they were doing a good job.

That was something my father had taught me. He wasn't one to hand out praise willy-nilly, but he'd always said, credit where credit is due. And every time I'd been on the receiving end of his praise, I'd been on a high about it for weeks.

It was hard to suddenly turn that off. I knew I'd done the right thing, walking away from my father after he'd disrespected Addie. By pushing me into choosing between the woman I loved and my family, he'd forced my hand. But I found myself searching them out in the crowd. Still foolishly hoping I'd see their familiar faces. Still hoping my relationship with them could be saved. Praying he could change his ways.

I shoved my hands deep in my pockets when I couldn't see them. As the lights dimmed and the first rider was called, I realized how stupid it was to hope I could have it all.

---

*A*ddie waited for me by the buses after the rodeo. She jogged over, grasping my biceps in both hands and ran a worried gaze over me.

"I'm fine," I assured her.

Her eyebrow shot up somewhere near her hairline. "Are you sure? Because that fall..."

Had hurt like fucking hell. There was no doubt about that. I'd been off my game. No matter how hard I tried to pull my head out of my ass, it hadn't been enough to come away with two clean rides. I'd managed to hang on for the first one, though without any of my usual style, and had earned myself a low score. But hey, a score was still points on the board, and in this sport, sometimes just holding on was all you had to do to rank. My second ride had been a disaster from start to finish, though. I'd somersaulted over the bull's horns, landing on my back in the dirt, with the wind knocked out of me. Rem and Abel had managed to direct the bull away, and I was grateful because it had taken a long time for me to get back on my feet and stagger to the edge of the ring.

"I'm sure," I assured Addie, putting an arm around her shoulders and steering her back to the bus.

"You two aren't going back to the hotel again, are you?" Rem whined, jogging up beside us.

The face paint he wore in the arena had been wiped clean, and he'd changed into jeans and a shirt, like most of us had. "We're going to a honky-tonk. Come with us, it'll be fun."

I started to say no thanks, but then Addie tilted her head curiously.

"A honky-tonk? I've never been to one."

"You want to go?" I asked her.

"I'd like to see what it's all about...but if you're tired..."

I ran my hand through my hair, realizing something. "I'm an asshat, aren't I?"

"What? No!" Addie said, at the same time Rem said, "Yeah, pretty much."

I shot him a look, and with a laugh he backed away toward the buses.

Addie seemed worried again. "Why would you say that?"

"Because I've basically kept you chained to our hotel room for months now. You've barely done any sightseeing."

Addie's worried expression smoothed over into a grin. "You kept me chained to our bed, not our room. There's a difference." She winked. "I was pretty happy to be there, you know."

My manly pride liked that. A lot. But I was still an asshat who needed to take his girl out on the town. "Let's go with them tonight. Maybe I'll even dance."

She raised an eyebrow. "Isn't dancing mandatory at these things?"

"God, I hope not, 'cause I was totally joking about dancing."

She elbowed me in the ribs good-naturedly, but my wince was real.

"Shit! You are hurt!"

I tucked her arm into mine and led her toward the bus. "Just bruises. Nothing that won't heal by itself."

"Nothing that's going to stop you from dancing, then," Addie said firmly.

I groaned, but it was in fun. If she wanted to dance, then that was what we'd do.

The bus dropped a dozen off us off out the front of the honky-tonk bar Rem had heard about from the receptionist at the hotel. Though I'd grown up seeing little country bars back home, The Winding Road was not like any I'd ever seen before. The outside of the building was lit up by neon lights that shone on the old brick walls. A huge acoustic guitar was mounted on the wall above the bar's name, and Addie pulled out her phone.

"Take a selfie with me!"

She put her arm around my middle, and I slung mine across her shoulders. We turned, and she held her phone so our grinning faces were in shot, tinged purple and green by the reflecting lights. The bar sign, and the small crowd waiting to get in were behind us.

We had to take multiple photos from various angles, but when she was satisfied, we joined Rem, Abel, and the others in line. Live music floated out the doors as we waited to get in, and I let the familiar sounds of country music wash over me.

"You like this music?" Addie asked.

I shrugged. "I don't much care one way or another. I'll listen to pretty much anything."

"I love it," she said, staring dreamily up at the large guitar and the night sky. She closed her eyes briefly, her body swaying.

My breath caught. She was so damn beautiful. I loved seeing her at peace like this. And I hated that I hadn't realized until now how much she liked music. I would have taken her to a bar every night if it meant seeing that look on her face.

Her eyelids fluttered open after the crowd in front of us moved forward. "I love country music especially. It's all storytelling, you know? It's what I love to do—tell people's stories—but songwriters are so clever. Being able to express all that emotion, and put it to music, too."

We shuffled forward, and I nodded to the security guard at the door before I focused back on Addie. Her eyes lit up when she spotted the trio playing on a small stage in the corner and the dance floor full of people. She immediately found the rhythm of the song, nodding along to the beat, and her hips swayed while she tugged me toward the bar.

"Let's get you drunk first, huh?"

I followed eagerly, because being drunk would definitely help my dancing skills. We found an empty spot at the bar, chancing two seats after another couple left and laughed their way onto the dance floor. Addie watched them go with a small smile.

"Did you ever think of learning to play?" I asked her while we waited for the bartender, who looked completely frazzled and run into the ground. "Maybe write your own stuff?"

"Oh no." She laughed. "Haven't you heard my singing in the shower? I'm woeful."

I'd heard and thought her off-key singing adorable. "You don't need to sing to write," I countered.

But she shook her head. "I'm happy with reporting the news. Well, mostly happy."

The bartender arrived, and we ordered beers. The man took two bottles from the refrigerator behind him and popped the tops off with a bottle opener mounted beneath the bar top, before pushing them across to us. Addie grabbed hers, and I handed him enough to cover the cost.

I hadn't realized how thirsty I was until the cool liquid hit my throat, and I swallowed several mouthfuls while Addie's last comment rolled through my mind. "What do you mean by that?" I asked finally. "That you're mostly happy?"

She swiveled on her stool so she was facing the band and leaned back, resting her elbows on the bar. The beer bottle dangled from one hand. She lifted one shoulder without looking at me. "Sometimes the story I have to write is hard, you know? Sometimes the story is spilling a dirty little secret the person would have never wanted revealed. Sometimes it's reporting on a death of someone who was taken too young. I once had a story about a home invasion gone wrong, that ended with an elderly woman in the hospital. I hate those stories. But at the same time, they need to be reported."

I brought my beer to my lips again but stopped before actually tipping it back. "What would your ideal story be then?"

She didn't even stop to think. "One that made my name known to millions. Something big. Something I got the scoop on."

"You want to be famous?"

She thought that over for a moment, then shook her head. "No. I don't think so. I probably would have gone into broadcast journalism or something if I'd wanted people to see my face everywhere. Not that there's many jobs like that back home. But maybe that's what I would have tried for. I don't need recognition in that way. I just...I want my words to matter. I want my stories to matter. I want to make a difference and an impact." She ducked her head and stared at the floor. "Sounds pretty stupid now that I say it out loud."

I tilted her chin up so she was forced to meet my gaze again. "Doesn't sound stupid to me at all. I think we're a bit the same like that. That's partly why I want to win. I don't need to be famous, and the money is great, and necessary, of course. But I want more. I want my name in the record books. I want to be the youngest to take out the title, or to be the man who tamed the wildest bull. I don't need them all, I just need...something."

The trio changed the tempo to a slower, country song that was older than I was. The familiar chords washed over me, and in an instant I was transported back to my childhood home. My mother singing that song while she baked, my father humming it tunelessly as I sat on his lap behind the wheel of a tractor.

"You know this one?" Addie asked, and I realized I'd begun to sing the lyrics beneath my breath.

I blinked at her. "Yeah, I do. My parents used to play it when I was a kid. It was their wedding song."

Addie seemed a little surprised, but then she recovered and clinked her beer bottle against mine. "Maybe we should dance, then? Since they aren't here."

"You want to dance in their honor?"

She shook her head. "I want to dance with my man."

The look in her eyes grew heated, and I abandoned my almost finished beer to the bar, taking hers with me. She let it go, her fingers opening as I grasped it, and then landing on my arm instead. I grabbed her fingers and led her through the crowd, finding a slightly darker spot on the edge of the dance floor, where I could pull her close and press my luck by stealing a kiss when the song ended.

She wrapped her arms around my neck, and we easily found the beat together, swaying back and forth. She rested her head on my shoulder, and I held her tight, still not quite believing she was mine, even after months of dating.

"Relax," she whispered, swaying. "Just listen to the song. Feel it."

And so I did. I took a page out of her book and allowed the melancholy song wash over me. It wrapped around us, and the memories it invoked rushed in.

"Why can't he see that I'm happy?" I murmured.

Addie lifted her head. "Your dad?"

I nodded. "He was a good dad, you know? He spent so much time with me when I was a kid. Taught me all about cars and tractors and the animals on our farm. We'd spend weekends beneath the hood of his truck, spilling oil all over the place, and earning disapproving looks from my mother when she came out to check what we were doing. But he was my best friend. Until I was old enough to realize his thoughts and ideas weren't all right."

We swayed back and forth. "You realized he wasn't perfect."

I nodded. "Far from it." I glanced around the packed dance floor, noting multiple other black people, besides Addie. "Nobody else cares," I said in her ear. "Nobody here cares that you're wrapped in my arms right now. We're not hurting anyone. Why can't he see that?"

A lump grew in my throat.

"I don't know, baby. I don't know. I wish I did."

Her words were meant to be soothing, but I heard the edge of guilt in them. I pulled back to study her. "This isn't your fault, Addie."

She bit her lip, even as she nodded. "I know. But I also know what it's like to come from a broken family. To have no roots. No ties to the people who raised you."

"I don't need them," I said firmly. "All I need is you. Anyway, you turned out perfectly, so I'll be just fine without them." And I meant every word. I didn't want to lose my family. But they'd made their bed and now they had to lie in it. Because I would keep choosing Addie. Every time, through every barrier life put in our way. I'd keep choosing her. Over and over again.

"I love you," I whispered against her hair. "So much."

She laid her head back down on my chest. "I know."

30

ADDIE

"*B*abe! Guess what?" I looked up from my phone and bounded across the room to where Kai was sprawled out on the couch. Too excited to control my energy, I threw myself onto his lap and kissed his lightly stubbled cheek.

With a startled grunt, he pulled off one side of his headphones and put his iPad down on the coffee table. His arms snaked around my waist and linked against my hip.

"Not that I'm complaining about you suddenly being in my lap, but it's not often you launch yourself at me like that. What did I do to deserve such enthusiasm?"

"Your story is in tomorrow's column! I just got a message from my editor. They're finally running it."

It was about time. With less than a month left to go on the tour and only three rodeos, including the grand finale in Las Vegas, I was beginning to think they weren't going to run the piece at all.

"Did you ask why it took so long? It's been months since you handed it in."

"Something about it making a bigger splash now that you're top three going into the last weeks of qualifying."

He gave me a little squeeze. "I'm really proud of you, you know? You've been killing it with that column. They'd be crazy not to ask you to do it again next year."

My smile faltered, and I had to force it back onto my face. "Thank you."

"Addie…" Kai warned.

"What? I'm fine."

"They will ask you back. I promise."

I tried to force my voice to sound lighthearted. "You can't promise that, though."

He placed a searing kiss on my lips. "Too late. Already did. It's going to happen. Now, don't you have an interview to get to?"

"Yep." I pushed up off Kai's lap and yelped when he swatted my backside. "I'll be back for dinner, okay? Maybe we can go out?" I wrinkled my nose in disgust at his sweats and wifebeater. "All that bull study is great, but I think you need fresh air. And a shower."

Kai sniffed at the collar of his T-shirt and made a face. "You're right. I don't think I've left the room in three days. The tour coach sent me so much footage I've never seen before."

"How is that even possible with someone who studies as much as you do?"

He shrugged, pulling on his headphones again.

"Shower, food, and fresh air, Kai Hunt," I said dryly. "Don't forget."

He saluted me, and I blew him a kiss.

I loved his dedication to his sport, and I knew it would all be over in three and a half weeks. Which would give him more free time. The only question now was, with the tour wrapping up, would I be able to stay in America with him? If my contract didn't get renewed at the end of the tour, I had no idea what would happen with the two of us. I was pretty confident we wouldn't break up. But what would a relationship look like with me back in Australia and him in the United States?

I shrugged off the uncertainty. Focusing on the positives. If we were separated, it would only be until the Australian competition started up again. Kai would surely come over for that, and even if I was back working at the dinky little Lorrington newspaper, we could fly in and out to see each other on weekends.

And we could have amazing phone sex in between.

With that smug thought in my mind, I left the hotel and strolled down the city sidewalk until I reached the café Brad Pruitt, head of the WBRA, had suggested for our interview. I'd put off interviewing the big man for too long, but with such little time left, I really wanted to give my readers a well-rounded view of what went on behind-the-scenes. And that meant talking to Brad Pruitt, even if the guy irked me.

I couldn't really put my finger on why I'd never liked him. I knew Bowen and Paisley had had run-ins with him on the Australian tour, and every time I'd crossed his path, his conversations had felt disingenuous. He was a good busi-nessman; I'd give him that. But my gut said he put his busi-ness over his riders. And that didn't sit well with me.

I spotted him through the glass windows of the New Leaf Café. His plaid shirt stretched across his barrel chest and a huge, black, ten-gallon hat perched on his head. He sat deep in his chair, reading a newspaper, something hot in the mug clasped between his fingers.

My phone jingled in my bag, and I took a few steps out of the doorway to take the call, knowing I was early to meet

Brad anyway. I shuffled a tissue pack, some loose coins, and a coral-colored lipstick to the side and pulled out my ringing phone.

Private number. I debated answering it, but knowing the alternative was going in to start my interview with Brad, I figured I may as well.

"Hello?"

"Addie, it's Mathew Radcliffe. The private investigator? We spoke a few months ago?"

"Oh!" Surprise jolted through me. "Did you find something?" I couldn't help the eagerness in my voice, even though I'd been warned not to get my hopes up. I'd checked in with the man twice since he'd taken my case, and both times he'd said he was still investigating leads. I'd been a little worried I'd been taken for a ride, considering the slow progress, but after checking with Rem, he'd assured me that was just the way Mathew worked, and that I needed to be patient. So I'd stopped calling him and pushed my curiosity out of my mind.

But now it all came flooding back in with a rush. Last time, he'd said he had leads on my birth mother. I had to lean back on the brick wall of the building to steady myself. This could be it. This could be the moment I found out my mother's name and where I came from. Maybe he even had a photo he could send me? I'd always wondered if I looked like my mother, or my father. And if our personalities would be similar, because we shared the same genetics, or if I would be completely different because I'd grown up away from them.

"I did find some things," the investigator said slowly. "I would have preferred to tell you this in person, but with your traveling, that would be impossible."

"It's fine. Just tell me. Please." I couldn't stand the

suspense. I dug my fingers into the hard wall behind me, despite knowing I was ruining the manicure I'd gotten just a couple of days ago.

"I did find your birth parents."

My heart stopped.

"Their names are Georgie and Ralph. They are still living together, though they were never married. They did confirm that they gave up a baby girl at the time you were abandoned."

"That has to be them, then? Right?" Excitement flooded my veins. Georgie and Ralph. I had parents. Two people who had created me, and they were both still alive. I'd been so nervous I'd started my search too late. If they'd died, I would have never gotten to know them, and I would have hated the years I wasted being too scared and angry to try.

"Can you tell me more? Can I meet them?" I held my breath while I waited for him to answer.

Mathew sighed heavily. "This is the part I would have preferred not to say on the phone. Unfortunately, they don't want to meet you, Addison."

"Sorry?" I choked out. My gaze blurred with tears. "No. Wait. That can't be right."

"They made that very clear. They didn't want me telling you their surnames or where they live. For what it's worth, I got the impression that it was an old wound they didn't want to open again. There seemed to be a lot of remorse there."

Remorse? I rubbed my eyes with the heels of my hands, not caring if I smudged my eyeliner.

"They don't even want to talk on the phone?" The words were small, weak. Sad. Words of a little girl, rejected by her family for the umpteenth time. I went right back to all those years in foster care. All the times I'd never felt loved or taken care of. All the times I'd dreamed of my real family swooping in and taking me away and living happily ever after. Somewhere, deep inside me, I'd held on to those little girl dreams. And thought maybe I deserved more.

I'd been wrong.

"Sorry, no. They said they didn't want any sort of contact."

Without saying goodbye, I hung up. I walked past the café door, not noticing or caring whether Brad saw me or not. I didn't care I was standing him up. I just kept on walking.

Maybe if I walked far enough, I could leave the stinging rejection behind.

31

KAI

*B*y the time I finally got to the last video on my to-watch list, my eyes were crossed and my brain mush. I pulled my headphones off, put my iPad down, and stretched out on the couch, twisting and popping all the tight muscles in my back. Shit. I'd been way too sedentary the last couple of days and I desperately needed a workout.

Addie had said she wouldn't be back until dinner, and though it was already six-thirty, I figured I could probably squeeze in a thirty-minute run on the hotel treadmills before dashing back upstairs for a quick shower and shave.

With my sneakers laced up, I took the stairs down to the hotel gym and set a treadmill to a punishing pace. With every stride, my muscles contracted and loosened, and finally, my head cleared. Like always, when my head wasn't dominated by bull riding—and even sometimes when it was —my thoughts turned to Addie.

I'd never had something so good in my life. This thing we'd built together over the past few months had been fast and hot and heady. But I'd never loved someone the way I loved her. Never had that complete soul-to-soul connection or that voice that screamed, "She's the one!"

A grin curved my lips. We hadn't had such serious conversations, but I knew. I'd known since the first time I met her that she was different. Though it had taken me a while to get here and to believe I could have her, I'd arrived.

And I wanted to stay right here in this spot with her. Always.

The ring sitting in a velvet box, hidden inside a flap of my suitcase was the proof.

Hitting the button on the treadmill, I increased the speed, pushing myself harder, but the grin never left my face. Shit. I was going to give myself away if I started grinning like a fool around her. I had the whole thing planned out. I had two tickets booked to Hawaii, and as soon as I could get her alone, by the water, with a huge orange sun sinking behind us, I was going to get down on one knee and ask her to marry me.

If I didn't fuck it all up and let it slip out before we got there, that was. I'd never been so excited for the bull riding season to end.

Addie still wasn't back by the time I got out of the shower, and I frowned at the clock that said it was already seven forty-five. I'd run for longer than I should have and had expected an annoyed Addie to be tapping her foot, waiting for me when I got back to our room. I'd been prepared to grovel for forgiveness, and make it up to her later, most likely naked. But that hadn't happened. There'd been no sign of her.

I shaved then sprayed on some cologne, the one Addie liked best, and pulled on a nice pair of jeans and a fresh white, button-down shirt. I rolled the sleeves to my elbows and slicked some gel through my hair, fussing with it in the tiny bathroom mirror. The whole time, I kept an ear out for the main door opening.

At eight, I sat on the neatly made bed, fully dressed and ready to go out. My stomach rumbled. "Need food, babe," I mumbled before picking up my phone and bringing up her name. I punched the 'call' button. By the time she got back and changed, I might have gnawed off my arm. Ordering some room service might be the better option.

I tapped my foot on the thick carpet while the phone rang out. I dialed again, thinking maybe she was somewhere noisy and just hadn't heard her ringtone. But when my third call rang out, I became officially worried. Restless, I pushed to my feet and paced the little room. Where had she said she was going? I'd been so engrossed in my stupid videos, I hadn't even paid attention.

Brad.

She'd said she was interviewing Brad for her column. Even if I didn't know where, I could call him and see if they were still together. I couldn't imagine how an interview could possibly still be going, considering she'd left hours ago, but maybe she'd started writing up the story afterward.

Relief washed over me. That was likely it. I'd seen her get lost in a writer's zone. She was probably still sitting at a café somewhere, engrossed in her story.

I hit the 'call' button beneath Brad's name and waited for him to pick up.

"Kai!" Brad boomed in my ear. "Ready for this weekend?"

"Yes, sir," I said on autopilot. But before he could get another word in, I asked what I really need to know. "Is Addie with you?"

"Addie? No, son. She stood me up. She was supposed to meet me at a café earlier today, but she was a no-show."

Unease spiked in my gut again. "What do you mean?" Though it was obvious. I just needed a moment to process. Brad seemed to grasp that.

"What's going on, Kai?"

I shook my head and resumed my pacing. "I don't know. She left earlier and said she was going to interview you, and that she'd be back for dinner. But it's past eight, and she's not answering her phone."

"Shit," Brad said, following it up with a sigh. "Look, I'm sure it's nothing, but you keep trying her, okay? She probably just forgot about our interview or got held up doing something else. You let me know when you hear from her."

"Yes, sir," I mumbled and hung up the phone.

I tried Addie five more times, all to no avail. Where the hell was she? My unease rapidly turned to worry and then to panic. It was well past dark outside, and I didn't have a clue where she was.

Taking to the hallway, I thumped on the door of every other rider on tour, hoping Addie was with one of them, conducting and interview or chatting with their girlfriends. By the time I got to the end of the hall, a group of the guys trailed me, murmuring about going out to look for her. No one had heard from her since this morning.

"Fuck this, I'm calling the police." I didn't care if she'd only been missing a few hours. We were in a city that neither of us knew well, and anything could have happened to her. She could have been mugged or hit by a car or lost her purse and had no way of getting home without cash or a phone. A million different scenarios raced through my head, each one more terrifying than the last, until I gave myself a mental shake and forced myself to get a fucking grip. Panicking wasn't going to help. But I *was* calling the police.

I'd just unlocked my phone when her name flashed up on the screen. I'd never hit the 'answer' button so quickly in my life. "Addie!" I yelled. "Are you okay?"

There was a long pause. "I'm fine."

The line was full of static, and her voice sounded small and far away. Despite her hesitation, I waved the other guys away, mouthing thank you at them, and returned to my room. "Where are you? Did something happen? I was just about to call the police."

"Sorry I worried you."

Why did she sound so stiff and formal? So unlike herself? Despite the fact I was no longer imagining her dead in a gutter somewhere, a fresh wave of worries plagued me. "Don't worry about that. Just come back, okay? Where are you? I'll get a Lyft and come meet you."

"No...I. Kai, I just need a moment."

A moment? What did that mean? "Okay," I said slowly. I paced over to the kitchenette and gripped the lip of the countertop so hard I was surprised when it didn't rip straight off the cupboards below. "I'll wait up for you."

"Don't. I don't think I'm coming back. Not tonight."

My heart froze. "Addie. What's happened? You need to tell me. I'm really fucking worried right now."

"I know. And I'm sorry."

"Stop saying you're sorry!" The words came out a little snappier than I'd meant them to, my fear over what had happened to her in the few hours we'd been separated giving my words a sharp edge. I sucked in a deep breath and tried to calm down. I made sure my next words were gentler. "Please, baby. Come home. We can sort this out."

"I will. I promise. Just not tonight. I just need some space to get my head together. Please, let me have that."

"Okay," I whispered. Silence echoed in my ear, then the

call disconnected. It was even longer before I lowered the phone and accepted that whatever Addie was going through, she didn't want my help.

I jerked awake, sitting bolt upright in the armchair I'd fallen asleep in sometime around 3:00 a.m., when I'd given up all hope of Addie returning. With bleary eyes, I glanced around the room, wondering what had woken me. Nothing seemed out of the ordinary. I'd left the hotel room blinds open, and I blinked at the early morning sun streaming in.

Three quiet knocks came from the front door.

I sprinted across the room and threw open the door without bothering to check the peephole. "Addie!"

"Not so much," Rem drawled on the other side of the doorframe. Concern lined his forehead. "I guess she's not here then?"

I shook my head. "She didn't come back last night."

"Fuck."

"Yeah." I ran my hand through my sleep-tousled hair. "What are you doing here this early, anyway?"

Rem clapped a hand to the back of his neck and looked down at the floor. Tension crept across his shoulders.

"You read her column yet?"

"Her column? No, why?"

Rem sighed. "Hell, man. I think you better read it."

I backed away from the door, leaving it open, letting Rem follow me. He watched me pick up the iPad from where I'd discarded it yesterday and bring up the website she wrote for. I navigated through the website to the page called Rodeo Roundup and waited the second or two it took for it to load.

"What the fuck?" I whispered.

Rem cringed.

There in huge black letters was the column headline—Rodeo Racist: Kai Hunt's White Supremacy Ties.

And beneath it, three little words that made me do a double take. By Addie St. Clair.

The photo from the White Unite website, the one my father had gotten taken down, the one only Addie had known about, was right there beneath the headline, along with an article I couldn't even finish reading. I got the gist, and it made me sick to my stomach. It didn't just paint me in a bad light, it smeared my name right through the mud. With horror, I watched the column's comment numbers increase. Arguments broke out between faceless internet trolls who cheered for a high-profile figure being so open about 'white causes,' and those who called me a hateful animal who should be put down. There were a whole range of opinions in between. With sick fascination and the detachment that came with shock, I read every one. Numbness spread through me, chilling me to the bone.

"I don't understand," I finally said, without looking up.

"Don't understand what?"

My head snapped up. Addie stood in the doorway, in the same clothes as the day before. Straggly pieces of hair framed her face, and dark circles rimmed her eyes. But all I felt was relief.

I strode across the room and crushed her to my chest, burying my nose in her hair and breathing deep. "Thank Christ. I've been so fucking worried about you."

Her returning hug was limp, and she pulled away before I was ready.

She glanced over my shoulder at Rem, who cleared his throat. "Uh, I'm going to leave..."

"You don't have to," Addie said, dropping her purse on the floor by the door but not really moving inside.

"Yeah, actually, I do. I think you two probably need to talk. Or...something."

He hustled out of the room, only stopping to squeeze Addie's arm. "Call me later, okay?"

She nodded.

He closed the door behind him.

"Where have you been?" I choked out. I couldn't stop looking at her. My gaze raked her from head to toe, and my fingers itched to reach out and touch every inch of her body, reassuring myself she was home.

"Does it matter?"

My worry accumulated, only growing more intense by her lackluster attitude. "I don't know, Addie! Maybe? Yes? When you left yesterday, everything was great between us. And then you go missing and you don't come home, and then there's your column..."

"What about my column?"

I held the iPad in her direction, my wrist limp, the device dangling from my fingertips. She took it. I watched her expression as she read the article, but her features didn't change.

She handed it back to me. "Kai, I—"

"I know you didn't write it. You don't need to say anything. I don't know why your name is there beneath the title. Or how your editor found out all this stuff about me. But I know it wasn't you."

Her dark eyes met mine, tears flooding them and dripping down her cheeks. "You don't know everything, Kai." The words were barely more than a whisper.

I couldn't stand it. I couldn't stand to see her cry. I cupped the sides of her face. "I know you, though. I know you wouldn't do this. You have no reason to."

She blinked. "Don't I?" Her expression hardened into one I didn't recognize.

"I know you," I whispered again, fear wrapping icy tendrils around my heart. I didn't understand what was going on, or where the Addie who I'd had in my arms just yesterday had gone. The trust and love I'd seen in her expression, less than twenty-four hours earlier, evaporated quicker than I could blink, leaving nothing but the stony eyes of a woman I didn't know.

She pulled back. "I can't go back to that dinky little newspaper in Lorrington. I needed a story. A real one, that would put my name on the map." She pointed to the iPad. "You were it."

Shock punched me in the gut. "I don't believe you. All this time. We weren't just a fling, Addie!"

She shrugged, staring down at the floor.

"You love me," I challenged her, enclosing in on her space again, anger curling into fiery heat in my gut. "And I love you."

She took a step back until she hit the door, but I didn't stop. I caged her in with my body, my hands on the wall either side of her head.

"Look at me."

She didn't move.

"Look at me, Addie," I growled.

When she lifted her head, I slammed my lips down on hers. The sudden impact of our kiss sent fireworks through my body, lighting up every nerve ending. I shoved my fingers into her hair, tilting her head back and claiming her mouth. She opened, and I plunged my tongue inside, claiming, owning the kiss and stealing her breath. When I finally broke away, with my heart pounding and my chest aching, I was sure the Addie I loved would be back. I'd felt her in that kiss. I'd felt how right we were for each other. Just like I did every time we'd touched.

Her gaze focused on me, something flickering in the deepest depths of her brown eyes.

Then she stooped and picked up her bag from the floor. Shoving the straps up on her shoulder, she put one hand on the doorknob and twisted it, the door popping open an inch. She paused. "You were a good lay, Kai. And a means to an end. I'm sorry if I hurt you, but we were never going to be more than that. It would have never worked."

With that, she slipped out the door and closed it behind her.

And I let her go. It was all I could do to lean on the wall and try to breathe through the jagged hole opening in my chest.

32

ADDIE

I closed the door behind me and took two steps down the empty corridor before the steps turned into a full-blown sprint. I ran for the elevator and jabbed the 'down' button so hard it should have gone through the wall.

"Hurry, hurry," I urged the too-slow metal box, while hot tears blurred my eyes.

"Addie?" a voice said behind me, but I didn't dare look around, even though I recognized the concern in Rem's tone. He moved in beside me and grabbed my button-punching hand.

"Addie, shit. Stop. You're going to break your finger."

I couldn't look at him. Or talk to him. All I could do was desperately shake my head and pray I could hold myself together long enough to get away from Kai. My chest hurt so bad from holding my breath that I had to force myself to inhale. Passing out in the hallway before I had a chance to escape wasn't a smart move.

The elevator doors binged open, and I moved to step inside, but Rem blocked my way.

"Move!" I yelled desperately.

But his tall, broad frame didn't budge.

"No way. You're not running off while you're this upset. About-face. My room is right there. Come inside, I'll make you coffee."

"I don't want coffee."

"Yeah, you do. You're coming."

He steered me by the shoulders, and I gave up and let him guide me, focusing on my irritation with him instead of my heart breaking over Kai.

The inside of his room was exactly the same as the one Kai and I shared. Except there was no lingering scent of Kai's aftershave. There was no rodeo vest slung over a chair at the little dining room set. There was no iPad and head-phones discarded on the lounge.

There was no Kai.

A sob choked me.

"Ah, hell," Rem said quietly, pulling out a chair for me. "Sit down, will you? I'll find some tissues."

I did as I was told and waited while he ducked into the bathroom and grabbed a box of Kleenex. He set them down in front of me, then sank into the seat across the table. "Talk, Ads."

I shook my head. "I can't. It's too awful."

"Which part? The column?"

I shook my head. Then nodded. Because that was only part of it. "I just broke his heart." I looked up at Rem with huge eyes that felt raw. Just like my soul. "But I had to."

Rem sighed and folded his arms on the tabletop. "Spill it, lady. The whole story."

"My family doesn't want to meet me."

Rem's eyebrows shot up near his hairline. "Sorry, what?"

"My birth parents. The investigator found them, and

they don't want anything to do with me. I found out yesterday."

"Ah, shit. That fucking sucks. But that's their loss, Addie."

I shook my head. "People always say that. To make you feel better. But it's not really true. It's absolutely no loss to my parents, sure. But yesterday, I lost every childhood dream I'd ever had. All I ever wanted was parents who loved me, Rem. And for a few stupid moments, I let myself believe the fairy tale. I let myself think they'd accept me with open arms. And that they could give me what I've always needed."

Rem rubbed my arm sympathetically, but he didn't comment, letting me continue to pour out my story.

"Everything in that story about Kai is true. His dad is a racist. He is a member of White Unite, and Kai did go to gatherings as a kid."

Rem's mouth pulled into a taut line. "Kai isn't like that, though. I couldn't believe what I was reading when I looked your column up this morning. It just didn't compute."

"I know," I wailed. "I didn't write it, Rem. You have to believe me. That story is not the one I handed in."

"Sssh," Rem soothed. "I know. But why are you here telling me all this? Didn't Kai believe you when you told him?"

"I told him I wrote it."

There was no other word to describe Rem's face but flab-bergasted. He sat back in his chair, his eyes going wide, and he choked on his words, his normally deep voice coming out kind of squeaky. "Why on earth would you do that? Have you lost your mind?"

"No! Argh, I don't know. Maybe! But I need to let him go. That was what I realized last night, and what I came back here today to tell him. He has a family who loves him. And who he needs in his life. I'm coming between them and I can't do that to him. I love him too much."

Rem blew out a long slow breath. "Fuck, Addie. For a smart woman, you can really be dumb sometimes. That isn't your call to make."

I bristled. "I know what it's like to come from nothing. And to have no family to rely on. How did you feel when Abel was across the other side of the country and you couldn't see him?"

A shadow passed over Rem's face. "Pretty shit."

"And how did you feel about your mother, and Abel's mother, for keeping you two apart?"

Rem ground his molars together. "I see your point. We don't really talk much anymore. Christmases and birthdays at best."

"See? You resented her for keeping the two of you apart."

"It's different with you and Kai."

I shook my head sadly. "I let myself think it was, too. But it's not. He'll come to resent me, eventually, if we stay together. I don't want him to wake up one day and feel the way I felt yesterday when I realized I was never going to have anything to do with my parents. I have no family, Rem. None. Nobody to celebrate holidays with. Nobody to call every Sunday night. No father to have my back, no mother to be proud of me. And that's exactly what Kai will have if we keep this up. Nothing. He'll feel the same way I felt yesterday when I got that call. And I wouldn't wish that feeling on my worst enemy. I know this whole thing isn't my fault. I do. It's just a shitty set of circumstances. But I love him enough to want the best for him. I want him to have everything. And everything includes his family. There's no replacing them. I knew I'd have a hard time getting him to see all that, but I was prepared to argue. But then the story....

It just seemed the easier option, to let him think it was me who wrote it."

Rem shook his head. "You want him to have everything? Everything doesn't include love? Doesn't include you? How is that everything? You aren't replaceable either, you know!"

I swallowed hard, not wanting to voice the single thought that broke me more than any other. But I had to say it, as much for my own benefit as Rem's. "But I am. Girl-friends come and go. He'll find love. He'll just find it with someone else. He's twenty-two. He's got a lifetime of love ahead of him."

Rem rubbed his eyes with the heel of his hands. "You know what? I need that coffee. With whiskey in it. Because damn if that isn't the saddest thing I've ever heard."

Tears welled in my eyes again, and he shifted around the table to put his arm around me. I laid my head down on his shoulder, and he kissed the top of my head. "You're a good egg, Addie St. Clair. Not too many women I know would break their own hearts to see someone else happy."

"You can't tell him."

Rem didn't say anything.

I lifted my head sharply. "Rem! You can't tell him, or our friendship is officially over. I swear to you, I will hang you up by your balls from the center of the Las Vegas arena if you utter one word of this to anyone."

Rem's eyes widened, and he held his hands up in mock surrender. "Shit, Addie. You're scary."

I laid my head back on his shoulder, satisfied he wouldn't say anything.

I wasn't scary. What was scary was the thought I'd just let go of the love of my life.

33

KAI

*I*f I'd thought Addie walking out of my life hurt, Rem coming to my room hours later and picking up all her stuff was like rubbing salt in the wound.

"I'm so sorry, Frost. This is so fucking awkward. But she asked me to..."

I nodded and stepped aside. I stared out the glass windows that overlooked the city while he threw her things in a bag. I wanted to rip each and every item from his hands and put them right back where they belonged. Here. With me. Just like she did. But I couldn't do that. She needed her things. Even if seeing them piled into a suitcase was torture.

Rem paused in the doorway. "You going to be okay?"

I didn't answer. "Is she staying with you?"

"For now. The hotel is booked out. Next stop she'll get her own room again. She already organized it with Brad."

Fuck. That had happened quick.

"You know I'd never..."

I glanced over my shoulder at him. His expression reeked of awkward worry. But I knew what he was saying. He wouldn't try to hit on her. He didn't need to say it aloud.

He was a good friend, and I trusted him to look after her while I couldn't. "Yeah, I know."

"So, we're good?"

"We're good. Just..."

Rem waited.

"Just tell her I love her."

The tiniest of smiles flickered at the corner of Rem's mouth. "I'll tell her."

With that he closed the door and left. I sank down on the floor by the window, too numb to continue standing.

You were a good lay, Kai. And a means to an end. I'm sorry if I hurt you, but we were never going to be more than that. It would have never worked.

If I hadn't heard the words with my own ears, I would have never believed they'd come from her mouth. Despite what she'd said, I did know her. And I knew she wasn't telling me the truth. She was a mighty good actress; that much was for sure. But I didn't believe a word of it.

My phone ringing startled me, and I pounced on it, hoping it would be Addie. An unknown number flashed up, and I answered it warily.

"Kai Hunt? It's Bill Granger from Rodeo News—"

I hung up before he could get any further.

The next time my phone rang, it was my parents' number on the screen. I ignored it, uninterested in talking to them. Time ticked on. My phone didn't stop ringing, but it was never the one call I wanted it to be. My mother's cell was one of the most frequent callers, but I ignored them all.

Eventually, I put a movie on and slumped on the couch, but I couldn't focus on the story.

"Kai?" a voice called through the door.

I glanced over in surprise. "Mom? Is Dad with you?"

"Just me," she called from the hallway.

With effort, I pulled myself up and opened the door for her. I didn't go in for a hug like I would have once upon a time. Instead, I left the door swinging and went back to the couch.

Her nose wrinkled as she stepped into the room.

I wasn't in the mood for more of her judgments. "Why are you here?"

"I read the article..."

"Oh. That."

"When you didn't answer your phone, I got on a plane. I came straight from the airport."

"You shouldn't have bothered."

"You're my son. Of course I should have."

I shrugged.

She perched on the edge of the couch by my feet, picking at a loose thread on the purse she placed delicately on her lap. "What's going on with you two?"

I gave a bitter laugh. "I haven't a clue, Mom. All I know is she broke up with me. But I guess that'll make you and Dad real happy, huh?"

Mom shook her head. "No, actually, it doesn't."

I scoffed. "Right. Go home, Mom. I don't know why you came here. I'm not good company at the moment."

She opened her mouth to protest, but I cut her off.

"Please. I don't have it in me to get in another argument with you. Just leave me alone."

To my relief, she stood slowly. As she passed my head, she reached out and brushed a strand of hair off my forehead, like she had when I was a kid.

"This isn't what I wanted," she said softly.

"Yeah, well, looks like neither of us got what we wanted, did we?"

I stared blankly at the TV until long after the door

clicked closed.

For the next two days, it was more of the same. My cell phone rang night and day, and my voicemail got so full of messages that it stopped taking new ones. The hotel phone was no better, and in a fit of irritation, I yanked the plug from the socket and threw it against a wall.

If only I could do the same with my cell. But stupid, dumb hope stopped me from dropping my cell from the balcony of my tenth floor hotel room. Because if Addie called...

That was all that kept me going. Trying to work out what the hell had happened between the two of us and conjuring up plans to fix it. But after two days of giving her space, praying she'd come to her senses, I was losing it. I couldn't do it anymore.

I stormed down the hallway to Rem's room and paused at the door, my fist poised, ready to knock. And then laughter came from inside and had to clutch the doorframe for support. I pounded my fist on the door.

The laughter inside stopped.

"Addie! I need to talk."

Nothing.

I rested my forehead on the door. "Addie, please." I was begging like the desperate man I was. And I didn't care who heard me. The hole in my chest that had opened the day she left was rapidly consuming me. Knowing she was so close, just on the other side of the wall, was torture.

The door opened a crack, and I stood straighter, but it was Rem who slipped outside, closing the door behind him. I stepped back into the middle of the hallway. "Please, Rem. She won't talk to me."

Rem blew out a long breath. "You just gotta give her time, man."

"I can't. I know something happened to her, and it's fucking eating me alive. It's all I think about."

"She doesn't want to see you. Have you looked at yourself in a mirror? I don't think you really want to see her like this either."

I hadn't. But I knew I probably looked like I'd gone on a week-long bender. Had I even showered since she'd left? I knew I hadn't slept.

"Did you tell her I still love her?"

Rem looked like he was in physical pain. "Yeah, man, I told her."

And it still hadn't changed anything. I wanted to double over with the pain, but I forced myself to nod. "Okay."

I stumbled back to my room defeated, Rem's eyes staring hard into my back.

"Kai, you know we have a rodeo tonight, right?" he called.

I shrugged without turning back to him.

"Fucking hell," he muttered.

His heavy footsteps echoed down the hallway, his long legs making short work of the space between us. He snatched the room key from my hand, and I blinked at him in surprise.

"What are you doing, motherfucker?" he hissed.

"Huh?"

"Get your shit together. Go take a shower. Drink some coffee because I can smell the freaking alcohol on you. And get your ass ready for the rodeo."

"Why do you care?"

"Because you're my friend, asshole. And so is she. And when you two sort this gigantic mess out, how guilty do you think she's going to feel if you threw away your shot at the title because you were moping over her? You're not throwing that away over a woman."

I leveled him with a glare. "Not just any woman. *The* woman."

Rem stared at me. "Do you mean that?"

"Of course I fucking do! I'm so damn in love with her I can't even think straight."

Rem ran his hands through his short hair. "You two are as bad as each other," he muttered.

"What?"

"Just go get ready for the rodeo, will you? And when you get out there tonight, remember what you came here for."

I'd never been booed before. And even though I'd expected some sort of backlash over the column, I hadn't quite realized the extent of my sudden loss of popularity. The protestors who often lined the streets outside the rodeo, not only held signs about outlawing bull riding, but now they also held signs condemning me for being a redneck racist. I'd been glad for the darkly tinted windows of the bus. But there was nothing to hide me from the crowd inside the arena. From the back of the bull pens, I gazed around the crowd, watching as they called my name. Some still cheered, probably unaware of the scandal, but the boos were there, loud and clear.

I didn't think I cared about what the public thought of me. Turned out, that wasn't true either. My stomach churned with nerves I wasn't used to feeling. I'd let everyone down. But especially Addie. I'd let her down in the worst way. She didn't feel I could be trusted with her secrets. And that was on me.

Rem's kick up the ass earlier might not have worked wonders, but it hadn't been completely in vain. He'd been right. I'd had my time to mope. Now it was time to start fixing everything in my life that was broken.

And the first thing was rodeo. That might not have been broken yet, but I'd been on my way to letting the whole thing go.

I wasn't going to do that.

Instead, I was going to ride tonight, knowing Addie was somewhere in the crowd. I was going to show her I was still the man she'd fallen in love with. That I was still strong and determined. That I could carry the weight of both our burdens, if only she'd let me.

I sucked in a breath, letting it expand in my lungs before making my way to the bucking chute.

The boos grew louder, but I blocked them out. They didn't matter. The bull I was about to ride didn't care whether the people in this crowd loved me or hated me. And if he didn't care, then neither did I. There was no room for that sort of thought. I climbed the railing, putting one foot on the bull's broad back, warning him I was coming, and my spotter grabbed my vest. He'd hold it until I nodded, in case the bull got antsy in the chute. But he didn't. He stood still, barely shifting his weight, and I settled on his back, strapping my hand in good and tight. I tried to focus. I needed to nod to the guys on the gate so they'd pull it open and set the bull free with me on his back. But instead of focusing on the beast beneath me, I sought out the woman I loved. And like two magnets drawn to each other, she was the first person I saw when I looked into the crowd. Our gazes locked. Her expression wasn't the cold, hard one that I'd last seen. It was the warm one, the one that said she was nervous for me and was hoping I'd do well.

"I love you," I murmured with no real idea whether she'd be able to read my lips from such a distance. But it didn't matter. Because it was exactly what I'd needed. That moment of connection, where I got a glimpse of the woman I loved. She was still in there.

And I was going to get her back.

I nodded, and the gate flew open.

The bull leaped into the arena, jerking hard to the left, beginning his spin. The crowd around me became a blur, one giant wall of noise and color that faded into the background. Dirt flew up from beneath the bull's hooves, getting up my nose and in my eyes. I dug my fingers hard into the rope, my glove protecting me from burns, but doing nothing to ease the force crushing against my bones while I tried to fight gravity and stay atop a bull who was doing his darndest to put me on the ground.

My thighs clenched, and my body jerked, muscles moving in time with the animal beneath me.

He was a good bull.

But I was better.

The eight-second buzzer sounded, and a whoop that was unlike me bellowed from my chest. I ripped the ropes from my hand and let the force of the bull's next kick propel me off his back. I landed easily on my feet and sprinted for the fences, hoisting myself up in one easy pull, to a height where horns couldn't take a piece out of me.

"Kai Hunt with a very impressive ninety-two!" the announcer called. "We'll be seeing you at the Las Vegas finals, Frost! Congratulations!"

Surprise punched me in the gut, and I spun around to look up at the leader board. Sure enough, my name was in the number one spot. Even if I screwed up my next ride, I'd done it. I was through to the finals and in contention for the title.

If there was any booing in the crowd now, I didn't hear it. My shock turned to triumph, and a grin stretched my mouth so wide it hurt. There was only one person I wanted to share this moment with. I found her again in the stands and pointed at her. She stood with everyone else, clapping, a tiny smile lifting her lips.

That ride had been for her. And for me.

It had been for us.

The moment shattered when Rem jumped up beside me and slapped me on the back. "Too fucking good, Frost!" he yelled. "I'm buying you a beer tonight. No arguing, okay?"

For once, I felt like celebrating. And so I found myself agreeing.

34

ADDIE

I couldn't go back to the hotel on the team bus. There would be no way of avoiding Kai if I did, and I couldn't see him right now.

Not after that moment in the arena.

I hadn't been prepared for him to glance my way while he was getting ready for his ride. That wasn't what Kai did. He was laser-focused, always. He kept his head down, his gaze trained on his bull, his attention on what came next.

I'd thought it safe to drink my fill of him in those moments. And I had. I'd drunk him in like a woman who'd just found water in the middle of a desert. Two days I'd spent locked in Rem's room, terrified I was going to run into Kai. Because I knew if I did, I'd crumble. He'd give me one look, and I'd fall straight back into his arms.

I couldn't let that happen. So I'd hidden, hoping if I avoided him long enough, I'd forget. Forget the way his touch set my soul on fire. Forget the way I wanted to drown in his blue eyes. Forget the way my heart was so broken, I doubted it would ever heal.

But in that moment in the arena, I'd let my resolve falter.

I'd watched his lips as they'd formed the words, I love you, and my heart had broken all over again. That was when I should have gotten up and left. I should have run for the bathroom and cried for everything I was letting go. But I hadn't. Maybe because I'd done nothing but cry for the past two days.

Maybe it was because his gaze had pinned me to the spot, leaving me incapable of movement or coherent thought.

I blamed that look for the way I leaped to my feet when he slayed his ride. I blamed those mumbled words of love for the way I'd cheered when he'd officially qualified for the finals. I blamed my stupid heart for the way it doubled in size when he'd pointed right at me.

I knew what that moment had meant. I'd seen the other guys do it. It was a gesture of dedication. Their way of saying, "that one was for you."

And that was why I was avoiding the bus like the plague. I'd gotten swept up in the night and lost my resolve. I needed time to find it again. So instead of heading for the buses along with everyone else, I lurked in the shadows, watching Kai go pink with embarrassment over all the attention he was receiving.

"Why did that article have your name on it?"

I spun around and laid eyes on Kai's mother. Shock stole my voice.

His father was nowhere to be seen, and without him casting a shadow over her, she seemed different. Bigger somehow. Stronger. She didn't look mad exactly, but the way she contemplated me was forceful.

I swallowed and forced out the same lie I'd told Kai. "Because I wrote it."

She shook her head. "I have my suspicions on who fed

the media that piece. And I know it wasn't you. So that's why I didn't ask if you wrote it. I simply asked why your name was on it."

"With all due respect, Mrs. Hunt, you don't know as much as you think you do." I knew I was being rude, but this woman and her husband were the reason both her son and I were hurting so much. And I had no time or patience to explain myself to her.

She sighed. "I deserve that, I suppose." She moved a little closer, and we stood side by side, watching Kai with his friends. "But I don't believe for a second that the same young woman who braved coming to our home, where she knew she wouldn't be welcome, solely to ask for that photo to be removed, would then go and print it in a national publication."

"Well, I did."

"I don't believe you. I saw the way you love my son. And despite my husband's misgivings, I don't have any reason to think you're anything but a truthful, upstanding young woman, Addie. I don't think you'd hurt him like that."

I didn't trust myself to say anything. I just stared blankly ahead.

"My children are the most important thing in the world to me, you know. I've already lost one. I can't lose him, too."

Irritation prickled inside me. I didn't need her guilt or her shame that I was breaking up her family. "Look, I don't know what you want from me. I don't want Kai to lose his family. Despite the way you've treated me, I don't want that for you either. Kai told me about your daughter. I'm sorry for that. But I walked away so he could have you back. Don't ask me to fix it for you. I opened the door, but it's between the three of you now."

I'd had enough. I stormed away, but the shorter woman followed me, grabbing my arm.

"Addie, please! Wait! Just hear me out. That's what I'm trying to tell you. I want my son back. But not like this. I don't want the broken shell of a man who lost the love of his life because his parents were stupid old fools, who were stuck in their ways. There's nothing that hurts a mother more than seeing your child suffer. And he's suffering right now."

My heart ripped a little more. He wasn't the only one.

I stared the other woman down, confused as hell. "So... what? You want us to be together now?" God, my stupid hopeful heart fluttered at the thought. Then the hope died in the next second, because it was false. Nothing had changed. And nothing ever would. People like his father didn't suddenly grow a conscience. Not for anyone. Not even their own son.

"He'll never accept the two of you," Mrs. Hunt said, confirming my exact thoughts. But then she squared her shoulders, pulling them back and standing tall. "But he doesn't speak for both of us. Not anymore. And that's what I came here, alone, to tell you."

"You came without him?"

She nodded. Slowly, she reached for my hands. "I don't know if Kai will ever forgive me. I want to ask his forgiveness, but I know I need to ask for yours first. I'm sorry, Addie. I'm sorry for not standing up when I should have. I know Kai loves you. And though I don't know you, I suspect you might love him the same way. I raised a good man..."

I nodded. Because I could give her that. "The best."

She smiled. "If he loves you, then I know you're worth loving, Addie. You're worth having in my life. In my family."

My stomach clenched. They were the words I'd wanted my own mother to say. Yet she hadn't. And she never would.

She was the weak one, I realized with a start. Both my birth parents. They were the ones who'd had a little girl and hadn't wanted her enough to try. They hadn't bothered to find me a good home. Even now, twenty-two years later, they still didn't want to make room for me in their lives.

But here in front of me was a woman who was admitting she was wrong. And saying she wanted to do better. She wasn't weak. She was strong. She was standing up for her child. And for me.

A lump grew in my throat. "I don't know what to say."

She squeezed my fingers. "Say you'll let me try. I know I've hurt you, and I can't expect your trust. Not yet. But I will try, Addie. I'll keep trying, every day. Until I prove myself to you, and to him."

"What about Kai's dad?"

She shook her head sadly. "His decisions are his own. But they'll no longer influence me. Just like they don't influence Kai. They haven't swayed Kai in a long time. I think you know that."

I nodded, blinking back tears.

Mrs. Hunt squeezed my hands again. "I think someone might want to talk to you."

I glanced up through wet eyelashes.

My heart stopped.

I pulled my hands away from Mrs. Hunt and took in Kai's tall frame, standing just a few feet away. He studied the two of us intently. "Mom? Addie?"

I suddenly felt like I couldn't breathe. It was all too much. "You two should talk," I blurted out.

Mrs. Hunt's face fell.

"I'm sorry, I..." I didn't know what. All I knew was I

couldn't process any of this with Kai so close to me. The temptation to fall straight back into his arms was all too real. So instead of doing what I really wanted, which was step into his embrace, bury my face in his chest, and beg him to take me back, I turned on my heel and walked away into the darkness of the night.

35

ADDIE

I woke up with a fluffy white towel in my face.

"Get up," Rem demanded.

He stood at the end of the couch in his hotel room, still wearing the clothes he'd worn the night before, his arms crossed over his chest.

I blinked blearily, my eyes feeling red, raw, and sandpapery, just like they had the last few mornings in a row. Crying yourself to sleep would do that to you. Since Rem hadn't come back to the room last night, I'd cried longer and harder than ever. I'd drifted off to sleep in the early hours of the morning, after tossing and turning and agonizing over everything Kai's mother had said last night. I didn't know if I could or should trust her. I'd been let down by so many parental figures in my life, it was hard for me to believe anything she'd said.

But I wanted to.

I wanted to believe that Kai and I could live in a world where he didn't have to give up everything in order to be with me. I missed him. God, I missed him so much. The few hours of sleep I'd gotten had been full of dreams of Kai. His touch. His love. All of him.

I groaned and threw the towel to the floor. "Go away, Rem. I'm not in the mood." I just wanted to wallow in my own misery for a bit longer.

He bent and snatched the towel back up. It landed on my face again.

This time I sat up, pissed he wasn't listening. "Seriously, Rem. Stop it."

"Nope. Get up. Have a shower. We're having breakfast in ten. Move it."

I narrowed my eyes at him. "Have you only just come home?"

He nodded. "Yep. And I'm hungry. So hurry up."

"You're not going to go away until I agree, are you?"

He turned and stalked into the single bedroom he'd tried to insist I take. I'd refused. "See how well you know me? Now hurry up, my stomach sounds like a jet plane taking off." He closed the door, leaving me alone in the living area.

My stomach growled, reminding me it had been a long time since I'd eaten, too. Breakfast actually sounded pretty good.

Rem was waiting for me when I emerged from the bathroom twenty minutes later, freshly dressed and towel drying my damp hair. He hurried me out the door before I could even protest the lack of time to blow-dry. We walked down the sidewalk toward the main street where all the cafés were, and I scraped my hair back into a high ponytail, grateful for the hair tie I had around my wrist.

Rem walked so briskly, I had to jog every few steps in order to keep up with him.

"For someone with a hangover, you sure do move quickly," I complained. "Where are we going anyway?"

Rem stopped me, grabbing the tops of both my arms. He was tall enough I had to tilt my head back in order to look up at him.

"Why have we stopped?" I asked.

"We're here. It's the café behind you."

I went to turn around, but he shook me a little, drawing my attention back to him.

"Before you go in there, though, I need to give you something."

My eyebrows furrowed. "What do you mean before *I* go in there? What about you?"

He shook his head, reaching for his back pocket and pulled out a length of skinny rope. It was worn and frayed, and I suspected it was probably one of the ropes they used to hang on to a bull. He shoved it into my hand and folded my fingers over it.

"What's this for?"

Rem grimaced. "For hanging me up from the Las Vegas arena by my balls."

I let out a laugh that felt strange after crying all night. "Why would I do that..."

Then I got it. *If you tell Kai, I'll string you up by your balls from the Las Vegas arena.*

"No," I hissed. "Rem! You didn't!"

He screwed his face up, a mixture of remorse and determination settling on his handsome features. "Yeah, sorry, Ads. I did. I told him everything."

The blood drained from my face, and I slapped him hard in the chest. "What kind of friend does that? I told you that stuff in confidence."

He let me slap him for a moment, but then he caught my

hands and leveled me with a serious look. "I'm the best kind of friend. I'm the kind who will keep your secrets and take them to my grave. But I'm also the kind of friend who will blab them to the man who loves you, when you're being too damn stubborn and selfless to tell him yourself."

I scowled at him.

His lips lifted at the corners. "Scowl all you want. But you know it should have never been me who you confided in. It should have been him."

I opened my mouth to argue, but he put a finger over my lips and turned me around. "You can be angry at me all you want later. But right now, you've got a breakfast date."

Through the glass of the café window, Kai stood, biting his lip, looking more worried yet hopeful than I'd ever seen him before. My resolve to stay away from him melted. Unlike Rem who looked, and smelled, like he'd been at a bar all night, Kai was freshly showered, his short hair slicked to one side, his jeans and shirt clean. He stood there, with his guard completely down and hope written all over his face.

I couldn't walk away. Not again. It was all I could do not to run into his arms.

I held the rope up in front of Rem's face and shook it, then shoved it into my purse. "Just in case I need it later."

"You kinky fucks—"

I whirled back around and glared at him. He was laughing his head off.

"I meant for stringing you up, asshole."

"Yeah, yeah, sure, sure. Just go get your man, would you? I want my couch back."

I couldn't help the slight smile, and Rem rushed forward and kissed my cheek. "You're both good people, Addie. You deserve to be happy."

"Thank you," I whispered against his shirt. I lifted a hand in a half wave as he loped away, and then I turned to face the man I loved. He was still watching me through the window, and with a deep breath, I opened the door and walked toward him.

36

KAI

"So Rem told you everything?" Addie asked, as she settled into the seat across from me.

She was too far away. I hated, even after everything Rem had told me last night, there was still such a distance between us. I hated we were on opposite sides of the table when we should have been sitting right next to each other. I hated we weren't touching when all I wanted to do was pull her into my arms and hold her and never let her go again.

"Don't be angry at him. In his defense, I got him drunk then badgered him until he talked. He put up a valiant effort."

She huffed out an annoyed sigh, but I could tell she was fighting back a smile.

"He's dead to me," she joked.

"Harsh."

"That's what happens when you betray me."

I went quiet. "Is that what I did?"

Her smile fell. Her arms followed. She leaned forward on the table. "No," she said quietly. "You never did anything wrong. I just want you to have your family. I don't want to waltz into your life and demand you give everything up for me. That's not who I am."

I grabbed her hand, and relief poured through me when she didn't snatch it back. Instead, she let me link my fingers through hers. Her hand still fit perfectly in mine, like it always had. Like it always would. I just needed to make sure she knew it.

"Why didn't you tell me about your parents?"

She looked down at our fingers. "I don't know. I'm not used to having anyone to confide in. I never had any sort of family. I've never even really had friends. Not close ones. Not the kind you tell your secrets to, anyway."

"But you had me. You *have* me, Addie. Always. I want to know your secrets. No matter what they are."

A tear rolled down her cheek. "But your family…"

"You're my family, too. You and me? That's what a family is. Two people who accept each other, warts and all. If my parents, and yours, are too stupid to see how good we are, and how much love there is here, then we don't need any of them. All we need is each other."

"I didn't want you to resent me."

My heart squeezed. "You know the only thing I would resent?"

She shook her head.

"You walking away from me before I really got to tell you how I feel. So I'm going to tell you now, in case you're planning on walking out that door without me by your side. I love you, Addie. I love you more than I've ever loved anything or anyone. You're the sweetest, most big-hearted woman I know, and you're all I need. The way I feel about you, makes everything else—my parents, bull riding, everything—it all pales into insignificance when you're holding my hand."

I stared deep into her brown eyes, and the noise of the other customers around us died away, until it felt like it was just the two of us in the room. "Rem said something to me last night. He said, remember what you came here for."

I smoothed a lock of hair that had fallen loose of Addie's ponytail behind her ear, noticing the way she shivered when my fingertips brushed the soft skin of her neck. "He was talking about winning the finals. But I realized something last night. That I might not have come here for you, but I found you along the way. And I damn sure intend to leave with you."

Addie's breath hitched, and her gaze grew glassy, her eyes filling with tears. "Are you sure?" she whispered.

"Never been more sure of anything in my life." I couldn't wait another moment. I leaned across the table, one hand snaking to the back of her neck, and tugged her forward until my lips crashed onto hers.

I kissed her hard, branding her, claiming her yet again as mine. My lips moved, proving to her I wanted this. I wanted her, no matter the consequences. Because the alternative— not having her—was unthinkable. I could live without all the rest, but never without her.

Everything I gave to her, she gave right back. Around us, I was dimly aware of the rest of the café cheering, and when we pulled away, Addie's cheeks were pink.

"Oh my God," she whispered with a laugh. "We made a scene."

I leaned in and kissed her again. "I don't care. As long as you know I love you."

She nodded, her smile turning wide. "I do."

"And no more thinking anything is more important than you, okay?"

She grinned, but then she lowered her voice. "No one has ever said that to me before. I want to believe it."

"Believe it, baby," I whispered back. "Because I mean every word. And I'm going to spend the rest of my life making sure you know it."

"I want that."

"I do, too."

The box in my pocket dug into my leg. I'd grabbed it from my drawer on impulse, determined one way or another to prove to her I was serious about us. But now it didn't feel right. Not because I didn't want to marry her. God, I still wanted that more than I'd ever wanted anything. But it didn't seem big enough. My proposal to her wasn't going to be a desperate bid to get her back. But it would be soon. There was just one thing I needed to do first.

37

ADDIE

*T*he morning of the Las Vegas finals, I woke with Kai's big hand splayed out over my lower back. He rubbed slow circles on my naked skin, and I wriggled on my belly, angling my head so it was propped up on my hands. My bare breasts pushed into the soft mattress, and I blinked at Kai sleepily.

"Hey, you. How long have you been awake?"

His hand on my back turned featherlight, tracing up and down my spine, tickling the skin as he went. "A while," he confessed. He shifted onto his side, a mound of pillows propping up his head. "I was watching you sleep."

"Creeper."

"I just like looking at you."

"I like you looking at me," I said boldly. Because I did. Even now, with a sheet over my ass and my breasts covered up by the fact I was on my stomach, I liked the way his gaze rolled over me. Too many people in my life had turned in my direction, seen the color of my skin, and judged me on that alone. But Kai never had. He saw my skin as beautiful, then went beyond that, searching into my soul and my heart, seeing the real beauty beneath.

We'd spent the last week since we'd reconciled discovering each other all over again, and I'd never been so happy.

Or so turned on.

Kai's touch sent ripples of pleasure straight through my skin and into the depths of my body—to other places, I wanted him to touch a whole lot more than where he was touching me right now.

Our need for each other was always in sync, and the next time he trailed his hand down my spine, it went lower, beneath the sheets, brushing over the top of my ass, and then on the next pass, lower still, cupping my ass cheek and squeezing it gently.

"Fuck, I love this. So bitable." And to prove it, his lips followed the path of his fingers, kissing his way down my spine and over one ass cheek, his teeth grazing my skin as he went.

I squirmed, wetness gathering between my legs already. I wanted more. I wanted to spread my legs and beg for his mouth to get between them.

But the responsible side of me won out. "Hey, hey there, cowboy. You've got a bull to ride tonight. You haven't got time for this."

Kai ignored me, his lips still trailing down my body, below the swell of my ass to the backs of my thighs. "What if I'd rather ride you?"

His hands parted my legs, and despite my weak protests of a second ago, he barely had to encourage me before I was opening myself up to him. I wanted him. And he knew it. His strong hands massaged the backs of my thighs, his thumbs kneading higher and higher, until they were brushing over my sex.

He dragged his fingers over my outer lips, driving me mad for wanting him to part them and get to the good stuff inside. But he took his time, drawing out the sensation until mewling noises of need escaped my throat, and I subconsciously rocked back, trying to get more friction where I wanted it most.

Eventually, one thick finger spread me and brushed over my clit, making me moan. But he didn't linger there, he moved it to my entrance, slicking through the wetness.

"What if I want to ride you here?" he asked quietly.

In answer, I raised my ass in the air, gasping when his finger invaded my pussy. "Yes," I moaned. I rocked forward, burying my face in the pillow before pushing back again, taking his thick finger deep. He brushed my G-spot, and I moaned hard.

I almost cried when he pulled his finger away.

He chuckled and kissed my lower back. "So eager," he murmured, and my face went hot. I was glad it was still stuffed into the pillow.

But it was the truth. I was always eager for him. In any way I could get him.

I especially liked when he took his time with me, like he seemed to want right now. I whimpered at the loss of him, but he slid his wet finger higher, between the cheeks of my ass and over the puckered star of my asshole.

"What about here?" he asked, teasing at my back entrance. His fingertip nudged inside, like he'd done several times before, knowing how much I liked it when I was turned on. "What if I ride you here?" he asked.

My core throbbed at the thought of his thick cock penetrating me there. The thought was a little intimidating, but as he pushed his finger deeper into my ass, the beginning of my orgasm built. He used another finger to enter my pussy and then, matching the rocking of my hips, he finger-fucked me in both ways.

"Yes," I moaned, loudly. "Yes. Fuck me there."

I meant it. I trusted him not to hurt me. We'd been playing all week. Building up to this, and I wanted it. I wanted to give him all of me. In every way.

"You sure?"

"So sure."

He turned away, but I didn't dare look. I heard him fumble on the bedside table, then there was a crinkle of a condom and the pop of a tube of lube opening.

He got behind, pulling my hips up to meet his. I ached for him to be inside me. His cock notched at the entrance to my pussy and then thrust inside, hard and long, filling me and stretching me, making me yell out all at once.

His finger returned to my ass. As he rocked his cock in and out of my pussy, his finger entered me. Pleasure exploded through me, and I came hard, clenching around him, but he didn't stop. He rode out my waves before adding another well-lubed finger.

"Is it enough?" he asked, his movements gentle.

But I shook my head. I could already feel another orgasm building. "I want it all," I whispered back.

For a moment, everything disappeared from my body, and I cried out at the loss, immediately wanting him back inside me. In whatever way I could get him.

Then his cock pressed against the place his fingers had been just moments earlier. Only a slight pressure, but I was so turned on by the orgasm that had just rocked me to my core, I just wanted more. I pressed my hips back, taking the head of him.

"Fuck, Addie," he groaned. "Fuck."

He didn't move, letting me control the show. Slowly, I

pushed myself back, his cock sinking inside a place I'd never let another man go. But Kai was different. He was forever. And I trusted him with everything I had. I knew he loved me. And I wanted this. Perhaps more than he did.

It was uncomfortable at first, but it was only moments before I enjoyed the feel, pleasure taking over me. We both moaned.

"Kai," I panted. "I want this."

"Me, too, baby, me, too. I got you."

He reached around and played with my clit while his hips moved back and forth, slowly thrusting into my body. After a few more thrusts, I adjusted and set a faster pace. My arousal dripped from between my legs and his fingers spread it over my clit, rubbing circles on it.

"You're so fucking tight," he groaned. "You feel so good."

"You do, too," I whispered. "Stop holding back. I need to come."

He didn't need telling twice. He picked up the pace, his hips pistoning while his fingers worked my nub. My second orgasm barreled down on me so hard and fast, if Kai hadn't had a hold on me I would have faceplanted onto the bed.

"Ohhh!" I screamed sensation rushing through me. "Kai!"

My vision blurred, and my legs wobbled. Kai thrust into me once more before he yelled his own release. His grip on my hips tightened as he poured into me, and I snuck a glance back at him.

He was a thing of beauty, lost in his release. His body slick with a fine sheen of sweat, his abs contracting, and he worked the last of his erection into my thoroughly well-sexed body. His head tipped back, his beautiful lips parted slightly to let out the groans of pleasure I could never hear enough of.

His gaze caught mine as he pulled out.

"I'll be back," he said softly.

I nodded and collapsed down onto the sheet. My body ached, my ass in particular for sure, but it was the good ache that came after a marathon morning of excellent sex. And I knew I'd want to do it again.

Water ran in the bathroom, and then Kai was back, scooping me up from the bed and carrying me into a hot shower.

"Oh," I sighed after he set me down on my feet. The hot water poured over my body, delicious, warm rivulets sluicing between my tender parts. "That feels amazing."

I leaned against his broad chest, letting his hand roam over me, washing me gently. "Are you okay?" he asked, his voice full of concern. "I hadn't really expected it to be so..."

"Full-on?" I supplied with a sated smile.

"Yeah." His eyebrows furrowed with his concern, and I laughed, prodding at the crease in his forehead with my finger.

"I'm fine. Better than fine. I don't think I've ever been so fine in my life."

His anxiousness disappeared, and he dropped a kiss on my forehead. "I love you. You're kind of amazing, you know?"

"Because of the anal?"

He choked out a laugh. "Well, that, too. But I just meant in general. I love you."

"You, too."

He turned the water off, and I groaned. He nudged me with his hip. "We've got things to do."

"We do? Do you have training or something today?"

He shook his head. "Nope. Gotta get there early. About four. But there's something I want to show you first."

I wrapped myself in a fluffy white hotel towel. "What's that?"

He smiled. "You'll see."

———

*K*ai herded me out onto the Las Vegas streets, pulling me into an already busy crowd of mismatched tourists. Kai didn't even stand out in his wide-brimmed hat and boots. There were others in the crowd dressed just like him, and he nodded at each of them, like this was a small town and we were out for a Sunday morning walk.

I stifled a giggle. "You can take the boy out of the country..."

Kai shrugged. "What? I'm just being polite."

I tucked my arm around his waist, but he jumped aside like I'd electrocuted him. I raised an eyebrow.

"Sorry!" he stuttered. He moved around me so I was on his other side and put his arm over my shoulder. "I just...I have an injury on that side."

I frowned. "Since when? You were fine after last week's ride."

His cheeks went pink. "Since...this morning."

I snorted on my laughter. "Sex injury? Okay then."

He laughed, too, but he didn't slow his pace. We dodged around a few older couples who were obviously walking too slow for Kai's liking, and he practically jumped out of his skin when I begged to stop for a take-out coffee.

"Kai Hunt, are you nervous about tonight?" I asked, walking beside him again.

"What? No."

I squeezed his hand. "I think you lie. You're so full of

nervous energy, you're making me twitch. Chill out. You've got this in the bag."

"I'm not nervous about tonight. Swear. I just really want to see some of Las Vegas while we have a few hours free."

"Okay, but what's the rush?"

He slowed his pace just a fraction. "Nothing. I just wanted to show you something. It's just up here actually."

We stopped in front of a little chapel that boasted Elvis weddings. Its walls were washed white, a little patch of green grass that looked too perfect to be real, with a cute wooden picket fence at the front. I took in the pink and yellow flowers growing in brightly colored pots and fished around in my pocket for my phone to take a photo. An Elvis impersonator stepped outside the chapel and walked a few steps away from the door, leaning on the wall and lighting up a cigarette.

"You kids getting married?" he called to me as I snapped a picture, and I laughed, shaking my head.

My face went hot, and I hoped Kai wouldn't read anything into it. "No, no. Just doing the tourist thing."

A wide grin split the man's over-tanned face. "You sure about that?" He jerked his chin.

I turned around, prepared to laugh the whole thing off with Kai.

Only to find him down on one knee.

"Kai—what?" A tiny sound of shock escaped my mouth, and I glanced around, not exactly sure what I was searching for. Hidden cameras perhaps?

He grinned up at me, appearing calmer than he had all morning. Older somehow. More confident. And it was sexy as hell. He pulled off his hat, running a hand through his short blond hair, and then took my hand. "I love you, Addie. I always have, but more now than ever. I had this whole thing planned out. I was going to take you to Hawaii and do it on a beach at sunset."

My heart flip-flopped. I was vaguely aware of Fake Elvis and other tourists, slowing their paces to curiously watch us, but my gaze never strayed from Kai's. I couldn't have looked away even if I'd wanted to. Not in that moment. Not with his expression so sure and confident yet open and vulnerable at the same time.

Kai produced a silver ring from his pocket, and I gasped. The mid-morning sun hit the diamond just right, sparkles glinting off the edges.

"I don't want to wait. I want to be with you. Always. And we don't have to get married here, even though I booked Elvis over there to marry us in..." he checked his watch, "about fifteen minutes. We don't have to do that. We can go anywhere in the world and have a huge wedding if you want to. But there is one thing I need to know now. Addie, will you be my wife?"

I've never nodded my head so fast. "Yes," I choked out, tears building and spilling onto my cheeks. "Yes, I'll marry you. Anywhere. Anytime."

Fake Elvis cheered, and Kai pushed to his feet, grasped my face between both hands, and kissed me hard.

"Yes?" he whispered when he pulled back, his eyes wide. "Really?"

I laughed against his lips. "Of course, yes." I wrapped my arms around his neck and kissed him again. "Did you really book the chapel?"

He grinned. "Yeah, I did."

"Bit presumptuous of you!"

His cheeks went pink.

God he was cute. "I love when you get embarrassed. I'm

going to really enjoy seeing you blush for the rest of my life."

He held me tight again. "And I'm going to really enjoy loving you for the rest of mine."

I would have probably swooned if he hadn't had such a tight grip on me.

"So, Vegas wedding," I said when I stepped back, my brow furrowed. "We don't have a witness, though. Do they provide one? Or is that just a movie thing?"

Kai paused. "Actually, I have that covered." He linked his fingers between mine. "Come on."

Fake Elvis held the door to the chapel open, and after we signed some forms in the reception area, he led us through another door.

A gasp escaped my lips. "Kai!"

It was the most beautiful chapel I'd ever seen. While the building was quite small, it had high ceilings with a glass-paneled roof that let in streams of light. The sides of the room were beautiful old wood, and full-sized trees and plants grew in large beds. A long aisle led to an altar, where Fake Elvis took his spot. Behind him, a waterfall ran from the ceiling down to the floor.

"Do you like it?" he asked with a smile.

"It's gorgeous! I was not expecting this at all."

Kai tugged me down the aisle, and I went after him, still gaping around me at the beautiful space. It took me a moment to realize there were other people in the room. "Mrs. Hunt? Jacqueline?"

My eyes had to be saucer wide, my gaze bouncing between Kai's two mother figures.

They stepped forward from the front row of seats, Mrs. Hunt wearing a broad smile that matched her son's. Kai kissed her on the cheek, then stepped away to stand with the third woman I didn't recognize.

I turned back to Kai's mom. "I can't believe you're here," I said, my fingers shaking.

"And miss my only son marrying the love of his life? Never."

"How did you know I'd say yes? After last time we saw each other..."

She smiled knowingly. "Mothers know these things. And I meant what I said to you that night, Addie. You're a part of my family now."

Neither of us mentioned the fact Kai's dad wasn't here. But the fact she was...

"Thank you," I said, hugging her.

For a moment, she froze, but then she hugged me back with such gusto I thought my ribs might break.

"You make him happy," she said quietly into my ear. "So, thank you."

I awkwardly turned to Jacqueline, remembering the way I'd fled Sunny's funeral. But she smiled, instantly putting me at ease. "Don't look so worried! It's your wedding day!"

I bit my bottom lip. "I hope you understand..."

The older woman patted my on the arm. "Kai called. He explained everything and asked for my blessing."

My breath caught. She didn't need to say anything else. She was here. At our wedding. That said everything.

Jacqueline pulled me into her embrace. "Kai is just as much my son as Sunny was. He'd be happy for the both of you. As am I. I hope you'll allow me to continue being a part of your lives together."

Her voice wobbled, and I held her even tighter, hoping

she could feel how much I truly meant what I was about to say. "I wouldn't want it any other way. Thank you."

We separated, both of us with tears shining in our eyes.

"Okay, let's get married!" I declared, making everyone laugh.

"Just one more thing before we do," Kai said, stepping forward and taking my hand. He led me to the other woman in the room. "Addie, this is Kawana."

I held my hand out to the older woman. "Nice to meet you."

Kawana grasped my hand tightly. Her dark-brown skin matched mine, and when she spoke, it was with an Australian accent. "You look just like her," she said, choking on her words a little.

I glanced at Kai in confusion, then back at Kawana. "Sorry? Who do I look like?"

Kai came to stand beside me. "Don't get mad…"

I glanced at him sharply. "Nothing good ever comes from a man starting a sentence like that."

Fake Elvis muttered something that sounded distinctly like, "Ain't that the truth."

I ignored him.

Kai's expression was distinctly guilty. "Rem gave me the number of the private investigator you used to find your family."

I shook my head. Bloody Rem. I was seriously going to do some permanent damage to his balls the next time I saw him. Meddler.

"I asked the investigator to go wider than your birth parents." Kai took my hands and squeezed them. "You and me, Addie, we're family. And you're all I'll ever need. But I know how important finding out where you came from is to you. And I want you to have that knowledge."

I glanced over at Kawana, then back at Kai. "Is she...." My bottom lip trembled. I didn't know who to look at, but Kawana rushed forward and placed one warm hand on my arm.

"Sssh. No. I'm not her. Not your mother. Your mother is my sister. I'm your aunt." She gave me a hopeful, warm smile.

"My aunt? I have an aunt?"

The woman nodded eagerly. "You do. And an uncle, and cousins. They're all very excited to meet you when you get back to Australia."

The room around me felt like it was spinning with the overload of sudden information. "Sorry, I think I need to sit down for a moment." I slumped into one of the white wooden chairs with a gauzy bow tied at the back.

Kawana came and sat beside me, and Kai fetched a chair from the row in front to flank my other side. "I'll tell you anything you want to know about your birth parents. We have all the time in the world for that. But the main thing I wanted to say to you today, is that they're fools. They run their own lives, and I run mine, but my family is never too big to include another. And I hope you won't hold your parents' bad choices against us. I've thought of you often through the years, Addie. And I'm honored to sit here at your wedding today. As your family. If you'll have me."

A fresh round of tears dripped down my face, and I wiped them away with the back of my hand. "I need to stop crying. My eyes are going to be all puffy in my wedding photos."

Kai leaned in and kissed my temple. "You'll still be the most beautiful woman I've ever seen."

I sucked in a deep breath. Kawana gave me a steadying

smile, which helped propel me to my feet. My gaze met with Mrs. Hunt's, and she nodded her encouragement.

I held my hand out to the man I loved. "Time to get married."

He pulled me in and gave me one last kiss as we headed for the altar. "And then live happily ever after?"

Sounded like a plan to me.

EPILOGUE

REM

*T*his wasn't my first rodeo. Hell, throughout the years I'd been a bullfighter, or rodeo clown if you preferred, I'd racked up hundreds of nights of running in front of bulls, distracting them from destroying the rider who'd just come off their back. I didn't get nervous often.

Except in Las Vegas.

Every year, the grand finale was held in this arena, and every year, I stood backstage and stared out at the massive crowd and let it really sink in I'd survived another three hundred and sixty-five days. Another year where I was still walking, still breathing. I hadn't taken a hoof or a horn to a vital organ. Sure, I was a little older, a little stiffer, a few more minor injuries to add to the ever-growing list. But I wasn't dead.

With my history, and now the way I liked to get my adrenaline rush by jumping in front of bulls, being alive was something to be celebrated.

I just had to make it through one more night.

"Rem!"

I spun around and grinned when Addie rushed up and

threw her arms around me. She hugged me hard and then stumbled back to stand with Kai, who was watching, looking pretty darn pleased with himself.

"What was that for?" I asked. "Not that I'm complaining."

She held up their linked fingers. One of hers shined with a sparkly new diamond ring. My eyes widened as I glanced between the two of them. "Is that what I think it is? You're engaged?"

Kai laughed, the sound deep and throaty. "Actually, we skipped that part altogether."

"Huh?"

"We just got married!" Addie yelled.

The two of them were grinning like naughty schoolkids who had just gotten away with sticking their hands in the cookie jar.

"Holy shit, you're not joking?"

"Deadly serious! Oh, hey, can you take a photo of us?" Addie passed me her phone, and before I had even really caught up to what was going on, she had her hands fisting in Kai's shirt, pulling him close to kiss him. He responded immediately, dipping her backward. I snapped off a few shots, and when she came up laughing, I handed the phone back to her. She flicked through them. "This one! Aaaand send!"

"Who'd you send it to?" Kai asked, trying to peer over her shoulder.

"My editor. I'll be making sure she prints that, along with the real story I wrote about Kai Hunt, world famous bull rider, and the man who is about to take the championship buckle home. Or I'll sue." She beamed up at her new husband, and I couldn't help but feel a smug sense of satisfaction. I'd had a little something to do with getting the two of them down that aisle and I was a bit cocky about it.

"Make sure you include the part about Remington James, and how he single-handedly got the two of you back together."

Addie shot me a smile that was so sickly sweet I was immediately on guard.

She stepped in closer to me and said softly, "Don't push your luck. I've still got that rope in my purse and your balls are right there." She moved her knee swiftly toward my junk, and I jumped back on instinct.

I held my hands up in surrender. She had a point. "Okay, fair call." Then I winked at her. "Just print how devilishly handsome I am then. Did you ever find out who was behind that first story?"

Kai grimaced. "We think it was my dad. Mom believes he fed it to the newspaper to try to break Addie and me up."

"Lucky you had me around to prevent that, huh?"

Kai rolled his eyes, and I scooted out of the way before Addie's next attempt at my balls actually connected. "Seriously, though. I'm glad it all worked out. See you out there, Frost. You got this in the bag."

Looking decidedly un-Frost like, he turned back to his wife, seemingly unworried the biggest night of his career was about to go down.

The arena went dark, and the crowd cheered. I let the noise soak in, riling me up for what I needed to do tonight. When the pyrotechnics started up, I plastered on a huge smile.

"Give it up for our bullfighters, Rem, Abel, and Eric!" the announcers called.

The three of us ran out into the arena, and I threw in a

backflip just for kicks. The crowd cheered louder, just like I knew they would.

"Show pony," Abel ribbed me.

I grinned wide. I was. I knew it. And I didn't care. I loved this job. I loved the adrenaline rush and the crowd cheering. Sure, the bull riders got most of the glory, but over the last two years, Abel, Eric, and I had become more and more popular with the crowds. Especially since I'd started throwing in some acrobatics and really owning the 'rodeo clown' tag, even though that hadn't been our official title for a long time.

People could call me what they wanted. Wannabe bull rider? Sure, go right ahead. Clown? No worries, I could own that. I had the most dangerous job in the sport. There was nothing people could say to diminish that. I lived for the rush.

Kai slapped my hand as he ran past to take his spot in the riders' line up, and huge bursts of flame lit up the darkness of the arena, while upbeat music poured through speakers, getting the crowd on their feet and cheering louder than I'd ever heard before. It was deafening.

There was nothing like the finals. It was like every other rodeo of the tour, all rolled into one massive night, and the excitement was palpable.

When the lights came up, all the riders left the floor, but Abel, Eric, and I remained in the ring, walking to the side, ready for the first bull of the night. Trickles of adrenaline pulsed through my veins.

Bring it.

For the next two hours, that was what we did. We watched the riders while bouncing on the balls of our feet, getting in close to the bull, but not so close we got in the way. Then the second the buzzer went; it was our turn. We rushed in, circling the bull, moving on quick feet, distracting him and, when necessary, protecting the rider.

That was my job. Protect the rider at all costs, even if it meant sacrificing myself. And I was happy to do it. Not only was it the biggest rush, but these guys had become my family. Abel was my brother, but so were the other guys. I didn't want to see any of them hurt. And it was my job to get them out of that ring safely.

I gave each rider my full attention, just like I always did, but tonight, I was on edge, waiting for Frost to ride. I could admit, that grumpy asshole had really gotten under my skin this year. He was a good guy, and talented. He had the girl. He just needed the championship buckle now.

I wanted it for him.

I also wanted the nice sum of cash I'd collect if he won. But that was just an added bonus. I'd put a bet on him the very first week of the tour, my gut instinct and years of watching telling me the whiz kid had the skills to go all the way.

"Last rider of the night, competition leader, Kai 'Frost' Hunt!" the announcers called.

There were still some boos in the crowd, that frankly pissed me off, but I had a feeling once he and Addie went public with their relationship, the newspaper Addie worked for would be eating their words, and Kai would go back to being one of the crowd favorites. How could he not be, with his handsome face and that whole broody, mysterious thing he had going on.

It would never work for me, but obviously some people liked it.

"You think he's got this?" Abel said while Kai strapped his hand.

A broad smile spread across my face. "Let's see."

The gate flew open, and Kai's bull bucked out into the arena, skittering hard to the left. Abel and I to both jumped up the fence behind us to avoid getting a body slam from a fifteen hundred pound animal. But Kai was hanging on like the pro he was. The bull settled into his spin, throwing his head back and kicking out as he went, and Abel and I both climbed down from the railing with wide grins.

Nothing like the unexpected to keep you on your toes.

Kai waved his free arm, jerking his body in complete unison with the beast beneath him. It was easy to get lost in the rhythmic move of rider and animal, dancing in perfect sync around each other. Kai made this shit look effortless in a way nobody else did.

I didn't dare glance at the clock, knowing it could cost me my life if I lost focus for even half a second, but I knew he had to be close to that golden eight-second buzzer.

"Come on, come on," I muttered.

The buzzer sounded, and I ripped my hat off, whooping it up. I didn't even need to see the score. I knew he had it in the bag.

Kai dismounted on the force of the bull's next kick, landing safely on his feet and scuttling for the fences. Eric was closest to the bull's head, and he rushed in, distracting him and getting the big guy headed in the right direction. It all went like fucking clockwork.

Kai stood high on the railings, pumping his fist in the air while the crowd screamed around him. His score flashed up. Ninety-eight.

"Kai Hunt with the top score of the entire competition, ladies and gentlemen. And what a day to do it. This young gun certainly knows when to pull out all the stops."

When Kai got down, the three of us rushed him. Abel

and Eric slapped him on the back, but I was a hugger and I didn't hold back. I slung my arm over his shoulders.

"Too fucking good, Frost. Too fucking good."

The asshole grinned and elbowed me, but then he hugged me back. "You're a good friend, Rem. Thanks for always having my back. Inside and outside the ring. "

I knew exactly what he meant. "Don't get sappy on me."

He shoved me. "Fuck off, then."

We both grinned at each other.

But then Frost's smile fell. "What the hell?"

His gaze focused over my shoulder, at the tunnels that led into the arena from the backstage area.

I spun around, every muscle tensing up in case a bull had escaped from their enclosure and was coming back for round two. It didn't happen often, but the few times it had were always a reminder that you were never really off duty, if there were large, dangerous animals around. You always had to be on your toes, until the very last of them had been loaded onto a truck and were headed home to their barns full of straw and chow.

But it wasn't a bull. A swarm of uniformed police stormed the ring, looking completely out of place among the jeans, plaid, and chaps.

What the fuck was this? A Village People reunion? We already had the cowboys. We just needed a chief and a construction worker...

A hush fell over the crowd as the police surrounded Kai and me.

"Remington James?" a big guy at the front barked out.

I took a step forward. "Yeah, that's me."

Three guys moved in quicker than I would have given them credit for. Kai was pushed out of the way, protesting loudly.

The officer grabbed one wrist, yanking it up behind me. "Remington James, you're being placed under arrest."

"For what?" I yelped, struggling with the man, trying to yank my arm from his grasp. "What the hell is this?"

"Don't struggle. You'll only make it worse for yourself," another officer snarled, coming in to seize my other wrist.

Fuck not struggling!

"Then tell me what I've supposedly done! Ow, fuck!"

The first guy yanked my arm so hard I was afraid my shoulder might pop out. He forced me down onto the ground by kicking out the back of my knees. Gasps erupted around the crowd, and from the corner of my eye I saw Abel and Kai being held back by other officers. There suddenly seemed to be bodies everywhere. More cops rushed from the gates, as well as rodeo officials and riders. An alarm sounded from the speakers, and the crowd pushed toward the exits.

"Get off him!" Abel yelled. He struggled with the men who held him back. "He hasn't done anything!"

Cold metal cuffs were slapped onto my wrists before I was hauled to my feet by the back of my shirt. "You can't arrest me for no reason," I yelled at the guy shoving me toward the gates. "This is illegal."

He leaned in close to my ear. "You're one to talk about illegal. Did you really think the past wasn't going to catch up with you, huh, Viper?"

I stopped struggling. Nobody had called me Viper in a very long time. And it was a name I had never wanted to hear again.

My gaze met with Abel's. "Call a lawyer."

The officer behind me chuckled. "Smart move. You're going to need one."

THE END

*T*he story continues in Sexy Dirty Cowboy! Preorder now!

*G*et a sneak peek at the next generation of cowboys in a FREE bonus scene! It features not only Kai and Addie's kids, but Johnny and Isabel's (from 25 Reasons to Hate Christmas and Cowboys) too! Click here or check out the bonus material section on my website! www. ellethorpe.com

ALSO BY ELLE THORPE

The Only You series

*Only the Positive (Only You, #1) - Reese and Low.

*Only the Perfect (Only You, #2) - Jamison.

*Only the Truth - (Only You, bonus novella) - Bree.

*Only the Negatives (Only You, #3) - Gemma.

*Only the Beginning (Only You, #4) - Bianca and Riley.

*All of Him - A single dad anthology, featuring Only the Lies. Only the Lies is a bonus, Only You novella.

Dirty Cowboy series

*Talk Dirty, Cowboy (Dirty Cowboy, #1)

*Ride Dirty, Cowboy (Dirty Cowboy, #2)

*Sexy Dirty Cowboy (Dirty Cowboy, #3) - Preorder now!

*25 Reasons to Hate Christmas and Cowboys (a Dirty Cowboy bonus novella, set before Talk Dirty, Cowboy but can be read as a standalone, holiday romance)

Add your email address here to be the first to know when new books are available!

www.ellethorpe.com/newsletter

Join Elle Thorpe's readers group on Facebook!

www.facebook.com/groups/ellethorpesdramallamas

ACKNOWLEDGMENTS

Woah. Here we go again. I love this part.

The first person I want to thank is my husband. He's a proud Aboriginal man. I'm white. We've been an interracial couple for nineteen years, and have three Aboriginal Australian children.

While Addie and Kai's story is nothing like ours, there is one thing that Kai and I share. That initial need Kai has to protect and fix things for Addie is something that I pulled from myself.

I remember once going into a sporting goods store when we were first dating. The clerk took one look at my husband and accused him of trying to steal a pair of soccer gloves.

I've never been so outraged in my life. How dare she? My husband is the hardest working man I know, and the thought of him stealing anything was ludicrous.

I made a scene. Just like Kai does with his parents.

And then my husband put his hand on my arm and said, "It's okay. I'm used to it."

And that broke my damn heart. But then I watched, as

he calmly explained to the clerk, and the manager, who eventually apologized, and we left with our purchases.

I realized he didn't need me to fight that battle for him. He knew how to handle it better than I did. Just like Addie did. What he needed me to do was support him. And that's what I've tried to do every day since.

I know Kai is doing the same thing with Addie. :-)

But anyway, I have more people to thank!

Thank you to Jolie Vines, Zoe Ashwood, Emmy Ellis and Karen Hrdlicka who make up my stellar editing team. And an extra thanks to Jo and Zoe for being my author besties too!

Thank you to Sara Massery for the chats, sprints and graphic design advice.

Thank you to Shellie, Ally, Karen, and Alyssa who always beta read my books and give such great advice.

Thank you to my kiddos for being troopers when I'm being boring and just sitting in my room writing.

Thank you to all the amazing reviewers, bookstagrammers, bloggers, my readers group and to everyone who read Talk Dirty, Cowboy and liked it enough to read this book too. Just wait for Rem's book....it's a good one!

Love, Elle x

Love, Elle x

ABOUT THE AUTHOR

Elle Thorpe lives on the sunny east coast of Australia. When she's not writing stories full of kissing, she's a wife and mummy to three tiny humans. She's also official ball thrower to one slobbery dog named Rollo. Yes, she named a female dog after a dirty hot character on Vikings. Don't judge her. Elle is a complete and utter fangirl at heart, obsessing over The Walking Dead and Outlander to an unhealthy degree. But she wouldn't change a thing.

You can find her on Facebook or Instagram(@ellethorpe-books or hit the links below!) or at her website www.ellethorpe.com. If you love Elle's work, please consider joining her Facebook fan group, Elle Thorpe's Drama Llamas or joining her newsletter here. www.ellethorpe.com/newsletter

- facebook.com/ellethorpebooks
- instagram.com/ellethorpebooks
- goodreads.com/ellethorpe
- pinterest.com/ellethorpebooks

Lightning Source UK Ltd.
Milton Keynes UK
UKHW011846280222
399339UK00002B/527